THE BETRAYAL
of
JOHN MACHELE

IAN M ROBERTSON

T

The manufacturer's authorised representative in the EU for product safety is Authorised Rep
Compliance Ltd, 71 Lower Baggot Street, Dublin D02 P593 Ireland (www.arccompliance.com)

This is a work of fiction. Names, characters, businesses, places, events
and incidents are either the products of the author's imagination
or used in a fictitious manner. Any resemblance to actual persons,
living or dead, or actual events is purely coincidental.

Troubador Publishing Ltd
Unit E2 Airfield Business Park,
Harrison Road, Market Harborough,
Leicestershire. LE16 7UL
Tel: 0116 2792299
Email: books@troubador.co.uk
Web: www.troubador.co.uk

ISBN 9781836281702

British Library Cataloguing in Publication Data.
A catalogue record for this book is available from the British Library.

Printed and bound in Great Britain by 4edge Limited
Typeset in 11pt Minion Pro by Troubador Publishing Ltd, Leicester, UK

Cover illustration by Jérôme Brasseur

THE BETRAYAL OF
JOHN MACHELE

To Aisha:
Sometimes a word is all
it takes.

Thanks
Ian

Ian M Robertson

For those who believed

CONTENTS

PRELUDE

Excerpt from the journal of Lieutenant John Clayson, HMS *Glenmore*:

Monday 29th August 1796

AM at 8 fired a Gun and made a Signal for a Court Martial to assemble on board at ½ past 9 the Court met to try a Midshipman of the Sandwich *for Disobedience of Orders and attempting to assassinate Mr Hill the 1st Lieut & to try a Marine for desertion.*

ALL MY OWN DOING

29th August 1796: HMS *Sandwich*:

THE NORE

I am John Machele.

This is my day and I intend to enjoy it. I've worked hard to make them organise this. From when I first got the idea, it worked like clockwork.

How to get myself out of the navy, which I never wanted to join in the first place?

I needed to plan it in such a way that I can save myself the trouble of putting a pistol ball in my brain and make someone take my life for me. They have already interfered when I've tried to drown myself by jumping overboard, and since then I know they are watching me.

But how to make certain that they can see no alternative but to court martial me and then have me hanged?

I learnt very early on after coming on board that orders must be obeyed. Captain Mosse said that to me himself. Everyone does what they are told on a Royal Navy ship. They are ruled by the Articles of War, with so many offences punishable by death.

It was almost too easy a plan to put into motion. Firstly, I had to disobey an order, so I made certain that I was somewhere on the ship that I had no business to be and that an officer would see me and order me to go somewhere else. The order came and I ignored it. It was repeated and I told him I would not do as he said. They – officers and the people on deck – cannot believe that an order would be ignored. That I didn't even answer the first command. God, don't they just hate it when they are not replied to? And as for saying to the first lieutenant that I wouldn't obey his order… well.

I knew how much Lieutenant Hills had a reputation for running a tight ship, so open defiance, disobedience and contempt, especially by telling him that he was no gentleman, was guaranteed to ensure that I was put under arrest. This first step in my plan worked even better than I had hoped, because Captain Mosse came on deck and he ordered me to be taken below. Now I had Lieutenant Hills precisely where I wanted him. Captain Mosse had, in effect, come to his rescue. How shaming, being told he was not a gentleman and seeing his commanding officer take charge of my little engineered incident.

But that was just the beginning. They kept me under close watch whilst deciding what to do about me. It was important to me that I was being watched. I had brought on board with me a pair of pistols, good ones too, not like the ones in the ship's armoury. They had been given to me with the rest of my uniform and equipment when I joined the Royal Scots Greys. Not the ordinary ones issued to the troopers, but hand-crafted ones as befitted a mounted officer.

I knew that with them watching me they would see me take them out of my sea chest and that someone would be sure to raise some sort of alarm. Sure enough, it was Lieutenant Hills who was summoned and who took them away from me. I had not planned it to be him. Any officer would have done, but this was working out well. The man whom I had disobeyed and insulted by saying he was no gentleman had now removed something of mine from my possession.

I began to feel myself concentrate on Lieutenant Hills, and there was only one more step to take to make my court martial inevitable. I would physically attack him. It was quite laughable really. My midshipman's dirk had been removed, as had my pistols, and all I had left was my penknife. Still, it was a weapon of sorts and could inflict damage of some kind. I had no qualms about threatening to cut his throat, and it was only the marine sentry's quick response that prevented it as I grabbed hold of Mr Hills. Captain Mosse, who someone had alerted, intervened again and this time ordered that I was to be clapped in irons.

So that was how I made damn sure that I would be court martialled, and not just court martialled but tried for a capital offence. Simple really. A few steps culminating in attempting to kill the first lieutenant, even if I only had a penknife! Oh, well done, John!

I think it's still quite early in the morning. It's hard to tell where I'm confined. I can't hear the bells, but I suppose the marine sentinels are changed every watch. What a boring job for them having to stand guard on the other side of the door with nothing else to do. We can't even exchange words. That has become quite clear to me when not one of them has answered any of my questions. I am certain today is the day. My big day. I can hear footsteps and voices. The sentinel stamps his feet as he comes to attention. The door opens and a lieutenant I don't think I've seen before beckons me out.

'Come, Mr Machele. Time for you to prepare for the court.'

What does he mean by that? Prepare for the court? I have been preparing for the court for many days now, so what else am I supposed to do?

'I am to escort you to the gunroom, where you will find your best uniform has been freshly pressed so you may look your best for the court. It is most important that you look your best,' the lieutenant continued.

'Yes, sir. Thank you, sir,' I replied.

Apparently, this is all that is expected of me, and we make our way to another deck: the lieutenant first, me second and a marine bringing up the rear.

How do they manage to go up and down those stairs? Come on, John, how long have you been on this ship? Ladders, ladders… why can't they call things by their proper names? What was my point? Oh yes. How hard it must be going from one deck to another carrying a musket. Why a musket? Why not just a pistol, or are pistols for the officers?

The gunroom seems strangely quiet. Normally, it is full to overflowing with all the midshipmen eating, drinking, some trying to sleep, others reading and rereading about navigation, but today there is no one there. Yes, there is. It is the chaplain. What is he doing here? Surely I should not be needing his services until the day of my execution or perhaps the day before so that I can pray with him. Have I somehow missed my own trial or erased it from my mind?

'Oh, Mr Machele, it grieves me to see you in this state. I have written a plea of my own saying how I felt that that of which you stand accused is not of your true character and that I have not witnessed you acting like this before, and requesting the court to show mercy,' said the chaplain, looking at me expectantly, but what he thought I was going to say apart from an expression of gratitude, I don't know. I gave no answer and waited for him to continue, which he did.

'John, I may call you John?'

I nodded my acquiescence.

'What do you intend to plead in your defence?'

I looked at him as though I did not understand what he meant and then said: 'I have no intention of pleading anything.'

'But, John, you must. Everybody pleads for mercy. Otherwise, the court will think it very odd indeed.'

I know what the chaplain is really saying. He is saying without saying that only a madman would not plead for mercy when faced with being sentenced to death. I am not mad but am perfectly sane, so I will make a plea for mercy, which will be proof of my sanity.

'Very well, Chaplain, I will plead for the court's mercy but, like you, I shall make it a plea in writing and hand it to the court along with yours. Is there pen and ink here?' I sat at the gunroom mess table and pondered what to write.

I must sound regretful and claim my behaviour to be not of my usual character. I will gently tug at their heartstrings by talking of a troubled past but without giving any details. I will make no direct mention whatsoever of my actions against Lieutenant Hills and throw myself on the mercy of the court. That's it, John, just enough but not sufficient to change their verdict.

I thought for a moment and then wrote just the one page. I folded it, asked for wax and sealed it so no one else could read it, and also accepted the chaplain's sealed plea. I swore to present both to the court, which seemed to give the chaplain satisfaction.

'Thank you, John. May God go with you,' said the chaplain, as he turned and walked aft into the gloom of the 'tween decks, his duty done.

My uniform was laid out for me and I removed my rather dirty working clothes I had been wearing whilst confined and saw the ship's barber waiting to shave me.

This could be risky. What if I was to suddenly jerk my head forward as I feel the blade begin to scrape the stubble from my throat? Don't be silly, John. That would spoil everything. If I did that, they would undoubtedly think I was mad. Or would they? Maybe they would think I was afraid to face the court and its logical outcome. No. Let him shave me and then I'll get dressed.

'Very well, Mr Machele,' said the unknown lieutenant, who clearly thought it was now time to formally introduce himself. 'I am Lieutenant Roberts; Third Lieutenant of His Majesty's ship *Glenmore*, and it is my duty to escort you to that ship for your court martial.'

Oh, so we are going to another ship, are we? Why is that? Never mind. If that's what they do, then so be it.

We make our way to the main deck and climb down into the waiting boat. Even though the seamen at the oars are avoiding looking at me directly, I know I am being watched very closely in case I try to throw myself overboard. Why would I want to do that? The sun is shining, the air is the freshest I have smelt for many days, and I am on my way to my court martial, which I have so cleverly engineered.

The journey by boat hasn't taken very long. Here we are. The bowman has hooked onto the Glenmore's *chains. She's much smaller than the* Sandwich, *only being a frigate of thirty-six guns, but that means an easier climb to get on board. Up we go. An extra marine escort is waiting as I step aboard. Remember your manners, John. I turn aft and salute the quarterdeck before I am taken to the great cabin for the main entertainment of this day, the 29th of August 1796, and I do so like entertainment. Always have, haven't I?*

VAUXHALL GARDENS

1786

All the world's a stage. Did I think of that? Not sure. Maybe I heard it somewhere, but it's the truth. Are we all here to entertain and be entertained? Vauxhall. Yes, that's where I heard it. What a place. I think I went there twice. I tried to go there a third time, but something happened to stop me. Oh yes, it was winter, so it was closed.

Where was I? Pay attention, John, pay attention. I am playing the lead role here at, what is after all, my very own court martial, even though I don't get to say much.

I think I was about ten years of age, anyway, still not too big to be carried around on someone's shoulders. Who was that I was with? No idea now. Just someone else who was "looking after" me. How many had there been? No idea. They come. They go. I go to them. I leave them. They leave me. But some things I know are more important than them with me or me with them.

Oh, Vauxhall Gardens; the people, the plays, the music, the colours, the noise, the smells. There were women with painted faces and men as well. All their faces were like masks.

Sometimes they had what they thought of as real masks. These were on the end of a short stick or handle which they brought up in their hands to cover their eyes and noses but left the rest of them on full display. Everyone pretended not to know who was behind the mask but, surely, they knew by their hair, their clothes, their height, their build, their manner, their gestures and, above all, their voices.

I never wore a mask or, at least, not one they were aware of. You see, they pretended to be anonymous, or pretended to be someone else so they could behave and say whatever they wanted regardless. I could do that because being me was being someone else. I decided who I was behind my non-existent mask and acted that part.

Did you know some events or entertainments were called "masques"? It just meant that everyone taking part wore a mask. What made that so different from the usual except it was French and they could charge more for the supposed sophistication?

I'd never seen so many people in one place before. It had taken simply ages to get through the crowds simply to find the entrance. My carrier, who had collected me from my home at the time and who was very smartly dressed, showed the piece of card to the gatekeeper, who waved us in.

'What's that card?' I asked.

'That's our special ticket. Can't get in without one or paying half a guinea.'

He showed me a piece of card just over one inch long and nearly as wide. It was engraved and printed in brown, with the price of admission clearly marked on it.

'I thought it was one shilling to get in here?' I queried.

'Oh yes, young sir, usually it is,' he explained, 'but tonight's a bit special. This is the Jubilee.'

'What's a Jubilee?' I asked.

'Well, young 'un, it's a celebration. Supposed to be celebrating fifty years of the gardens being opened; only it's fifty-four really. Still, the day's right. The 29th of May, and it don't matter too much if it's 1786 instead of 1782, does it? They do say the Prince of Wales as well as other members of the royal family will be here. This won't be an official royal event, and when they attend things like this they prefer to be incognito, but everyone knows who they are regardless,' he added, with what sounded like a touch of pride in his voice.

'Gosh, will I get to see them, do you think?' I said, gazing around at the throng surrounding us.

'I couldn't possibly say, but you may do. You might very well.'

I peered down and to one side and I'm not sure, but I think he winked at me. No idea what that meant at all. He changed the subject quickly.

'I bet you can't guess how many people are going to be here today. Sixty-one thousand, that's how many. Sixty-one thousand. Don't seem possible, does it?'

I had no idea what sixty-one thousand meant, but it was clearly a lot and many of them were in domino costumes, some in ordinary fancy dress and others, like us, in our best clothes for the occasion.

'Why are so many people wearing domino costumes? Both the women and the men. And why do the women in those costumes seem to have different shapes to the others?' I had noticed this straight away but couldn't think of any reason.

'My, you do ask a lot of questions. Well, when this Jubilee was announced, it was suggested that people may well want to come in these costumes. They didn't have to, but many have. So, you've seen different-shaped women, have you?' He looked up at me a while as if deciding what to say next. 'Sometimes ladies, society women, dress to make themselves look more fanciable. They wear specials items of undergarments to make their… erm… bosom bigger than it really is, and this foreigner, an Italian called Sestini, I think it was, got women to wear something else, further down at the back to make their bums, I mean bottoms, stick out under their petticoats. Fancy you noticing that at your age. Now, where was I? Oh yes, Mr Tyers, who owns the gardens, said he wanted women dressed as dominos, and this is his own words. He wanted them to "depend only on the elasticity and rotundity of nature". And that's all I'm going to say about that, young sir, so let's just keep moving along a bit, shall we?'

'But what about that lady there? The one dressed like a milkmaid wearing all white except for the gold watch at her side. Why does she wear that?' I persisted.

'Oh, she's quite famous, and the watch means she's expensive too. You don't need to know any more, not at your age.' I knew he sounded a bit embarrassed but I didn't know why. Still, grown-up things are grown-up things. I'd learnt that long ago.

And move along we did, and it was then that something happened that had a great effect on me. A memory I have held on to all my life. The lighting of the lamps in Vauxhall Gardens.

My carrier knew all about the lamps used to illuminate the gardens. He told me that usually there were about 2,000 glass globes and bucket lamps hanging from boughs of trees, with smaller ones suspended from the arches and obelisks. He added that for this occasion an extra 14,000 lamps were being employed. With me still on his shoulders, he took us to where the original 2,000 began and said to me, 'Watch this, young John. This is like magic.'

I didn't know what to expect. Two men stood, one at each side of an avenue of trees reaching far into the dusky distance. They nodded to each other and one applied a burning torch to a fuse on one side and the other to a fuse on the opposite side. In a matter of seconds, the avenue was lit from one end to the other.

The crowd gasped and then, as one, cheered and cheered.

My carrier explained to me that originally each lamp had to be lit by hand, but someone had designed a system whereby each lamp was joined to its neighbour by a flaxen fuse soaked in a spirit so the lamps appeared to light almost simultaneously.

I was enchanted, enthralled, captivated by this. The sight of flames being created and controlled so easily. To have that power at your fingertips must be a wonderful thing. And what a colour. Most of the lamps were blue, and although some of the audience began to cough as the escaping smoke reached them, I relished it. The smell of whale or seal blubber oil might not suit everyone, but to me it said there were flickering flames nearby.

But back to that first visit on that man's shoulders. Apart from the noise, the people and the sights, I think I remember a rather curious thing happened. I had this sense that I was being watched. I'd had that feeling before, but that was when I was asking to be watched in those little entertainments I performed with other children in some of the houses I had lived in. But this was different. There was a man who was looking at me and not at the lighting of the lamps. He was staring intensely at me and my carrier.

'Best get down now, John,' said my carrier. 'Here, give me your hands.'

He held my hands and swung me across his back and onto the ground, where I stood looking at the gentleman coming towards us. I saw that he had detached himself from a group of exceedingly well-dressed men and women who waited some distance away. He seemingly had no need to weave in and out of the crowds. They parted before him and the people whispered and pointed at us as it became clear that we were his intended target.

He was an upright, slightly portly man who I believe I had seen more than once before. He came right up to us and stood staring down at me. He looked up, and he and my carrier exchanged nods. Well, I thought they exchanged nods, but if I remember correctly the nod from my carrier was much more than a mere inclining of his head. Could he be bowing but without the other people noticing it as such? I wondered.

'So, this is the boy, is it?' said the gentleman.

'Aye, it is, sir,' replied my carrier.

'How are you, lad? What do you think of all this?'

'It is very fine, sir, and the cakes look nice,' I replied. This seemed to amuse the gentleman no end and so I added, 'And the women keep hiding their faces behind masks or fans, which is very strange.'

'Oh yes, the ladies can be very strange indeed, but it's a few years before you need to concern yourself with that,' he chortled. 'Here, boy, a half guinea. See how many cakes you can buy with that. Well, I must take my leave. My party is getting restless. Good day to you both.' And he returned to his group of exquisitely dressed men and women who had waited at a distance and now, to my young eyes, were vying to be the closest to him as they moved off together in what I could only describe as a procession through the parting crowds.

'Who was that gentleman who gave me a half guinea?' I asked the man who was once again carrying me. 'I'm certain I've seen him before.'

'Never you mind who he was. All you need to know is that he is a very important personage who has your best interests at heart, and don't you forget he gave you that half guinea. That should tell you how important you are to him.'

We moved through the crowds to a small booth, which my carrier told me had been especially reserved for us. This was a very clever thing indeed, I thought. Someone had had the idea of purchasing old carriages and coaches that had fallen into disrepair and were going to be broken up and had had them cut in half from door to door. This made two private alcoves, with a roof and seats already in them. How clever!

Our one had the number 47 displayed on it, and no sooner had we seated ourselves than a waiter with the same number pinned to his coat came over and asked us what refreshments we wished to order.

'Well, John,' said my carrier, 'what are you going to spend your half guinea on?'

I ordered two cheesecakes, that was 8d; four heart cakes, another 8d, and six Shrewsbury cakes, which was another shilling. I loved sweet things then. I was going to share my good fortune with my carrier, so I ordered a dish of beef and some ham, both at a shilling each, and two quart mugs of table beer, which was another 8d. My carrier did say he would normally have had claret, but since he was looking after me then, he should only drink small beer, being not very alcoholic at all.

I was a bit surprised when the beef and ham came. It was sliced so thin you could see through it. I heard later that the cook who carved the meat boasted that he could cover the whole area of Vauxhall Gardens with the slices from one ham. Still, I had only spent five shillings, which meant that even after giving the waiter a sixpenny tip I was the proud owner of five shillings.

I didn't know what the cakes I'd ordered were made of, but the waiter was able to tell me. The cheesecakes – and they were quite large – didn't have any cheese in them at all. They were made from finely mashed potatoes with eggs and butter and loads of nutmeg whisked into them and the mixture poured into a dish lined with shortcrust pastry for baking. Who would have thought it? The heart cakes were sweet and buttery, flavoured with lemon and full of juicy currants. And the Shrewsbury cakes, well, they were like big fat biscuits, crisp and crunchy but soft in the middle.

This was a good place to sit and eat and watch the parading visitors. I saw many young, and not so young, men and women moving away from the brightly lit areas.

'What's down there? Where are they all going?' I asked.

'Well, young John,' replied my carrier, showing every sign of embarrassment yet again (I seem to have a habit of asking grown-ups questions they don't want to give me the answers to), 'there's the Druid Walk, the Lover's Walk and the Dark Walk, but you don't want to fuss yourself about that, not at your age.' He gazed around and, pulling his watch from a pocket in his elegantly cut coat, said, 'Well, my lad, 'tis time I was getting you back home, or your people will be wondering where we've got to.'

So saying, I clambered back onto his shoulders and we made our way back to the riverbank where our especially reserved wherry was waiting for us for that trip back up and across the Thames and so to my house at the time where he returned me to the care of my people. I never knew his name but wondered if I would see him again.

I do remember that I still had five shillings of my very own left over from that half guinea and all the cakes and sweet things I consumed. I also remember the amount of time I spent out of bed that night being sicker than I had ever been before or have been since.

MY CLEVERLY PLANNED
COURT MARTIAL

29th August 1796

All this pomp and circumstance here today and it's all because of me. Why does everyone look so solemn? They aren't on trial for their lives. If I'm not in the least concerned, unless they find me not guilty, which they can't possibly do, then why should they be? They wouldn't understand even if I told them, so why bother? Nobody understands or wants to know what I think and feel. Whoever asks me what I want? Any so-called conversations with me concerning my well-being are usually restricted to 'And how are you today, sir?'

All very polite, restrained, distanced. Governed by social niceties and acceptable manners, which are so important in polite society. No genuine interest in my responses at all and, on most occasions, I reply in a formulaic way, 'I am very well, sir, and you?' Neither of us is remotely interested in the health of the other. It is merely an accepted ritual before the real issue is raised. One day, I'll say what I mean: 'Not at all well, sir. If you knew what I was thinking, you wouldn't ask me how I was but probably keep well away from me.' Since they are stuck in a ritual where they only hear expected responses, that is probably what they would hear anyway. However, there is often something about my manner or tone of voice as I look them in the eye, something I am very good at, and appear to smile that would, maybe, slightly, momentarily confuse and even disturb them.

But back to today, my big day. What a scene! It looks more like a cleverly staged entertainment with each person where they are supposed to be and with a particular role to play.

Facing me and the rest of the great cabin on the Glenmore, seated behind a large table, are the captains sat in judgement over me. Shouldn't my dirk be on that table so that when they decide I'm guilty then the point would be towards me? No, I remember somebody telling me once that when an officer is court martialled, his sword is the first thing he looks for when the court reconvenes. That's right. Point towards the prisoner equals guilty; hilt towards the prisoner equals innocent. No such thing for me, though, because I am only a midshipman. Neither fish nor fowl. I do not hold the king's commission and am not even the holder of a warrant. I can be promoted and demoted at the captain's whim. Oh yes. I'm surprised they could find a table large enough to seat eleven captains behind, but there they all are: Captains Trollope (he is in the middle and seems to be in charge), Knight, McDougall, Daily, Ferrier, Duff (the captain of the Glenmore, so really this is his great cabin), Surridge, Ross, Mansfield, Bessell and Douglas. Captain Trollope is referred to as the president, which means he is presiding in a senior position to the other ten.

Trollope. Trollope? What sort of name is that for a captain of one of His Majesty's fighting ships? I've known a fair few trollops over the years, but none of them looked like him. Thinking back, I never really knew what some of them did look like. People look different in flickering candlelight, and most of those trollops weren't there in the morning and, come to think of it, neither was my purse on a couple of occasions. Mind you, I don't know how good a fighting captain this Trollope is but I've seen trollops fight: scratching, biting, pulling each other's hair. Always attracts a good crowd, that does. Just a minute, didn't one of the other middies say something about him when he sailed in and moored his ship, the Glatton, *within sight of us on the* Sandwich? *Yes, he is a fighting Trollope if the story is true. That middie, which one was it? It doesn't matter. Anyway, he said this Captain Trollope had fitted the* Glatton *completely with carronades. Nasty, short-muzzled things, fifty-six of them in total, thirty-two- and sixty-eight-pounders. That's the weight of each ball they can fire. According to that middie, Trollope is quite the hero. Only last month, July, he engaged on his own a French squadron of eight vessels: one of fifty guns, five frigates, a brig and a cutter. The* Glatton *punished them so severely that he was able to drive them all into the harbour at Flushing, where at least one of them sank. Nobody said how many French were killed or wounded, but the* Glatton *had only two men wounded, one of whom was the captain of marines, who died later from his wounds. Yes, that makes Trollope a hero. I wish I had been there instead of being stuck on the* Sandwich, *which didn't look as if it was ever going anywhere. I can imagine the glorious noise, the flaming flashes from the guns' muzzles as they belched forth their solid harbingers of death and, above all, the smell of the all-enveloping clouds of eddying smoke.*

Where was I? Oh yes. So much gold lace on display. I can tell who has made the most prize money out of them all by the freshness of their dress uniforms. Others, although wearing their best finery, have a degree of tarnishing to their bullioned epaulettes and salt stains on their faded coats. It doesn't matter how hard a captain's personal servant tries to keep best uniforms looking like best uniforms, because long periods on blockade duty in the unpredictable and unforgiving weather of the English Channel will always take their toll. Still, these are their best uniforms, and they are bound by tradition to wear them regardless of their condition, and they try to look their best in them.

Even I have been presented with my dress uniform, minus my dirk, of course. What on earth do they think I might do? Attack Lieutenant Hills again. Why would I go to all that trouble? I've done that already and that is why my plan has worked so well. No need to do it again. Anyway, it looks as though Lieutenant Hills has a very important role to play in today's proceedings. He is to be the prosecutor, and I'm fascinated to see how he will perform. Will he show himself to be gentlemanly in his questioning of the witnesses or show all assembled that I was perfectly correct when I said, 'You are no gentleman, sir.'

So, even I am wearing my dress uniform for what it is worth. It hardly seems worthy of the name. It is plain in the extreme. Navy blue coat, white waistcoat, black stock, white knee breeches, stockings and buckled shoes. Gilt buttons and those odd little white flashes on my collar saying I may look like an officer, but really, I'm only a midshipman. Plain, plain, plain. They should have seen me in my dress uniform when I was a cornet in the Royal Scots Greys. Now that was a uniform; I should have worn that today. More gold braid and lace on it than any of those captains have got on theirs. My God, that would make them sit up and take notice of me. I wonder where it went.

It's not really the plainness of my uniform I'm concerned about. Navy blue and white go very well together. It's that mark on my breeches that could embarrass me. I was so careful dressing in the gunroom, but I only had the dancing light of a lantern and that was being held by someone else. Couldn't I even be trusted with a lantern? Probably not, especially with all that tar and cordage about. What did they think I would do, set fire to the ship and take them all down with me? There's nothing that sailors fear more than a fire on board.

Why put me in a cell by the cable tier? It stank and I know what of. It was the smell of old mud and seaweed that couldn't be completely squeezed out of the anchor cables, no matter how hard the straining people worked at the capstan. To smell this bad, the cables must have been in use for years in so many different anchorages. The Thames wasn't the cleanest, either, with all sorts of waste floating in it, looking for a route to the sea or a way of sinking to the bottom to join that stagnant, oozing mass. I could tell, it was obvious really, that no sooner had the outgoing tide carried the rubbish away than the incoming one brought lots of it back to join the new rubbish.

So, that stench surrounding me in my cell. God, it stank in there, and the person standing guard, the sentinel, didn't smell much better. He shouldn't be called a sentinel but a "scent in hell". I like that. Very good indeed, John.

Oh yes, why was I put in that cell? They said it was for my own safety. I think what they meant was that being locked up on my own without any way of getting hold of any sharp instruments or firearms would save me from myself. They have no idea that I have no intention of joining my Redeemer by my own hand but am getting them to do it for me.

So, how did I get that mark on my breeches? I was marched out of the gunroom to a waiting boat under escort. Up a couple of decks, past some guns. Did I brush against one of them? What about the stairs, oops, get it right, John, ladders, they call them? I bet it's tar. How do I get that off? The whole journey was from darkness into light. I passed people. Seamen in their messes, my fellow midshipmen in the gunroom. No one said anything. No 'How are you?' or 'May you be lucky, John.' Just as though no one knew me. It was like they had never seen me before, but isn't that the way it has always been?

Well, let the show commence. This is really like watching an entertainment. It should be a dramatic play but I'm not so sure now. I can feel a sense of boredom coming over me already.

Why are the charges against me being read out? I know what they are because I was there.

Lieutenant Hills is calling a veritable string of witnesses to my behaviour. This should be good. Will they remember what happened as well as I do? I can always correct them if they get it wrong, I suppose, but as long as what they have to say means I'm found guilty then why should I bother? Who is coming to centre stage first? I wonder. Oh yes. It's that master's mate: Milner. George Milner. I'm glad I don't have to remember their names. So many on the ship I don't recall ever having met. I've probably seen them but never been properly introduced. I see how this works now. The witnesses are called one at a time by name, and then they have to swear an oath to tell the truth and after that Lieutenant Hills asks them questions.

Hills is asking him about the evening of 19th August, which was when I began all this. That was when I started to disobey orders by not leaving the deck when I was told to. This is what really annoyed the lieutenant more than anything else... when I told him he was no gentleman. This witness states on oath that he heard me say it. This all sounds very matter of fact. Not quite the way I would have described what happened, but then I can't expect these seamen to be the quality of actor that I am. I suppose the witnesses can only answer what questions are put to them. There's something else I've noticed. Those captains there can ask questions as well if they want to. I wonder how Lieutenant Hills reacts to that. Does he think that if he had asked the right questions then they wouldn't have to interrupt?

Who is next? Another quartermaster. Is he a mate as well? Why not just say he is someone's friend? Mate sounds a bit common to me. Which one is this? James Hockless. Same questions. Mostly the same answers but some a bit different. Agreed that I disobeyed the order to go below and that I insulted Lieutenant Hills, but Hockless adds that I was led away by the ship's corporal.

Not another quartermaster's mate? It's very important to get their rank exactly right. If you got them wrong, that would be nearly as bad as denying an officer was a gentleman, wouldn't it? What's this fellow James Ventriss got to say for himself? Nothing much that we haven't heard already, except two of them had to use force on me to remove me from the deck.

If only they would ask me what happened, I would be only too pleased to tell them, and in much more detail as well as in a much more entertaining manner. Everyone else here – and quite a few have come to watch – gives every appearance of being very interested indeed. Am I the only one here who thinks this whole affair should be moving along at a much brisker pace? There should be real drama, a sense of building to a climax with high emotion as the prisoner, me, is tried for his life. But no.

Next witness please. I've seen him before, probably been properly introduced and even had supper with him, but that's always been one of my problems, the old memory for names. Faces I'm good with, but names? Yes, Lieutenant Flatt. Will Hills be able to get any more detailed information from him than the previous witnesses? I wonder. I'm certain he will because – and I'm sure they are not supposed to – they are bound to have discussed what they are going to say today. Can't foresee one officer not fully supporting another. Not at all the gentlemanly thing to do.

How am I going to get this mark off my breeches? I mustn't rub at it. That will only make it worse. Anyway, people may wonder what I'm doing sitting here rubbing at myself.

Just a minute… Lieutenant Flatt clearly has an eye and a memory for detail. He was the officer of the watch that evening of the 19th and heard, and committed to memory, everything that happened. He's now quoting my very words when I was being removed from the deck. He really is very good. Very good indeed. He's reciting an exchange between me and Hills.

"'Mind, Mr Hills, you've collared me,'" and Mr Hills said, "I did not," and Mr Machele said, "You did, damn your eyes, and you shall repent it.'"

Very well remembered indeed. I am sorely tempted to applaud him for his performance but sense the court would deem that to be most inappropriate.

Hello, what's the president, old Trollope, asking him?

'Did you think the prisoner was perfectly in his senses and sober that evening?'

Now, what's he going to say to that? I wonder.

'I think in my opinion he was in his senses and sober,' responds Flatt.

Quite right. Well said. You have no idea how sober and in my right senses I was then and am now. Oh well, that seems to be all that is going to be said about the first day of my plan, and now they are moving on to the 21st of August. Didn't I do anything of importance on the 20th? Never mind, there's still lots of the story to come.

Gosh, here comes a collection of marines. Three of them. All wanting to tell their bits of my story. They always look like the toy soldiers I had as a lad in their red jackets and white cross belts. *They stand so straight they look as though they are carved from blocks of wood. They never look directly at you when being spoken to or when replying. They have been trained to look through people, not literally, but staring at a point just over your head.*

The first one is Thomas Halsey. He's duly sworn in and Hills is asking him if he heard me accusing Hills of taking some of my property. Halsey agrees this was so but does not know what I was referring to.

Time for the next one. Marine Shepherd. He confirms that I had collared Lieutenant Hills and heard my accusation that Hills had taken my property. He says he didn't know what was being referred to but was ordered to keep me there whilst Lieutenant Hills went to fetch Captain Mosse. Marine Shepherd tells the court that he was concerned about being involved in what was happening between a senior lieutenant and a midshipman.

What he actually says is: 'I was afraid of being in a hobble about the tussle.' *What a delightful expression. I've never heard that before. I wonder where he comes from. I'd like to talk with him for a while to see what other expressions he uses in his everyday chats with the other marines.*

Just a minute. Time for marine number three. That's it. March four paces, halt with a great stamping of feet. Why do they have to do that? It is so loud. Marine Mahalem takes the oath and stands at ease to give his version of events of 21st August. Even standing at ease is a noisy process. Why on earth is it called by that term? He's clearly not at ease being here and giving him permission to be at ease isn't going to help matters. The thing about the marines is that they do everything by numbers. There is a marines way and the wrong way, and heaven help you if you choose the wrong way. Oops, what's that he's saying? Yes. Yes, that's the same story so far, but now he's adding something else. This is something really important. The penknife. The good Marine Mahalem reports, whilst gazing at a point on the stern gallery above the president's head, that he saw me with my penknife and heard me say that I would run it into Lieutenant Hills. He then tells how he took hold of me and that the boatswain's mate removed the knife from my grasp. When the knife is produced for him to inspect, he agrees that it is the one I threatened Hills with.

Exit Marine Mahalem with much stamping of feet and a rigid posture that would have done credit to the mainmast of the Sandwich *on a windless day.*

There is no mention this time of what property of mine I was accusing Lieutenant Hills of taking, but never mind, I'm sure that will become clear in the fullness of time.

Here comes that boatswain's mate. Driscoll. Marines and sailors. They could be quite different species. No stamping about, never looking at whomsoever they are addressing. He is just standing awkwardly and shuffling his feet, whilst his fingers seem to be very interested in the seams of his trousers. What's he got to say? Ah yes, the same as the others, but he is saying that he heard – or rather he is more willing to say that he heard – me say to Lieutenant Hills: 'Hills, I will cut your throat.'

That's right, Driscoll. That's exactly what I said. Driscoll is also shown my penknife, which he identifies as the one he took from me.

I must pay more attention. Lieutenant Hills is asking Driscoll another question. What now?

'Did he appear, in your opinion, to be sober or in a sense of insanity?'

Why is he asking this? Another witness has already said I was sober and in my senses. Didn't he believe him? No, Hills, you certainly are not a gentleman if you question the word of a previous witness. Someone who has sworn an oath to tell the truth. Does that mean you are calling him a liar? Still, what is this boatswain's mate going to reply to this question?

'He appeared to me to be sober and I should suppose in his senses,' replies Driscoll.

Well said, Driscoll. You could see that I knew full well what I was doing. Driscoll is rubbing his hands up and down his trousers, and when he is told there are no more questions for him and he can "stand down", his sense of relief is almost tangible as he not so much marches but rather continues his shuffling to the cabin door.

Time for another marine by the sound of the marching boots and the thundering stamp as he stands in the "attention" position and then "at ease". An officer, no less. Lieutenant Thomas Young. He seems to be very accurate in recalling the events he was involved in.

Captain Trollope is leading the questioning. I wonder why. Does he think Lieutenant Hills is not doing the job properly? Surely not. Trollope doesn't seem overly interested in the details of the events but is following his own line of enquiry.

'Did you think him at the time of this scuffle in his

sober senses or that his conduct then was that of a man in a state of insanity?'

What is this all about? Why these repeated questions about whether or not I was either drunk or mad? I am not mad, so why keep on asking people if I am? They only have to ask me. Come on then, Lieutenant Young, how are you going to answer?

'I did not think he was a madman. I thought he was in his senses.'

Quite right, man. Quite right. Exactly what I would have told them if only they would ask.

I know this next witness. It's Lieutenant Johnson. Come on, swear him in and let us all hear even more about what I have never denied doing, shall we? What's this? Hills has only asked him if he saw me in irons and if he heard me say I would shoot him. He agrees to both of those, and I can sense that Hills has more questions to put to him, but Trollope has taken over yet again. Here we go. The same line he always takes.

'Did you think the prisoner at that time was in a state of insanity or in his sober sense?'

Johnson replies, 'I thought he was in his sober senses and no ways insane.'

Trollope isn't going to let this go, is he?

'How long has he been in the ship?'

'About two months,' answers Johnson.

Keep going, Trollope. Ask him in a slightly different way, why don't you? He really does want someone to say that I am mad, doesn't he?

'Have you heard of any symptoms of his insanity during that time?'

Trollope sounds so determined to get the answer he wants that there is a hint of exasperated impatience in his voice. He really should remember as the president of the court that witnesses are under oath and that they can be punished if they are found not to be honest in their answers.

'No, of none,' Johnson asserts.

He has a slightly puzzled expression on his face which I take to mean that he feels he has already declared that he did not consider me insane and that he is being pressured to alter his statement. Of course, why didn't I think of this before? This is a properly, legally convened court of law. It is governed by process and precedent. If it can be found that I am not responsible for my actions due to being insane, then I must be discharged on those grounds. Not one witness has been prepared to say that they believed me to be insane, so my plan is working well. I would be willing to place a wager of everything I have that the court has never experienced anyone like me before.

I don't think Hills has performed too badly. He asked what he thought were the right questions, but he didn't always get the answers he hoped for. It's amazing how people see and hear different things even though they are all in the same place at the same time. Why he should be surprised at that, I don't know. I could have told him that.

Ah. Captain Mosse has been called. This should be interesting. Look at him. The man positively reeks of discomfiture. Oh, Captain Mosse, all you can do is tell as much of the truth as you dare, which is not that much. The court wants to know how it was that I came to be on board as a midshipman in the first place. Do you know what, so would I!

So, I came recommended, did I? Who on earth by? I didn't ask to be here, so who did? Ah. So, he feels unable to answer that, does he? Very odd that he can't say, but doesn't that sum up very nicely how my life has always been run by someone certainly unknown to me, so why should anyone else know who it is? None of their business anyway. This is just another one of those things that happen to me. People I don't know make decisions for me. Still, that's why I'm here in this courtroom, isn't it? To put a stop to all that. This is my life. This is my decision being taken by me. Odd to see the way those captains looked at each other and simply nodded when Mosse said he could not disclose who had recommended me. I could tell that Mosse did not know the answer himself. What were they nodding about?

Hello, who's that captain staring at me? He's been doing that since this began. Short, wiry chap; third from the right. What's his name? Should remember. They were named at the start of the trial. Knight. That's it. Captain Knight. You stare as much as you like, sir, and I'll stare back. I don't know you and you don't know me. In fact, there's no point in us knowing each other because it will be a very short acquaintanceship indeed.

Their next question might give an answer to that. They are asking Mosse how long I've been aboard, and he's looking so confused that he stumbles over his answer and says I've been under his command for two or three months. That's rubbish. What must they think of him if he doesn't even know how long I have been in the Royal Navy? They ask him if he thinks I am insane, but when he tells them he thinks not, he does add that he knew me to be a 'violent young man'. *They seem very interested in the fact that when I was delivered on board it was a condition requested that I not be allowed ashore, and Captain Mosse states that I never asked to go ashore.*

I indicate by raising my right arm that I might be allowed to ask Captain Mosse a question. The court agrees and a hush settles over the cabin.

What do they think I am going to ask? A very simple question but one designed to completely throw him off course.

I ask him if I ever asked to go ashore, and he looks around the cabin as if seeking a rescue but eventually says:

'Yes, you may have done.'

I then ask him if he left instructions for the officer of the watch to that effect when he went ashore himself. Captain Mosse states that he had and, turning directly to the president, adds that the civilian who had brought me on board had told him that I was not to be allowed ashore.

That is what I wanted him to say. What sort of captain takes what are effectively orders from an unknown civilian about how he manages affairs aboard his own ship? Let us see how the court reacts to that. The next question should be telling indeed.

But there is no next question. That's odd, and Mosse has the look of someone very relieved indeed as he is told he can stand down. He has really not enjoyed this at all.

The president of the court, Captain Trollope, stares directly at me and says: 'Mr Machele, do you have anything which you wish to say to the court in your defence?'

I take three steps forward towards the table where that

coterie of captains sit and hand over both of the sealed, folded papers to him, replying: 'I believe that which I say is better read than heard in court. I give you also a plea on my behalf from the chaplain of the *Sandwich*, which he humbly requests you take note of sir.'

I like the way I put that. Very grown up. Clearly the words of a sane person indeed. Let there be no doubt in anyone's mind about that.

'Thank you, Mr Machele. We will retire to deliberate on our decision.' All the captains stand and bow to the room.

"Retire to deliberate on our decision" indeed. The next thing I know is that the court is ordered to be cleared, meaning everybody leaves and the captains stay. What an odd expression.

A marine enters, stamps his feet and indicates that I should follow him. As I turn, I spy my banker fellow, my friend as he now is, Mr Brooks. He's standing at the back waiting to be part of the clearing of the court. He nods and smiles at me in what I assume he believes to be an encouraging way. I nod an acknowledgement but do not smile back.

I'm not sure why he is here but here he is. What I do know is that we have been involved with one another on and off for a number of years and that now I class him as my friend. I was never certain of exactly how he came to be chosen for me as my man of business, but that is what my life has always been like. There are things I know, things I don't know, and things I very much would like to know. All that I do know with any certainty is that there are things that people, whoever they may be, will not let me know. Do they have any idea what it is like not to have any knowledge of who your parents are? Just to be constantly told that a certain personage has your best interests at heart but you are not permitted to know his name. There are times when I feel that I am not me at all but a puppet. Puppeteers pull my strings and I am manipulated to do their bidding. It has always been so. Somewhere in the background, away from my eyes, all is arranged for me and has been over the years.

BROOKS & BROWN

THE ARRANGEMENT

1792

The initial request to George Brooks had been to care for John Machele according to instructions that would be communicated to him as and when necessary. They always came in the same way. He would hear a carriage pull up outside his house and a plainly but immaculately dressed person in bottle green would hand him a letter, nod and say, 'Mr Brooks, the service you are providing does not go unrecognised.'

Respectability, responsibility and discretion were George Brooks's bywords, as would be expected of one of the founding partners of a private banking house in Chancery Lane, London, some eight years before, together with Richard Master, Edward Dawson, John Kirton and Ralph Clayton. Ralph Clayton had left the firm in 1791, and Dixon joined them as a junior partner, with the bank being named Master, Dawson, Brooks, Kirton & Dixon.

Respectability was established by his address in Green Street, Grosvenor Square, one of the most prestigious, fashionable and expensive areas in London. As a banker,

George Brooks was well aware of the class of people living in the area. There were thirty-seven peers (including those with Irish and Scots titles, which didn't necessarily carry the same cachet as English ones), eighteen baronets, fifteen "honourables" and thirty-nine "ladies". King George III's brother the Duke of Gloucester had a large, detached house in Upper Grosvenor Street, and there were also five non-royal dukes living in the immediate vicinity. Two foreign members of their own nobility had residences there: namely Baron Alvensleben of Hanover and the Duke of Orléans, more popularly referred to as "Philippe Égalité". From the army, bearing in mind that commissions up to a certain rank could be purchased and therefore rank was often an indicator of wealth, there were fifteen officers ranging from captain to general and one surgeon. The navy's presence, where commissions could not be bought, consisted of two admirals, three captains and also a surgeon.

Responsibility came with his firm's management of their customers' deposited funds.

Discretion was part of his everyday life as a banker, with details of customers' accounts sacrosanct. What happened between a bank and its customers, as far as the bank was concerned, had the strength of the rule of the confessional at its heart. Customers who had been refused loans or received requests for overdrafts to be cleared before any further advances would be made had been known to broadcast what they regarded as the "cheek" or the ungentlemanly behaviour of the bank concerned. Whilst their friends may have been a willing audience, often through a shared experience, customers who behaved like this found it cut little ice with their bankers and, strangely enough, when they threatened to transfer their business to another bank, found their custom, regrettably, declined without sufficient funds or unmortgaged collateral.

John Machele had first come into George Brooks's life in 1792, when John was sixteen.

Brooks well remembered the first contact with Mr Brown. He who, whatever the time of year, was always so well dressed in what could be described as a livery of bottle green but cut extremely fashionably by a tailor of repute. Mr Brown presented his request to open an account on someone else's behalf and the necessity for strict confidentiality.

'I can assure you, sir,' said Brooks, 'that an establishment such as ours would not be in the business of banking very long if our customers felt we did not offer a confidential service. I do have to explain to you, though, sir, that it is not in our interests to handle accounts for unknown parties who, and I'm sure you will not take offence over this, may use their access to their account to withdraw funds in excess of their deposits. This can place both us and the customer concerned in a potentially embarrassing position when, and this is an extreme measure, we as an institution have to refuse to honour the customer's bill drawn against us.'

'Sir,' interrupted Brown, 'you misunderstand me. My master, the personage whom I represent, does not, in any way, see himself as requesting a line of credit or even allowing this account to be overdrawn under any circumstances. Should the balance fall below an agreed level then, on being notified, I shall immediately arrange for the necessary funds to be deposited. The monies in this account are to be treated by your bank as a fund for investment on my master's behalf under your usual terms of business, with an additional percentage of, shall we say, five per cent, to yourself in addition to any expenses you may incur on our behalf. As I am sure you will understand, the agreement, in writing, will concern an account in my name and not that of the personage concerned, and all deposits will be in coin of the realm to lessen any possible, inadvertent or accidental breaches of confidentiality stemming from the use of bills drawn on other banks.'

'Well, Mr Brown,' said George Brooks, looking him full in the face and thinking that this was not so very out of the ordinary, 'this all seems very clear to me, and you can rest assured of the bank's best intentions in this matter. The opening and managing of the account present no problem whatsoever, but surely I get the impression that there may be certain requirements attached to our acceptance of your custom which at the moment have not been spoken of.'

'Indeed, sir,' continued Brown. 'There is a young person of sixteen years by the name of John Machele whom my master wishes to see well equipped for adult life and with that in mind has decided to enrol him in Mr Bettesworth's Naval Academy so that he is fitted out for a profession as an officer in the Royal Navy, a profession for which my master has a particular fondness. A requirement of this account being opened with your bank is that you,

Mr Brooks, be prepared to be named as having the care of him, and that all correspondence from the academy regarding this young man goes via yourself. That is all you are required to do, apart from meeting whatever expenses are considered necessary. I trust you feel able to do this?'

'Yes, sir, I do,' responded Brooks, with a hint of puzzlement in his voice. 'It seems a duty more usually carried out by a lawyer acting in parentis, but I see no problem with this.'

Mr Brown gazed around the room as though thinking of the best way to proceed. 'I think that we, that is the personage on whose behalf I act, will be requiring a very personal service regarding Master Machele. I understand when you say that having the care of someone is usually a duty carried out by a lawyer, but we are seeking to minimise the number of people directly involved. A lawyer would certainly serve, and he could be responsible for drawing on funds and making necessary payments. However, in our experience, lawyers get bogged down in the legal niceties. They have too many "*heretofores*" and "*in future to be referred to as the party of the first, second or even third parts*" to allow for the main considerations of our proposed agreement to be simple, fluid and flexible,' said Mr Brown, almost conspiratorially, hoping to draw Brooks in more as a partner than an agent.

Mr Brooks supported his chin on his steepled fingers and gave his visitor a quizzical look. His left eyebrow seemed to rise of its own accord.

'Mr Brown, what is it precisely that you are requiring this bank to do that needs our services to be flexible and fluid, and what exactly do you mean by these words, sir? As I have said, as far as things have gone at the moment, I see no major difficulties, but I detect there is considerably more which you are going to add.'

Mr Brown fixed him with a look that conveyed the message, *Trust me, I am going to be completely honest with you*, a look that George Brooks had seen before from many of the bank's customers, which invariably meant, *I am going to lie to you.*

'You are, of course, correct in your assumption. It is this bank and you in particular who has been deemed the most appropriate business and person to be entrusted with this task. The bank, of which you are a partner, has a most excellent reputation, as you have already stated to me, and you, as a gentleman, have received the strongest of all recommendations. It is not just a question of probity, but your observed approach to business matters indicates that you are someone who can respond rapidly to changing circumstances and almost invariably take the right steps to deal with them.'

'That is all very nice to hear, but I fear you are not yet addressing what may be called the nub of the matter, sir,' interjected George Brooks. He had been flattered many times before in his position as a partner in a firm of bankers and was only too aware that, without fail, it presaged a request that he was unable to grant.

'There is, as you so rightly point out, something more. The core of the matter is this,' continued the man in the bottle green suit. 'By having the care of Master Machele, there will be certain requirements of a more personal nature for you to perform. I say you, sir, and not one of your partners and certainly not one of your clerks. The additional five per cent we are offering is, if you wish to see it as such, a fee for these services. Should you agree to these terms which we, or rather the personage on whose behalf I am here today, are putting before you, which are advantageous to both the bank and yourself, then these services will not go unrecognised.'

Brooks found himself beginning to lose patience, feeling a lot was being said whilst nothing was being said. He rolled his eyes towards the ceiling in frustration.

'Sir, Mr Brown, we need to be more explicit. What role apart from managing the account and meeting whatever expenses are incurred do you actually want me to carry out?'

'Very good, sir,' responded Mr Brown. He took a deep breath and prepared to tell all he felt permitted to.

'John Machele has grown up being looked after by a succession of different carers. Families who have been paid for their services. He has no knowledge of his own parentage, and under no circumstances will I disclose any information pertaining to it to you. This same principle has been applied to all his carers. He has been well educated by private tutors and coached in good manners that he may progress in society. He is not aware of the plan for him to go to the Naval Academy, but he has previously shown himself to be amenable to moving from one place to another. Once our agreement has been signed, then we will arrange for him to meet you to explain that you will be managing his affairs for him, in effect, having the care of him.'

'But the specifics, the specifics, man,' interrupted Mr Brooks, controlling his temper with great difficulty, placing his hands flat on his desk and half rising from his chair.

'You will be required, on a second meeting, to acquaint him with the decision that has been taken for him to send him to the Naval Academy, with a view to his having a career as a naval officer. He should take that fairly well, as I said before. We would then like you to escort him to meet Mr Bettesworth, the proprietor, and supervise his enrolment. That is all there is to it. Keep an eye on his progress and be prepared to perform any similar services in the future. This proviso is to form part of our agreement, which will remain in place until he reaches his majority. There, does that fully explain things for you, sir?'

'Indeed, indeed, Mr Brown,' George Brooks replied, sitting back in his chair. 'I assume you will require the reports on Master Machele's progress to be held here for you to read at your master's pleasure?'

'Quite so, quite so,' agreed Mr Brown.

'And' Mr Brooks continued, feeling the time was right to finalise the details of the agreement, 'if I need to contact you with some urgency, then how should I do that?'

'Ah, Mr Brooks, a good question, and my reply to you should be taken in the spirit of good humour in which it is offered,' his eyes twinkling as he continued. 'Mr Brooks, you should leave a message at Brooks Club for a Mr B. Green. The club will send a messenger direct to me and I will respond direct to you. Did you like that, sir? Mr B. Green. Not Mr Brown but Mr Bottle Green, like my suit.'

He laughed out loud at his cleverness, and Mr Brooks smiled, more in tolerance than amusement.

Mr Brown continued. 'Excellent. Then we are agreed. I wish you good day, sir, and leave you to draw up the agreement on the basis we have discussed. Shall we say Monday next at midday to sign the agreement and make the initial deposit?'

'Indeed, sir,' acknowledged Brooks.

Mr Brown moved towards the office door and then turned back to George Brooks and handed him a brochure. 'Here is a copy of the services offered by the Naval Academy to peruse at your leisure. I bid you good day until next Monday. Good day.'

Mmm, thought Brooks. A little light reading. A title to inspire and captivate the imagination: *A plan of the naval & commercial academy at Ormond-House, Paradise-Row, Chelsea; for qualifying young noblemen and gentlemen for the Royal Navy, By J. Bettesworth, and able assistants.* He settled down to read it and extracted the core contents.

In 1782, John Bettesworth and H. Fox, who were tutors at the Maritime School in Chelsea, felt the curriculum to be too restrictive and left to establish their own naval school based on the principle that sailors needed to learn *humane subjec*ts in addition to mathematical ones and that no education could be called *liberal* without the juxtaposition of both. They initially described their establishment as a *Naval & Commercial Academy at Ormond House*, ironically also in Chelsea*, for qualifying young noblemen and gentlemen for the Royal Navy.* In 1792, the year John Machele was enrolled, the claims for the academy were made in an advertisement in the *Oracle & Public Advertiser*. The establishment offered a broad curriculum, with particular emphasis on *Nautical Studies* encompassing navigation, astronomy, tactics and naval mathematics. For practical seamanship, the academy had a ship mounted on a swivel which it was claimed was large enough *for 24 young gentlemen to go aloft at any one time*. The world of commerce was also catered for, with subjects including bookkeeping, commercial law and the importance of calculating exchange rates. They also offered a service *to see Gentlemen qualified to pass for officers in a few days*. All this for between twenty-five and forty-five guineas a year, with each young gentleman having his own bed.

The agreement, having been drawn up by one of the bank's senior clerks, was duly signed the following Monday, and it was arranged that John Machele would be brought to meet Mr Brooks on the Thursday at eleven in the morning.

WHEN I FIRST MET THAT BANKER FELLOW

1792

There doesn't seem to have been a real pattern to my life, unless being constantly on the move from place to place is a pattern. I stay just long enough to get to know the people I'm living with a little and then off again. Sometimes that man in the bottle green suit, what's his name, oh yes, Brown, just arrives and takes me off. That man? Is he a pattern? What makes a pattern?

I've looked at wallpaper for many hours in many houses. Some paper has pictures, which makes it simple for me to create a story. Other paper has various shapes or stripes and colours. So, I have worked out that what makes a pattern is when I can find something that begins to repeat. I have to check by counting the pictures, shapes or stripes as they come around again and again because I might have been mistaken the first time and chosen the wrong starting point and that would be unlucky. So, can I call that man's recurring appearances a pattern?

He is the one who is there at each beginning, and he is

there at each finishing, and that is a pattern, isn't it? In his bottle green suit, he invariably arrives in a plain carriage and we equally invariably leave together in that plain, unliveried carriage with my worldly possessions packed in trunks and neatly stored for our journey to the next place for me to stay in. As far back as I can remember, he always introduces himself to me as though I have never met him before. Either that or he thinks me quite addled in my senses and incapable of remembering who he is. Mark you, I know who he is, but I don't know WHO he is. I do know that he represents someone who, he says, has my best interests at heart, but he never says who that person is or why he takes this interest in me, and I've never asked. I've never even asked why if he is that interested in me he has never introduced himself to me instead of sending Mr Brown.

When I was much younger, I thought there was nothing odd about all this toing and froing, and now it seems a bit late to start asking those sorts of questions, I suppose.

Still, he has pulled up yet again in his carriage, so it must be time for me to move on. I'm not sure how many months I have been here. But I do know one thing. Nothing has happened to mean the people "caring" for me no longer feel able to continue doing so or, at least, I haven't been accused of anything, not like in some of the places I've been. Every time there has been a candle or a lamp knocked over, fingers get pointed at me and it's not always my fault, at least, not here, even when it has happened.

Ah. He's rung the bell and one of the maids has gone to open the door. She recognises him, or at least his name, and has clearly been told by her master that there is no need for any meeting or discussion between them but that he is to be shown directly to the reception room, where I will be waiting. There is, however, the maid informs him, the promise of a glass of wine for my caller following our meeting.

The door to the reception room opened and the maid said, 'Mr Brown for you, Master John.' She curtsied and ushered my visitor in. I got up from where I had been pretending to study a book on mathematics and walked towards him with my hand extended.

You see, I am very well versed in the niceties of social behaviour. A knowledge of this is invaluable in that it keeps people at a certain distance. You never need to show your real self, which can be very risky indeed.

'Master John, it's me, Mr Brown. I trust I find you well?' he said, shaking my hand.

This is something he has done since I was ten years old. There must be a rule about when a little boy can begin to be regarded as having the beginnings of becoming a man. He stood there as immaculately dressed as ever. Bottle green suits him well, but I wonder if I will ever see him wearing any other colour. Him wearing that colour is his own pattern, I suppose.

'Perfectly well, Mr Brown, sir. And yourself?' I enquired.

Actually, I think we look pretty well together. Him in his bottle green and me in a mustard-coloured jacket and buff breeches.

'I am well, thank you, John. I have a matter to discuss with you now that you are getting older,' he said.

I'm not sure I like the sound of this. Has he heard about my "adventures" in the hayloft with that other maid?

'What would that be, Mr Brown?' I replied as nonchalantly as possible whilst indicating that he should be seated on one of the couches positioned either side of the fireplace.

He duly sat, spreading the tails of his coat either side of him, and waited until I had made myself comfortable opposite him.

'Well, John, as I said, you are a young man now, and gentlemen have a man of business to look after their affairs. Not someone like me but a person more concerned with ensuring that you receive the best possible advice and guidance for your future until you reach twenty-one, your majority. I have arranged a meeting for you with just such a person for the day after tomorrow. A Mr George Brooks. A banker. A thoroughly reliable and trustworthy fellow. What do you say to that, John?' He looked at me expectantly.

What was he expecting from me? An outburst of "What, someone else interfering in my life?" Well, if he was, then he is to be disappointed.

'I shall anticipate the meeting with pleasure, sir,' I responded, with what I thought was my most engaging smile.

'Excellent, John. Excellent. Shall we say ten in the morning the day following tomorrow? I shall have a glass of wine with the person who currently has the care of you and will see you as arranged. Good day, John.' We shook hands again, and he didn't bother ringing for the maid but left the room to make his own way to my carer's study at the rear of the house.

A banker! Good Lord! A damn banker! What on earth do I need a banker for? And this fellow will look after my affairs and have my best interests at heart, will he? I can picture him now. A short, fat, fussy man with little gold-rimmed spectacles and a terribly outmoded style of wig. How on earth will he know what is in my best interests? Will he consult me to get my opinion about anything? No one ever has before, so why should anyone start now?

Is it any wonder that I so often feel that my opinion about really important things, things which directly affect me, like where I live or who I live with, is never considered? How old do I have to be before I have a say in what happens in my life? It is MY life. Me, John Machele. Does it matter what I am called? I know that I am me, but is my name me or am I my name? How often have I seen my name spelt in a different way? They always get "John" right. That's the easy part. But Machele? I've seen Mashell, Marchell, Marshall and occasionally Machell. I try to make things easy for most of the people I come into contact with, and I've heard Mr Brown introduce me on many occasions. Perhaps he should have a card printed with my name on it then there would not be any excuse for all the different spellings. I don't have to sign my name very often but, and this is to save other people's embarrassment, I have devised a signature in which the last "e" in Machele reaches skywards and may be taken for a second "l". That is how considerate I am. I help people to spell my name probably as they think it should be. What's in a name anyway? I'll tell you what's in a name. I am John Machele and I know who I am because I know my own name. I am not where I live. I am not what other people *care to name me. I am John Machele, and the older I get, the more I become John Machele.*

So here we are. Just the two of us. Me and Mr Brown in that personal carriage of his in the heart of London's money and legal centre: Chancery Lane. We pull up outside number 25. I peer out of the carriage window to see what the place of business of this banker fellow looks like. First impressions are so important, are they not? I know this only too well. I can be as polite and well behaved as the next fellow initially. What an odd expression. Why do people assume the next person is so good without knowing who the next person is?

The name of the bank is written in golden script over its frontage, starting to the left of the door and finishing to the right of it. Very well balanced. Aesthetically pleasing, I feel. That's a good word, John. Aesthetically. Design and balance are essential in life. Creates a good impression. What does it actually say, though? Master, Dawson, Brooks, Kirton & Dixon. No shortage of names, and who is it that I am to meet? Ah yes, Brooks, that's right, Brooks.

'Come along, John. Out we get,' said Mr Brown. He continued. 'Having a banker to manage your affairs means you have really grown up. Not come of age, of course, but pretty well grown up. Listen to what he has to say and be sure to take advice and guidance when it is offered. He knows his business well and has been chosen most carefully.'

After the coachman had come down from his perch, pulled down the step and opened the door, we left the coach.

'Very good, Mr Brown. I am certain Mr Brooks has been chosen most carefully, and I will certainly do my utmost to follow whatever advice he offers,' I said, as we approached the door to the bank.

Again, it was all show. I responded to Mr Brown in precisely the way he hoped, nay, expected me to, in the way of a young gentleman. My thoughts did not in any way match my words. I was thinking to myself that even though Mr Brown was probably doing what he felt, or rather that someone else who I never seemed knowingly to have contact with, felt, was in my best interests, still, I was not being asked what I thought. I was never asked. Regardless of the way in which things were put to me, and every effort was made to make it sound as though I was involved, the undeniable fact was that I was always simply being told what was going to happen to me and when. Why should this be any different? Mr Brown has told me that having my own banker as my man of affairs is a sign that I have grown up. Does he have any idea just how condescending he sounded when he talked to me the other day and also just now? Talked to, that's right. Not talked with but talked to.

As we entered the bank, we were approached by a fairly short, slightly podgy, bespectacled figure with a deferential air about him.

Almost exactly as I had imagined this fellow Brooks to be, except he had no wig, fashionable or otherwise, and was much younger than I thought him in my mind.

'Mr Brown and Mr Machele?' he queried, looking from one to the other myopically.

Mr Brown nodded but made no effort to offer his hand or to introduce me at all.

'Come this way, gentlemen, if you please.'

He guided us to the rear of the large open space, cluttered on one side by a bevy of clerks doing whatever it is that clerks do. Clerking, I suppose. He raised his hand and knocked on a solid oak door and in response to a cry of 'Come in,' he opened it fully and indicated by an inclination of his head that we should enter this inner sanctum.

'Thank you, Dodd. Please ensure that we are not disturbed,' said an authoritative voice from the figure behind a large and fairly imposing desk. Dodd, whoever he was, and he most certainly was not my Mr Brooks, left the office and closed the door behind him. This rather tall, elegantly dressed gentleman stood up and came from behind the desk, extending his right hand.

So, this must be Mr Brooks. Not at all what I have been expecting. No glasses, certainly not podgy, and no wig either. He has his hair swept back from his forehead and as he comes towards us, I can see it is in what is becoming the new fashion, tied at the back with a black silk ribbon. Very smartly dressed indeed. I wonder who his tailor is.

'How do you do, sir? A pleasure to see you again,' he said, as he shook Mr Brown's hand. He turned towards me and we shook hands.

What a firm grip and those eyes. He stares at me as though I am the most important person in the room. What a change that makes.

'And you must be Mr John Machele. I am George

Brooks, one of the partners in this establishment, and I look forward to a long and fruitful relationship working with you. Come, take a seat, both of you,' he continued, as he made his way back behind his desk and settled into his chair.

Gosh, this is not what I was expecting! He is treating me genuinely like a real person. Like an adult, and me just sixteen. He's talking about us working together. This has never happened before. Am I now to actually be involved in the decisions affecting my life? What is our relationship to be like? I am convinced there is a business arrangement underlying all this, but if he, in one way or another, is in effect being paid, does that make him like a servant to me? No, that's silly, John. This is real business, and we approach it more as partners in my future than any other kind of relationship.

All was politeness, as I would have expected. It was arranged that I would meet Mr Brooks without Mr Brown being present to discuss just how matters would progress.

Just me and him. Two men together having a gentlemanly discussion. I'm beginning to believe that perhaps it is true that at sixteen years of age I should have a say in what happens to me.

I was very quiet in the carriage on the journey back with Brown, or rather, Mr Brown, as he always reintroduced himself to me. Not that we really talked very much anyway. He would say what he wanted to say and I would respond as appropriately as I felt able to. It's an odd thing, my relationship with Brown. Oh yes, in my mind, he is always just plain Brown. Never Mr. I have a sense that he is really, for all his smart, fashionable appearance, somebody's servant, so why can't I, a soon-to-be gentleman, treat him as such? When we are together, I feel that I am the servant, the one who has to do what he is told.

'How did you find Mr Brooks?' asked Brown, interrupting me in my reverie.

'Very much a gentleman, sir. Not at all what I was expecting.'

'What were you expecting, John?'

'Well, some fusty, petty-minded chap. I thought the clerk was the banker first of all, and I wasn't at all happy about that. But Mr Brooks... well.'

'So, what did you like about him?' continued Brown.

'He had a firm handshake and looked me in the eye like a gentleman should. That's important, isn't it?'

'Indeed, it is, John. Indeed it is. And tomorrow, John? Tomorrow, you will be meeting him man to man. I won't be there, so it will just be between the two of you. And whatever Mr Brooks has to say, just remember that he said he was looking forward to working with you. There will be decisions to be taken, but I believe Mr Brooks's intention is that they will not be taken without your involvement and consent.'

'I understand, Mr Brown, and may I say how much I appreciate being treated with such delicate consideration.'

That's very well put, John. Very well put indeed. I can always tell when Brown is concealing something from me and I fear this is no exception. I like what I have seen of Mr Brooks so far, but was he pretending that we were simply going to discuss things in general when we meet tomorrow?

Lots of things have been done to me over the years and they always mean moving yet again, and I never know where I'm going until I get there and it all starts over again and it's always Brown who does it. Always. Maybe he has got tired, like I have, of all these changes. Is he telling me that I am to have my own man of business as a way of finding someone else to do his duties for him? I wish I knew who his master is. He never says anything more about him except the usual response of 'He is a personage who has an interest in you.' If I'm nearly grown up, shouldn't I be told?

'This is where we part, John, and I wish you every joy of your meeting with Mr Brooks tomorrow. Don't forget my carriage will be yours for the day tomorrow. Good day, John.'

BETTESWORTH'S NAVAL ACADEMY

1792

Of course, now I think about it, this isn't my first time in the navy or something like it.

I remember being "requested" to go and see that fellow Brooks at his bank one day when I had just become sixteen years of age. I've never quite understood who he was and what his relationship to me might be. When I ask him, he always replies that he has the care of me. Odd because if he really does "have the care" of me, then surely I would be living with him like I've lived with all those other people through the years. Coming and going; going and coming. I lose count of the number of places I've lived.

Uncle this, Aunty that, Mr this, Mrs that. It would certainly be quite a list if I could put the effort into making one, but why should I? Once they've gone, they've gone. I turn my back on them as soon as I've moved somewhere new. Not worth remembering their names. They're only doing a piece of work for somebody. Why won't they ever tell me who for? They get paid for it anyway, so it's not as though they are caring for me out of love or even a sense of duty, like they might if they were part of my family. What was always obvious to me was that they had families, not always in the same house, often grown up and living elsewhere, and I was not a genuine part of it.

On the other hand, how would I know if I was part of a family? I've only watched people in families. Always an outsider for as long as I can remember. I suppose it's that that has kept me sane. I've seen what families do to each other. All polite and contented, happy with their lot when people are watching but then, when they think they are unobserved, they argue and hurt each other with their petty jealousies and vying for attention to see who can gain the most favour.

You see, I have seen all that. I have been an observer who sees so much but is not seen to be seeing. I have been there but not there. It is not me who has detached myself from their lives but they who do the detaching.

'Oh, that is just John. Don't worry about him.' And if they don't worry about me then why should I worry about them? I have learnt not to attach myself to people, but I do sometimes, when I see families being close, being affectionate to one another, wonder what it would feel like to be like them. But then I see the other side, the darker side, and understand why I think the way I do. Keep your distance, John. Keep your distance. I would. I do. But there have been times when I know I have liked someone I have been living with and I think they have liked me, but something always happens that means I have to move on. I really mean being moved on. One day I am there, something happens, I

believe it to be something very bad, but I never know what and nobody tells me, and the next thing I know is that I am somewhere else. I am with someone else, and it always starts so well because they want the money for "caring" for me and I, not knowing what these bad things I have actually done are, show myself to them as someone quite presentable. I do my best to be biddable, to learn the rules of the new house and carers, but I'm still mindful of the fact that really I am there as a form of paying guest (well, I don't pay but someone does) and that I will, in all probability, not be there very long anyway.

Do these people I get moved to know everything about me, or are they just given the minimum of information with no details of the badness? Would they take me if they knew what I was supposed to have done when with all the other people who "had the care" of me? Would I want to carry on moving from one set of carers to another if I knew what I'd done? Those who I believe do know are the ones who look at me and just don't believe that this presentable, well-mannered lad before them can be the same one. And maybe that is the challenge. I am not the same one, or at least, not immediately.

I may not remember everything that happens around me and there must be a lot. There are so many things to remember, but why are they necessary or deemed important and by whom? I decide what is important to me, not anyone else. The other things I just forget about as if they never happened. There are some things I can summon into my mind, usually as a result of what someone says, not necessarily about or to me. A word, a glimpse, of somewhere *that reminds me of somewhere else, or maybe it is that place. Smells are useful. Especially the smell of smoke. I can bring back so many experiences with smoke and often flames. I have a sense that people who have "had the care" of me in some way share that memory. If I think very hard indeed, I connect smoke and flames with moving, or being moved, from one place to another. There never seems to have been any difficulty finding fresh places for me to live in. Someone must pay them very well for the time they spend just watching me. I don't understand why people say they "have the care" of me. What do they think "care" means? Somewhere to sleep? Somewhere to be fed regularly? The food is always good but then I don't think I know what bad food actually is. What do poor people eat? I've seen what I am told are poor people, but I've never seen them eat. What makes poor people poor? I wear good clothes and go to school. Well, I think I went to school once or twice with lots of other children, but that stopped suddenly, like so many things. School now comes to me with a succession of tutors, none of whom last very long.*

There are so many things I don't understand at all. One is friendship. People seem to think it is so important to have friends. I have no idea what friends are for. What purpose do they serve? I have me: John Machele, and that's quite enough. People who "have the care" of me have said they think me different to other people, but they can't tell me why. I, John Machele, am different, whatever that means, and make of that what you will.

Do I really concern myself with the opinions of other people? Not usually but I'm not a boy any longer and if people don't want me to hear things then they should not say them when I am there. Perfect, to them anyway, is not something I will ever be, not even to myself. Especially not to myself.

The other day, I heard someone use the word "mad". Were they talking about me? I'm not mad. I know what "mad" means. Mad people are locked up in Bethel, or Bedlam as we call it. People pay to go and see them. Am I in Bedlam? Do people pay to see me? No. I am not mad, but I wish people would not use that word in my hearing.

Where was I? Oh yes; I was talking about having been in the navy before, or at least something approaching it.

Mr Brooks and I duly met the following day.

'John, come in. Good to see you. Take a seat.' Mr Brooks seemed his usual courteous, affable self as he always showed himself to be with me, but this time, I felt it to be a veneer. He stepped around from behind his desk and we shook hands.

'Are things well with you, John?' he asked, rubbing his hands together and looking at me quizzically.

'Yes, sir; very well indeed,' I lied as usual, when asked this purely social question. I know the rules and do my utmost to stick to them.

'And you, sir?' I responded in my best interested yet ingenuous manner.

'Tolerably fine, John, tolerably fine. So, John, you've reached the age of sixteen, nearly a man and time to think about a career,' he said in a falsely jolly tone whilst gazing down at his desk.

Is it? As soon as he said that I knew what was going to

come next. I was going to be moved again, wasn't I? I wasn't aware of having done anything wrong or out of the ordinary. A career? What does he mean by a career? So now I am sixteen years of age, am I? How does he know? When was my birthday? I've seen quite a few birthday parties for other people but never had one for myself. When is my birthday, or is this just another one of those things that nobody tells me? Or doesn't anyone actually know? Am I the only person in England who doesn't know when and where they were born and who their parents are or were?

'A career, sir? I haven't thought about it,' I replied.

'Well, John, what are you good at? What do you like doing?' He was smiling in what he seemed to think was an encouraging way, but the smile was rather fixed and I had the sense that something had already been decided for me and that he, Mr Brooks, had been tasked with the job of presenting me with a fait accompli and he wasn't sure how I was going to react.

I couldn't really tell him what I liked doing most of all because I sensed he would disapprove of what I called my "dalliance" with Meg, who was a maid where my present carers had the care of me. There was a stable block with an upper floor where bales of hay made a very private place for us to frolic and romp.

My God, that was a new discovery for me but not for Meg, who was quite old, must be at least twenty. She was giving me an education beyond my wildest imaginings.

'Well, sir,' I replied, 'I'm getting very good at riding.'

Careful, John, you'll be telling him about Meg before you know it.

'I write a fair hand and can speak a little French. My arithmetic is good, and I have been reading the Greeks, sir.'

'Good, John, good.' Suddenly Mr Brooks began to take a lot of interest in the way he was holding his hands and then had a need to separate them and rearrange his ink well and quill holder. 'Have you considered a career as a naval officer in the service of His Majesty?'

'Not really, sir. I've never been on a ship. Seen them, of course. Oh, I did once go sailing with someone on the Thames, but that was some time ago now.'

Do I want to join the Royal Navy and serve my king? It has never crossed my mind, but it would certainly make a change. Join the navy? Where did that idea come from? Am I to be shipped out without so much as a by-your-leave?

Mr Brooks eyed me appraisingly from the other side of the desk and continued. 'Nobody is suggesting you join the navy right away, but we had an idea the navy might appeal to you. Do you have many friends, John?'

'No, sir. I don't usually stay in one place long enough to make friends. I have had acquaintances, sir.'

And now I have Meg, but that's not what he needs to know.

Mr Brooks gave the appearance of a man satisfied with the way the conversation was now going and ceased being preoccupied with his hands or the way things were arranged on his desk and he continued. 'John, I have a professional gentleman friend, a Mr Bettesworth. He runs a very highly thought-of naval academy in Chelsea on the banks of the Thames. It's a school where they teach not only the usual subjects in which you appear to have reached a satisfactory standard but also specialises in subjects that are necessary for a naval officer or a midshipman. I also believe they have some sort of replica boat or ship to teach you about rigging and sails and whatnot.'

Ah, it's not the navy but a school where I would be trained to join the navy as a midshipman. Not really sure what that is, though. Some sort of embryo officer, I suppose. Anyway, I get Brooks to visibly relax by saying that I am not averse to the idea, and his relief is positively palpable.

Mr Brooks continued. 'But Mr Bettesworth can tell you much more than I can. After we've had a spot of luncheon, we'll go over there and meet him. Don't be alarmed, John. I won't just introduce you and then leave you there saying I'll send your luggage on in a few days.' He chuckled as he said this. 'We'll have a talk. Mr Bettesworth will say whether or not he thinks you are suitable, and if all goes well you can probably consider starting next week and joining the other young gentlemen there.'

'Very well, sir,' I replied.

They've already decided what's going to happen to me, haven't they? This has all been arranged. Brown has arranged this and got Brooks to do it. Wait a minute, John. Wait a minute. What did Mr Brooks say just then? There was one word that could change everything. What was it? Oh yes. He said something about me being able to probably consider starting there. That is different if it is true.

'Excellent, John. I'm sorry. Most rude of me. Do you mind if I call you John?' said Brooks. 'It is not my decision to make and I cannot, and indeed would not, insist that you attend the Naval Academy. Let us have that luncheon and then we will go and see the academy and the proprietor, Mr Bettesworth, and see if he says he is willing to offer you a place.

'Now, John. Listen to me because this is most important. If you are in agreement that you wish to accept a place when it is offered, then there is every possibility that you can be enrolled there next week. But only if you agree to it. Do you understand that? Yours is the final decision concerning this.' Mr Brooks looked at me appraisingly, gauging my reaction.

This last statement of his had the effect of making me want to do as he wished. *If Mr Bettesworth offers me a place then I will certainly accept it. To my recollection, this is the first time ever that I have felt my future resting in my own hands. I, John Machele, have a decision to make about my own future at last.*

I've never been to Chelsea. What will this place be like? I know what will happen. I'll be on my best social behaviour and before I know it, I will be saying farewell to Meg and be one of the "young gentlemen" next week.

Is this what they call a fresh start for me? I have liked some of the places and people I have stayed with before but not very many, at least not in this way. I have met boys like me. Well, maybe not like me but around the same age, and I feel some could become more than just acquaintances. Would that make them "friends"?

What is so different here is that being at the Naval Academy is a business arrangement from the start, and all the young gentlemen are here on that basis. There is no pretence about Mr Bettesworth and his staff "having the care" of me, although that term is used about all of us. We know and the staff know what the caring means. They look after us as best they can, giving us a training for entry into the Royal Navy as midshipmen.

And we live by clear rules. They have told us that these rules are based on the Articles of War, which are the rules to be obeyed by everybody, officers and men, on board His Majesty's ships in the Royal Navy. The only difference is that we don't have the same punishments of flogging or death. Thank goodness. But to have a laid-down framework of behaviour to live by every day makes life understandable. I know where to be, when to be there and what to do. If this is what life will be like in the navy then at last someone has taken the right decision for me.

I've had my little ups and downs during the three months that I've been here. Nothing serious, I don't think. Had a bit of a disagreement with one of the instructors about just how quickly different types of fuses would burn when we were learning the basis of good gunnery practice. He looked like I had imagined a ship's gunner to look like. He was a squat figure, with thick forearms with various tattoos on them. His face was pitted with little black spots, which was the result of powder burns over the years. His pride was his pigtail, plaited and hanging down his back to his waist, although you couldn't really call it a "waist" since he resembled a barrel. When he spoke, it was more of a hoarse shout, and we often had to repeat anything we said to him due to his being half deaf from all the broadsides over the years. He demonstrated with different types of fuses and showed how the speed was controlled by a combination of gunpowder and the way the actual length of fuse was constructed. I challenged him over what I felt to be a valid point, which he didn't take very kindly to.

'Ah, Mr Machele, I see, has had two lessons in basic gunnery practice and already he is more of an expert than an ex-master gunner with over twenty years' experience at sea. Come on then, young sir. Show the rest of the class what you know.'

I gather now that the expectation was that I would be embarrassed and decline his offer to show off, but that would not have been my way, would it? I had the smell of smoke, very acrid smoke, in my nostrils, and if there was one thing I knew about, it was smoke, and anyway, he had shown us the bright flash when the fuse reached the small explosive charge. I could see how this worked well enough.

I came forward and he offered me a length of fuse and told me to instruct the class. He had that smug look on his face that experts have when amateurs think they can do better than they can. He had reckoned without John Machele.

'Thank you, Mr Masson. Right, you fellows. Watch this.'

I wasn't quite sure what I was going to do at first, but then the idea came to me. I remembered how all the lights were lit so quickly at Vauxhall Gardens all those years ago.

I put the fuse on the ground and poured a small trail of powder from the keg directly from where I was, some ten feet from the charge, to the charge itself. Retracing my steps, I took the smouldering slow match from the bucket where it was well away from any powder and, before Mr Masson could stop me, I called to the other young gentlemen, 'This is what it's going to be like firing a real gun on a ship. I call this the Vauxhall Method. Come here and watch this.'

So saying, I touched the slow match to the powder trail and instead of the slow progress to be expected from a handsewn fuse, the explosion was almost instantaneous. Not as loud as I was expecting, but the flash was the brightest thing I had ever seen. Like looking at the sun but not expected. Then it all went dark.

My eyes were open but there was nothing to see. I could hear the others yelling that they couldn't see, either. My God, John, you've really done it this time. You've blinded everybody. This will not end well for you.

I could hear Mr Masson shouting. He hadn't heard properly what I had called out to the others, and when he realised what was going to happen, it was too late for him to stop me.

He must have turned away, suddenly knowing what to expect so was unaffected. He did his best to calm everyone down and told us all to sit where we were and keep our eyes closed.

'It'll be all right in a while,' he said in his hoarse voice, the anxiety clearly showing in the way he spoke. 'I've seen it happen many times when people who don't know how careful you must be with explosives think they know it all. Let this be a lesson to you all, and especially you, Mr Machele. If you tried that on board, I shudder to think what would happen. That's endangering the ship, that's what that is. At the very least, the captain would have you kissing the gunner's daughter, and for those of you who don't know what that means, well… you'll be held over a cannon with your breeches around your ankles whilst a beefy boatswain's mate beats your arse with a rattan cane.

'Keep your eyes closed. It'll take a few minutes to clear. Then we'll have to inform Mr Bettesworth about this. No idea what'll happen now. No idea.'

What we all find a bit odd is that we're not allowed out after eight o'clock and it's lights out at ten. We're not children. We're young gentlemen. Still, I muse, maybe rules are made to be broken. There are three of us here who seem to get on well enough. That's me, Clarke and Wolferton.

We never use our first or Christian names, just family ones here. It seems that is what "gentlemen" do, and it's a tradition at the type of schools they go to.

Am I the only one here with a family name but no knowledge of his family?

I've had this idea for years, it seems. I want to return to Vauxhall Gardens. I was only ten when I went there first some six years ago, and now that I'm that much older I'm sure I'll see everything in a rather different light, and probably I have Meg to thank for that!

I asked Clarke and Wolferton if they had ever been, and they said they hadn't but had heard all sorts of stories about it and thought it would be a wonderful idea to go.

'Let's go tonight,' I said, rubbing my hands together in anticipation.

'We can't do that,' Clarke responded. He was quite

short and rotund and he had a habit of puffing out his cheeks when faced with any decision. 'We'd get into all sorts of trouble with old Bettesworth and, Machele, you've had several warnings from him already.'

'He's right, you know,' said Wolferton, his bony head bowing down from his gangly frame. 'He's watching you, and anyway, it's lights out at ten and we're supposed to be asleep.'

'Oh, come on,' I said, a little taken aback by their reluctance. 'We'll go after ten o'clock when they think we're asleep and be back before morning. They'll never know we've been,' I added, in what I hoped was a persuasive voice.

'And just how are we supposed to get there?' asked Wolferton.

'Easy,' I replied. 'We'll take a boat.'

Clarke was determined to show the impracticality of the whole scheme and said, 'We'll need to catch a wherry, and that means calling out for one and the wherryman calling back. We'll be heard and stopped before we even get on the boat.'

I had what I saw to be the obvious answer to their objections. 'No. What have we been taught here? Seamanship. We'll pretend it's a cutting-out expedition, only instead of going after an enemy ship and taking it out of the harbour under the nose of the enemy, we'll be taking a trip to Vauxhall Gardens under the very nose of Mr Bettesworth. We'll take the boat we've been training in and muffle the oars. It's an easy two-mile row.'

And it was also a two-mile row back some three hours later.

'Good morning, boys. Been taking a turn on the river?' Bettesworth stepped out from behind a storage shed accompanied by Mr Masson, the gunnery instructor, uncovering a lantern to illuminate the tableau of us three frozen to the spot. 'Off to bed with you now,' he continued, the mildness of his tone not fooling any of us for a minute. 'Be at the office next to my cabin in the morning at two bells, and for you who still can't remember, that means nine o'clock.'

We three didn't say anything, either to Mr Bettesworth or to each other, but went straight to our individual cabins.

I have no idea if the other two had any sleep. I did. It was an adventure and it had gone jolly well. Anyway, what is Bettesworth going to do about it? He is running a business here and if he throws us out then he will have to get three more to replace us and the fees. Well, that's how I see it.

We went to see Mr Bettesworth the next morning, each of us wearing our best uniforms and putting on what were meant to be extremely contrite expressions.

He made us stand to attention in front of his desk. He pushed back his chair and stood to address us.

'There are rules, and rules are there to be obeyed. If you had done this on a Royal Navy ship, it is likely you would be charged with theft of a ship's property even though you returned it, and you are well aware of what the Articles of War say about theft.' He continued. 'A good seaman is always aware of the weather conditions, which, luckily for you, were fine, and what other vessels are in the vicinity. It was dark and you were not showing any lights. That made you a danger to not only yourselves but to others. At best, your actions were reckless; at worst, they were bordering on madness. That's all. No excuses. This will be entered on your records here and I trust this will be a lesson to you all. Dismissed.'

There it was. That word again, and I knew he was referring to me in particular. Clarke and Wolferton weren't being referred to in that way. Just me. I saw the way his eyes settled on me when he used that word.

There was smoke and there were flames that night when the sails and rigging of the mock-up ship we trained on somehow caught fire.

I was moved on again then but, as usual, I was not consulted and simply told it would be best for me. People act quickly where I am concerned.

BETTESWORTH VISITS THE BANKER

1792

Mr Brooks's interview with Mr Bettesworth following his unannounced arrival was not the most enjoyable he had ever experienced. It was made perfectly clear to him that it was felt to be in the best interests of all concerned that Master Machele be removed from the academy immediately. Incidents were relayed as reasons, and Mr Bettesworth was adamant that John was to be expelled forthwith and was to be collected within two days.

The atmosphere was frosty to say the least as Bettesworth commented on his mock-up training ship having been set fire to and the problems he now faced with his insurers, the Sun Fire Office. He stated quite baldly that he would be pursuing compensation and recompense in excess of any monies paid by his insurers. He also made much of the friends he had who were newspaper proprietors and who would be only too willing to publish potentially damaging articles should the situation not be resolved both speedily and to his satisfaction.

Mr Brooks responded in an equally frosty tone that whilst he understood the situation as put to him, Bettesworth should be reminded that he, Brooks, although having the care of John Machele, was in fact acting as an agent on somebody else's account. Brooks assured the antagonistic Mr Bettesworth that he would make immediate contact with his client and arrange for John to be collected the following day.

Mr Brooks indicated he felt the interview to be over by moving from behind his desk and walking past Mr Bettesworth to the office door.

'Good day, sir. I thank you for the information, unfortunate though it seems to be.' Putting on a placating tone, he said, 'I am more than certain that this can be resolved satisfactorily very quickly indeed. I shall arrange for Master Machele to be collected and I shall be in contact with you as soon as any other necessary arrangements have been made.'

'And good day to you, sir,' responded Bettesworth. 'I shall await your communication with both interest and, I trust, patience.' He brushed past Brooks and straight out of the bank's door without giving the waiting clerk the chance to open it for him.

This was the first time Brooks had communicated with the man in the bottle-green coat by their urgent method. He was surprised at the speed of the response. Two hours later, Mr Brown presented himself at the bank and Brooks explained the situation in full.

'Very well,' said Mr Brown, giving every appearance

of a man to whom nothing comes as a great surprise. 'Things like this have happened before and may well do so again.' The way he sat with one leg crossed over the other and his hands folded in his lap conveyed an air of sanguineness. 'What I shall do, Brooks, is convey the news to my master and then look for possible solutions. When a decision has been made then I will request you to meet again with this Bettesworth fellow and put any proposals to him. I realise that this is not quite how you foresaw things working out, but Master Machele has ever been, shall we say, unpredictable. One day he is like one thing and the next another. I'm sure you understand. It is not always easy for any of us. So, I shall arrange the collection of John tomorrow, discuss the situation with my master later today and communicate his decision to you in the morning. I think that you will be pleasantly surprised tomorrow. Thank you again for the manner in which you are seeing fit to meet the requirements of our agreement. Until tomorrow then. Good day.'

He uncrossed his legs slowly, stood and bowed courteously to Brooks and on opening the office door allowed the waiting clerk to escort him out of the bank.

Well, thought Brooks, running his hands through his hair, *that was a very different experience from my earlier visitor. I shall look forward to Mr Brown's return tomorrow and trust the proposal suggested will be acceptable to Bettesworth. Otherwise, that will not be a meeting to relish.*

A SOLUTION TO THE AFFAIR AT THE NAVAL ACADEMY

1792

'Sir, if I may draw your attention to, and there is no other way of putting it, sir, a claim for compensation or recompense being made by Mr Bettesworth of the Naval Academy.'

Mr Augustus Brown was his usual deferential yet firmly insistent self. He knew exactly what the initial reaction from his master would be. What his master did not know was that he was being skilfully manipulated towards what Mr Brown felt to be the most positive outcome for all the parties concerned.

A puffing-out of his cheeks, a spluttering noise, a reddening of his face and an agitated striding up and down the room overlooking Grosvenor Square. This would be followed by standing stiffly to attention with his hands clasped behind his back.

Jutting his head forward in an antagonistic manner, he made the expected spluttering noise and brayed: 'D'you mean that damn academy fellow Butterworth?'

'Bettesworth, sir, Bettesworth,' said Brown patiently.

John Machele's interested personage's eyes protruded further.

'Bettesworth, Butterworth. I don't give a damn what his name is. Doesn't he have insurance for this sort of thing?'

'He does have insurance, but the insurers are questioning whether this act of young John's is covered by it,' went on the man in the bottle-green coat. 'There is the question of whether this was an accident or deliberate. In fact, there is doubt, amongst other things, that arson or, in other words, setting fire with criminal intent to create wilful damage is covered, sir.'

'Arson. Arson?' the personage angrily challenged, unclasping his hands from behind his back and advancing to the centre of the room. 'Who says it was arson? We don't know that John set this fire at all. We don't know it is not a coincidence!'

'Well, sir, it just may be coincidence that the young man happened to have been severely reprimanded for his behaviour only earlier that day and, as you know, there was the incident with the gunpowder a short while ago. If I may be permitted to say, sir, John does not take well to being disciplined, a trait which you may recognise, sir.' Mr Brown felt able to say this but understood that even with his close relationship with his master he was very near to pushing it to the limit. He waited to see the type of response that would be forthcoming.

'Can't this other fellow from around the corner in Green Street, the banker chap, ah yes, Brooks, that's it.

Brooks. Can't he sort it out? Isn't this what we pay him for?'

'Sir,' said Mr Brown, standing as nonchalantly as he could, knowing his next statement and carefully couched initial suggestion that would follow it would make his alternative solution so much more attractive.

He began: 'Sir, Mr Brooks is not a servant, as you know. As a banker, he has an agreement with us. We invest certain, but not excessive, funds with his bank and pay a fee of five per cent plus expenses for the services he renders. It is understood that the account will not be overdrawn and we will not ask for credit. In order to meet the financial claim being made by Mr Bettesworth, significant additional funds will have to be made available. Mr Bettesworth not only wants his piece of training equipment, namely the mock-up of a ship, to be replaced, but is also wanting a sum for his possible loss of income. This is because he cannot justify his fees if he is unable to provide in full the services which he advertises. There is the possibility that should his claim not be met then, being on friendly terms with a number of newspaper proprietors who have already printed the news of the fire, he may well be minded to publish another item saying how scandalous the situation is in which he now finds himself. There could be repercussions, sir, which may reflect badly on certain prominent persons close to yourself, sir.' Taking a deep breath, he continued with what he considered to be an initial solution acceptable to the personage.

'John has no idea you are his father, but he does know there is a person with his best interests at heart. Sir, try not to see Mr Bettesworth's approach to Mr Brooks as a threatening impertinence. He is unaware of your involvement so it cannot be so. See it more as a test of your willingness to continue in your support for the education and future of Master John. Consider allowing this payment to be made into our account with Mr Brooks so he may be able to calm the stormy seas before we run aground.' A seagoing or naval metaphor was usually guaranteed to sway his master and make him more amenable.

'Mmm,' said his master, visibly placated. He stroked the watered silk sash over his waistcoat and continued. 'Difficult times, Brown, difficult times. We will pay but I truly pray that this will be the last additional strain put on my finances for a while. People already seem to think I receive too much money, which they think I do nothing to earn. We must be careful, Brown. This must not come back to me.'

'Very good, sir. I believe this to be a wise decision taken after considering various matters. You can rely on me, sir. I will make the arrangements with Mr Brooks, and you can rest assured that you will hear no more of the matter.'

'Thank you, Brown, thank you,' said his master in a relieved yet resigned voice.

'Sir,' said Brown, feigning hesitancy as he coughed discreetly behind his left hand. 'If I might suggest something else?'

'Yes, yes. Let's hear it, man. Anything. Anything.'

'Well, sir, there may be an alternative way around this possibly embarrassing situation which will keep Bettesworth more than happy and also reflect well on yourself, although it goes without saying that your name will not be mentioned.'

'Out with it, man. Out with it,' interjected the personage impatiently.

'Yes, sir. What I have in mind with your gracious approval is this.' Brown continued in a confident tone as he began pacing up and down the room looking for all the world like a well-rehearsed public speaker in a lecture hall.

'I have been informed by Mr Brooks that Bettesworth's academy including its outbuildings, is insured with the Sun Fire Office. However, not only do they have a query about possible arson but there is also the question of whether or not the mock-up training vessel is classed as an outbuilding. It is a typical technical issue over a definition of terms. The training vessel is a fixture in the grounds of the academy, but is it a building? Now, sir, as we discussed before, Bettesworth, without this piece of equipment, feels he is unable to fulfil his advertised educational and practical training services for the young gentlemen destined to become naval officers. Let us think how the public regard the men of the Royal Navy. When fighting to preserve our country with their wooden walls, they are Hearts of Oak and Jolly Jack Tars. When ashore, they are given a wide berth. They are regarded as whoring drunkards and not fit to be seen in polite society. But what if they were seen to be doing something good? This is where you personally come in, sir. What if you with your attachment to the sea and the Admiralty put the suggestion to their Lordships that the crew of a small ship of the Royal Navy, say, a sloop, were to be set to work in

Chelsea reconstructing the training ship. This need not be viewed as compensation for Bettesworth but as an exercise for the navy itself, with the possibility of constructing such things in their own academies in the future.'

'This all seems very fine so far, but how does this work to my advantage?' queried his master who, although enjoying the pictures the proposition conjured up, was not fully seeing where the suggestion was going.

'Well, sir,' continued Brown, not at all fazed by his master's lack of imagination, 'Mr Bettesworth will withdraw his demand for additional compensation since the reconstruction will be an invaluable opportunity for his young gentlemen to observe how a ship's crew can work together on a task. They will see how an experienced officer and his petty officers, possibly a midshipman as well, give orders and carry out supervision. Bettesworth's young gentlemen can also be employed as part of the workforce. Excellent experience. Instead of Bettesworth placing a potentially damaging article in the press, he will be encouraged to write a highly complimentary piece praising our "Jolly Jack Tars". You, sir, will have saved yourself some money, the Admiralty will be seen in a positive light by assisting in the preliminary training of its future officers and the academy will be able to boast of its new mock-up training vessel. It works, sir. All we need now is a Royal Navy ship and its crew.' Brown stopped his pacing, faced his master and spread his hands out towards him.

'Damn me, Brown. Bloody marvellous. Bloody marvellous!' The personage's face burst into a wide grin and for a moment Brown was afraid he may be subjected to a full embrace. 'By God, this'll shut Butterworth up and no mistake! Call my carriage. Time to go to the Admiralty. At least I don't have to make an appointment. When the work's being done, I shall make an unofficial visit to the academy. Unannounced but known about. What? Splendid idea that.' He nodded in smug self-satisfaction. 'Don't mention any of this to Brooks yet. Tomorrow will be soon enough.'

'Very good, sir,' said Mr Brown, concealing his own satisfaction at a job well done.

BETTESWORTH BEMUSED

1792

The following morning at ten o'clock, Mr Brown was shown into Brooks's office where he described the proposal in detail, which brought a smile to Mr Brooks's face.

'He can't possibly refuse this,' he cried. 'A navy ship and its crew to reconstruct his training vessel and the possibility of a high-ranking personage, possibly from the Admiralty, to pay an unofficial visit to his academy. Astonishing. I shall go to him at once just to see the look on his face.'

'Ah, Mr Brooks. It is felt best that Mr Bettesworth is made to wait until tomorrow. Besides, John is being collected today so that should keep him happy for a while. It shows we are people of our word anyway. So, all will be well.'

Brooks shook him warmly by the hand. He looked him in the eye whilst doing so and said, 'Tell me, how has all this been arranged?'

'Come, Mr Brooks. I am not to divulge who my master is and you are not to ask. Let us just say that if my master was not who he is then these arrangements could not have been made.' He said this with twinkling eyes and tapped the side of his nose with his forefinger. 'Good day, Mr Brooks. Good day.'

On the following morning, Brooks's hired carriage pulled up outside Ormond House, the Naval Academy in Chelsea. There was the usual rather unsavoury smell from the foreshore of the Thames and the lingering aroma from the fire, which still permeated the atmosphere. There was that damp moistness in the air, the result of copious quantities of water being turned to steam as it hit the intense heat of the burning training ship. The flames had been encouraged by the tar coating the cordage and also the sails, which had been unfurled, giving yet another area to scorch and burn. *Still,* thought Brooks, *it's a fine day for all that and hopefully to get even finer for Mr Bettesworth and his academy.*

A servant opened the door to Brooks's knocking.

'Could you tell Mr Bettesworth that Mr Brooks would like a word with him?'

'Very good, sir,' replied the servant, knuckling his forehead like the retired sailor he was. 'If you would like to wait in here,' indicating a small anteroom, 'I'll ask if Mr Bettesworth can see you. I know he's teaching navigation to a group of young gentlemen at the moment, sir,' he said apologetically and then added, 'You may have to wait a while what with you not having an appointment.'

'Oh, I think he'll want to see me,' responded Brooks with a knowing smile.

True to his prediction, Mr Bettesworth entered the room just a few minutes later with an air of frustration and exasperation about him.

He nodded curtly at Brooks and said, 'Good day, sir. This is unexpected but I did hope to see you soon to see if there is any resolution in sight to this problem. Come through. Come through.'

He moved off down a passage with rooms opening off it on either side.

'The main classrooms, as you can imagine, but of course you've been here before.'

They went into Bettesworth's study, or *Captain's Office* as it said on the door, at the rear of the academy. The room overlooked the river, and prominent in that view were the charred remains of the pride of the institution, the mock-up training vessel. Bettesworth indicated a chair facing the window for Brooks to sit in whilst he made his way behind his desk and settled himself in his own, more comfortable, chair. It did not escape Brooks's notice that Bettesworth's seat of choice was what was becoming known as a captain's chair, and he had to fight hard not to allow himself a wry grin.

'Well, Mr Brooks, where do we go from here? I've left one of my assistants taking my class, so I'd like to be able to get back to it as soon as possible.'

He was leaning back in his captain's chair with his forearms and the palms of his hands flat on top of the blue leather inlay of his desk. He had fixed Brooks with what he hoped was an intimidating stare, with his mouth set in a grim line.

Brooks leant his head slightly to one side and raised an eyebrow.

'Mr Bettesworth, it is my belief that an accommodation can be reached to the satisfaction of all parties concerned with little or no further ado. I have had extensive discussions with my people and this is the proposal which I am authorised to put to you.'

Extensive discussions indeed. He had played no part in the proposed arrangements whatsoever. Mr Brown had delivered the entire proposed solution like a well-packaged birthday gift. It seemed so good to Brooks that he would not have been surprised if it had been presented with an elaborate bow in many coloured ribbons on top!

'Mr Brooks, let me hear your proposal, sir.'

There was more than a little antagonism in his voice and more than a hint that he was convinced that whatever was being offered would only be the beginning of a long and hard process of negotiation. After all, he was dealing with a banker, and as far as he was concerned bankers and insurers were cut from the same cloth.

'My dear Mr Bettesworth, I will not prevaricate,' said Brooks, as he spread his arms a little and leant towards the desk.

He was adopting a physical pose which from his long experience of dealing with the bank's clients he knew usually helped them to be persuaded of his sincerity.

He continued. 'This is the proposal. Your training vessel is to be completely rebuilt to your specifications by the crew of the Royal Navy sloop the *Atalanta* under the command of Lieutenant Hills. As soon as you confirm your acceptance of this, then the Admiralty will issue Lieutenant Hills with the necessary orders and the authority to obtain any stores and materials required.'

Bettesworth's jaw actually dropped, and he gazed at Brooks in utter disbelief. 'What? The navy is going to do this. Why? Of course, this is more than acceptable, but I don't understand how you have arranged such a thing, sir.'

'Mr Bettesworth, sometimes it is better just to accept that good fortune can sometimes outweigh any bad luck. Not that the fire could be referred to in those terms, of course,' Brooks added hastily. 'No excuse for that. No excuse at all. I cannot tell you of all the machinations involved in this arrangement but, although you may not be aware of it, the Admiralty has observed with interest your inspirational use of this vessel and feels this presents them with an excellent opportunity to assess the viability of constructing others themselves. It will be very good for the academy to be seen to be working directly with the Royal Navy, and your young gentlemen will gain great experience from their involvement in this.'

'Mr Brooks, I don't need to know how this has come about at all. All I know is that you have used your influence for my benefit and for that I thank you, sir.' He hesitated a moment and then, looking up, said: 'What do I do about the Sun Fire Office now?'

'Oh, come, Mr Bettesworth,' said a smiling Brooks. 'A minor worry surely. They are looking to reduce any claim you may have made, are they not? They are a business like any other. Ask them to make you a cash offer and then simply accept it. Just allow them to settle and then use the money as you will for the academy's benefit.' Brooks continued. 'Well, Mr Bettesworth, I must allow you to return to your navigation class. I dare say you will not be too hard on the slower young gentlemen today, eh?' He smiled and stood up from his seat.

Bettesworth came out from behind his desk and extended his hand, which Brooks shook warmly. They walked together to the front door of the academy and as Bettesworth showed his visitor out, he said, 'How is the young man? John Machele. I had no option but to expel him, you know. I felt him to be a danger both to himself and to others. It was odd but, and I don't know how else to say this, he seemed to enjoy the rules and regulations as if they were something that had been missing in his life, but what he could not abide was being disciplined or reprimanded. Strange.'

'Master Machele is uncertain what the future now holds for him, but I do know that he has very positive feelings about the three months he has been with you.'

Brooks sensed that Bettesworth was genuinely concerned about Machele's well-being and thought to himself that that boded well for the care of the other young gentlemen.

Brooks went down the two steps to his hired carriage and, turning back towards Mr Bettesworth, he said conspiratorially, 'It may well be that during the course of the work reconstructing your vessel you may receive an unofficial visit from a certain personage with an interest in all things nautical and also close to the Lordships of the Admiralty. Good day, sir.'

And, with that, he got into his carriage and tapped on its roof to tell the driver to move off.

Mr Bettesworth was left standing at the open door of the academy with his mouth agape.

AWAITING THE COURT'S VERDICT

29th August 1796

The marine escorts me to a small cabin which I enter whilst he stands outside the closed, but not locked, door. Nearly there, I think to myself. I wonder how long they will take deciding my fate. Not very long surely, unless they take refreshment. I've never known a coterie of captains… that's a good expression, John, a coterie of captains, I like that. I like that a lot… Where was I? Oh yes, I've never known a coterie of captains to hasten themselves when there is refreshment to be had. Actually, I have no knowledge of how a coterie of captains usually behaves, but there are eleven of them so I think that this decision will probably be a six-bottle one. Not enough to spoil their luncheon.

I know how to tell how long a coterie of captains takes to make a six-bottle decision or however many they manage to get through. I can't think why it should take much time anyway, or is it just a matter of form? They must be seen to have given my case serious consideration, although I have no idea what it is that they need to consider. I am guilty and there is no gainsaying that, no matter how the evidence is looked at. Oh yes, how long will they take? The life on board every ship in His Majesty's Navy is governed by two things. There are the Articles of War, which I am being tried under and, secondly, the sound of bells. Every half an hour, the ship's bell rings. The hour is signalled by even numbers of rings and the halfs by odd numbers. The watches change. They divide the day into four-hour chunks, so that at the end of every four hours the bell is rung eight times. Time to change the watch. I think that's hilarious. I picture people taking out their watches every four hours and then changing them for something else. Well, maybe not really hilarious but it appealed to me. Was that a bell I heard then? Not sure. I'll count from the next. After all, what's half an hour more or less today?

I learnt about the four-hour segments very early on after arriving on board the Sandwich. Then I thought someone was playing a joke on me when I was told there were two watches called "dogs". The First Dog Watch and the Second Dog Watch were only two hours each and filled the time between the end of the Afternoon Watch and the start of the First Watch. As far as I was concerned, that meant between four o'clock in the afternoon and eight o'clock at night. Never mind why the dogs are called dogs. What kind of system would call a working period starting at eight o'clock in the evening the First Watch? No idea. I found so many things so very odd about the navy. Mmm… I only found that the Dog Watches were an actual thing when I was the midshipman of the watch and had to be fetched from where I was dozing in the gunroom by one of the quartermasters.

When I reached the deck, I was made to stand to attention whilst a lieutenant, who was the officer of the watch, berated me most soundly whilst the ordinary seamen, the foremast Jacks or the people as I think they call them, God knows why, stood there grinning all over their faces. I really did think that time that I was going to kiss the gunner's daughter, but I was spared that humiliation at least.

The lieutenant started by being sarcastic, evidently to entertain the other members of the watch, by welcoming me onto the quarterdeck with 'I trust, Mr Machele, that you are well rested, and may I say how grateful we all are that you have deigned to grace us with your presence.'

I could appreciate what he was doing. It was a very entertaining performance and I so very nearly removed my hat and swept it downwards and forward across my breast in an elaborate courtly bow, accompanying the movement with a spoken response of 'Your servant, sir' but I managed, just in time, to remain silently at attention. The lieutenant's tirade went on apace and I soon changed from being Mr Machele to a middie and then a mere snotty. I don't forget things like that, and neither will I forget the experience that followed. I was the midshipman of the watch. The lieutenant decided that I would not be pacing the quarterdeck trying to look as though I was an alert officer in the Royal Navy but I would actually watch.

I was to spend the remainder of my watch watching from the masthead. I don't have a good head for heights and had dreaded every time I was sent aloft. Fortunately, when they beat to quarters, my place was on the platform, where the marine sharpshooters had their post when the enemy was being engaged. I still had to climb up to it and that was testing enough for me. It was a fairly gentle climb up the rigging, or the ratlines, pronounced "rattlins". Why can't people just pronounce things in the usual way and not keep changing things? Anyway, the ratlines looked like rope ladders, but the footholds are only thin pieces of rope tied between the shrouds, so they can be climbed as you would a rope ladder. I got no sense of security climbing it because I was never alone on it. There were always other people moving on either side as well as both above and below me, making the ropes quiver and shake in a most alarming way. The seamen had the advantage of me since they didn't wear shoes, which meant they could grip with their bare toes. And another thing. Why are some of these ropes called shrouds? I thought that was what you wrapped corpses in. Still, that's the navy for you. At least there was a real platform which gave, after a while, a slight feeling of safety and stability as long as I didn't look down too often. But for the remainder of this watch I was to go to the masthead. What he meant was not the top of any mast but the top of the mainmast. I was to climb all the way above the mainsail. I was to straddle the highest yard in the ship and stay there until ordered down. Then came the order I dreaded most of all: 'And, sir, I will be watching you. You will not, I repeat not, use the lubbers' hole.' That was punishment enough for me. This was even more terrifying than just being mastheaded.

At intervals up the ratlines there were access holes to the platforms around the masts. These holes were the "lubbers' holes". Seamen would scamper up the rigging, up and up, *and the most skilled of them, the topmen, would be going to their stations where I was being sent as a punishment. I was both horrified and filled with envy and admiration as I watched them, barefooted, run along the yards seemingly oblivious to the drop below them, where the members of the crew seemed like ants moving around. A topman would never even consider using a lubbers' hole but would continue climbing past the platform, which meant, for a while, they had to hang backwards so that if they missed their footing or their hands lost their grip, they would fall, after bouncing off the rigging, either onto the unforgiving deck or plunge into the equally unforgiving sea. And this is what I had to do. No lubbers' hole for me. I did it. Oh yes, I did it. It took me such a long time, and I never want to feel as frightened as that ever again.*

God, you're a fool sometimes, John. That was my chance to put this plan into action. I could have disobeyed the lieutenant's order and started this then and it would all have been over by now. So why didn't I? Well, very simple really. I hadn't been on board long enough to know that I had to come up with this plan. Things were still quite new to me and I have always liked new things. Well, for a short while anyway, and then they become just ordinary, and ordinary is not nice. So, I didn't think it necessary to leave this life whilst still at sea, even though being moored we didn't actually go to sea as such, and I was still trying to learn the ropes. That's good, John: to learn the ropes. That's one of the first things a midshipman has to do. So many ropes; each with its own name and each with its own purpose. Middies were tested by the officer of the watch, who would send them to check this rope or that rope, and heaven help him if he didn't know where to go. It was the same with the signal flags.

You were expected to be able to read signal flags, and there was a large book with illustrations of every flag that might be used which the signal midshipman had to have by his side when on watch or at quarters. I fairly enjoyed that because it was largely a matter of memory. I am really proficient at linking pictures to words or particular meanings. Words without pictures are just collections of letters. Nothing more. Where was I? Oh yes, the signal book. I realised very quickly that certain signals such as "All captains to report to flagship" or "Prepare to take on board supplies" were the quite common ones so I learnt them off by heart, for which I received praise for my application. I like praise. I feel myself standing straighter. I acknowledge it with a short 'Thank you, sir' and don't stammer and blush like some of the others, who are, mostly, somewhat younger than me. I accept praise as my due when I know I have done something well. Simple. Somebody says, 'Well done, John' and I say to myself, 'Well done, John' as well. I see nothing wrong with self-praise.

Mark you, there have been occasions when I have not read the flags as they were supposed to be read. I can be a little, just a little, over-confident at times. I was so sure one day of what a signal meant that, seeing the flags break out on the flagship... that's another odd navy thing. It's called a flagship not necessarily because that is where all the signal flags are flown from at all but because that is the ship with the admiral's flag being flown...

I reported to the officer of the watch, 'All captains

to repair on board', expecting to be ordered to relay this message to Captain Mosse.

Instead, the lieutenant fixed me with a stony glare, saying, 'Are you certain, Mr Machele?'

'Yes, sir,' I replied, without any hesitation.

'Have you read the signal orders for today? Have you actually bothered to open the signal book, or do you think that you know so much that you didn't need to?'

I remember that I, even I, blushed and stammered.

Silly boy, John, silly boy.

The orders on a separate sheet of paper inside the signal book detailed that certain signals were to have different meanings to their usual ones: a simple ruse to confuse any enemy who may be observing us and who would be as familiar as us with the meaning of certain combinations of flags. Another little ruse often employed for the same reason, but equally more often than not, designed to test the midshipmen's ability to select the correct flags to be hoisted, was being ordered to transmit lines of poetry or absolute nonsense. On one such occasion, I was told to send the signal "Ask Polly how to bake an apple tart".

It was a real test for me trying to put that signal together using the least number of flags, and God only knows what a spy would have made of it. Unless he wanted to know that as well!

Where was I? Ah yes. Not being allowed to use the lubbers' hole and how frightened I was and never wanting to be as frightened as that ever again. Still, I won't ever have to be, will I? I'm most certainly not frightened now. I know what will happen when I re-enter the court, but this is different, for I am in charge of my own destiny at last. I am not at the beck and call of everybody else. I, John Machele, have spun my web and can watch from the centre as people come and go, believing they are the ones who are governing what happens to me, totally unaware that I am using them for my own purposes.

Damn. I'm certain I must have missed another bell. Does it matter that much? Not really, I suppose. I was interested, for a while, in just how long a six-bottle decision would take to be made by a coterie of captains, but, well…

I wonder whose cabin this is. Probably a junior lieutenant. Whoever he is, he must be on watch. At least he gets to have an almost private place to himself even though this looks like there is only a piece of tarpaulin on this side and not a bulkhead at all. Still, it's a lot better than the midshipmen's berth. That gunroom with all those other middies in it. There's no privacy at all: eating, drinking, sleeping, even sometimes trying to study, not to mention the so-called "skylarking", which often results in the youngest and smallest being subjected to all sorts of maltreatment. Still, that's the way of the middies' berth. Everyone goes through it. Makes them grow up, so I was told. Never experienced it myself when I was growing up in all those different places, and I definitely wasn't subjected to any of this, but only because I am twenty years old. No wonder middies were also called "snotties". The young ones never seemed to have a handkerchief when they needed one, so they wiped their noses on their sleeves. Little beasts.

I didn't brush against one of them on my way here, did I? No, of course not. Even if I had, that stain on my breeches is much too dark to be caused by a runny nose, isn't it? So, what shall I do about it? I must look my best when they take me out to hang me. Perhaps I could borrow a pair of breeches from someone. I wouldn't need them for long and then they could have them back. Surely, they'd allow that. Treat it as a last request.

It's still a puzzle to me how I have finished up here in the Royal Navy. I know it was done without consulting me and because someone unknown thought it was in my best interests, but how do they know that? Only I know that, surely? There I was, enjoying life in lodgings, and there was that incident with the maid, and next thing I know I'm joining the bloody army.

How long ago was that, John? Think about it. Only a few months ago if I remember well, but things have gone so fast. I really must try to get what happened in the right order. It doesn't mean I'll forgive them for continuing to control my life, but I just want to understand. I'd also like them to understand what they make me feel like as well. That's important, John. Very important. You know they won't listen, don't you? Oh, they'll listen all right. The condemned man is allowed to make a speech before he is hanged. That is all part of my plan.

Oh yes, I'll be heard then all right. There will be no one to stop me. Just remember, John: the lodgings and that maid. That's what started all this off, isn't it, John? Ah yes, that bloody maid.

AT THE LODGINGS WITH MARY CHANDLER

February 1796

I have decided. Tonight, or maybe tomorrow night, Mary and I are going to spend the evening, and maybe most of the night, at a place of which I have fond memories: Vauxhall Gardens. It may be a little cold, it being February, but I'm sure I can keep her nice and warm. What are you thinking of, John? It's February. The gardens are usually only open from May to maybe September. All right, slight change of plan. Same outcome but I know of somewhere else just as suited to my purpose that can be very warm indeed.

I haven't actually asked her yet but that isn't really necessary. I am a gentleman and she is only a housemaid. A damned pretty one but still only a maid. I know that, like the others, she watches me whenever one of them isn't, but that is why she cannot refuse to allow me to escort her to the Theatre of Delights. She can watch me there just as well as she can here, and we can have such fun together. I'm certain she has never been anywhere like it before. It will be an education in diversion and enjoyment. She can sample the pleasures I have sampled, but this time it will be her with me. No strumpets or doxies to be paid for this time. No indeed. I shall be bringing my own. Pay the entrance fee. Buy a bottle or two of wine, better than she has ever had before, expensive but worth it this time. Watch her face light up in amazement at the entertaining spectacles. The ladies and gentlemen parading and then disappearing into their reserved rooms to commit whatever illicit follies they have in mind. Everyone safe in the shared knowledge that, if observed, the observer is engaged in a similar pursuit of pleasure and, therefore, will not be spreading the word around.

She will be knocking at my door very soon with my change of bed linen, and that will be the time to tell her of her forthcoming good fortune.

True enough, there is a knock at my bedroom door, and I hear Mary call out: 'Sir, Mr Machele. It's Mary. Can I come in, sir?'

'Yes, yes. Come in, Mary, come in,' I reply, in my most encouraging voice.

She looks around the half-open door and sees that I am seated at my desk by the window on the opposite side of the room.

'I've come to change the bed linen, sir,' she said. 'Won't take me very long. You get on with whatever it is you are doing, sir.'

So here she is. Mary, who has no idea of the pleasure that I am going to offer her tonight or tomorrow night. Mary, who I think is about the same age as me: around about eighteen or nineteen, possibly even twenty; not a classical beauty but good enough for what I have in mind; a bit shorter than me, not that I'm very tall. She is maybe 5' 4", and some would say a little plump. I would say she was wholesome in a manner that invites more than one little cuddle. Her cheeks are a bit flushed, but that is hardly surprising since I gather Miss Bywater, my landlady, keeps her so busy running errands up and down stairs. It's hard to tell the natural colour of her hair but, from the wisps that escape from her cap, it is probably a mousey brown. Now is the time to make my move and surprise her with the news of her good fortune.

Indicating the other chair, I waved her towards it. 'Come, Mary, sit here by me awhile. I have something to say to you.'

Mary moved across the room and sat in the chair, with a puzzled look of apprehension on her face.

Taking a deep breath, I continued. 'Mary, Miss Bywater works you hard, does she not?'

She pondered this question for a moment and then replied, 'No more than any other mistress, sir. And I do get Sunday afternoons off after me and the other servants have attended morning worship with her.'

'And what about your evenings? Which ones do you get off?' I continued, enquiring in what I hoped Mary would feel to be an interested and concerned tone of voice, but without her sensing where this conversation was heading.

'Oh no, sir. No evenings off as such,' she replied. 'I wait until madam says she won't be needing me anymore tonight and then I go to bed. It's a long day, sir.'

'Well, here is a surprise for you, Mary,' I said. 'Have you ever been to what may be called a house of delights?'

'No, sir, I have not,' she replied indignantly.

Mmm, I think. The poor girl has obviously never been, and why should she have, but even though she hasn't, she believes it to be a place of impropriety. Does she know what that is? I wonder. She clearly seems to think it is not a fit place for a decent girl to be seen in.

'Mary, Mary, it is not what you think. That is just what people call it.'

I fear I may have begun to give her the wrong impression, or, unfortunately, the right impression.

'It is an establishment where people go for sophisticated fun and enjoyment. There are entertainments; often plays and gaming rooms, but they are mainly for the gentlemen. There are also private dining rooms, and I am taking you there either tonight or tomorrow night after your mistress has retired for the night. There, what do you think to that, my girl? Tonight or tomorrow? You probably need time to put on your best clothes, don't you?' I finished with a smile and a flourish.

Mary looked down and fiddled with her apron. 'Oh, sir, thank you very much but I can't go with you. I'm a maid and you're a gentleman. You know about these things and how to behave and I don't. My best clothes aren't anything like those fashionable ones,' she said, beginning to look flustered.

Time for a bit of encouragement.

'Come, Mary. I am doing this for you. To make your life a better one. We can go in fancy dress as a groom and a maid. You'll be amazed how many people do that. It's part of the fun. Only, this time, my partner really will be a maid but no one will know.'

'Sir, I can't get away just like that,' she protested. 'It isn't as easy as you make it sound. What if madam needs me in the night and finds me not here? I would lose my position and she wouldn't give me a character, so how would I find another post?'

Well, here's a surprise. I thought she would be honoured and delighted. So pleased that I would do something as nice as this for her to make her life so much happier after all the drudgery all day long. There's something here I don't understand.

I got up out of my chair and paced across the room. Turning to face her, I said, 'So, are you saying you don't want to come with me, or you can't?'

I can sense an edge coming into my voice. I can almost understand why she can't, but that isn't quite the same as won't.

'But the idea, you like the idea, don't you?'

I can hear a pleading coming from me and I don't like it at all. If she can hear it, what will she think of me? I must not sound weak.

'Sir,' a slight tremor in her voice, 'sir, it would be madness if I went with you. It couldn't work. It would be crazy to try it.' Her voice was faltering and her eyes were flitting to the other side of the room where the door was.

Those words again. Madness. Crazy. Why do people keep saying them? It doesn't matter where they come in a sentence, and I most certainly know my grammar, it's the very words themselves.

I strode to where Mary was still in the chair at the desk and as I tried to make sense of what was happening, the effect of those words, I flung my arms wide and knocked one of the candles off the desk and against the curtain, which started to singe almost immediately.

There it is: smoke again. Are there going to be flames? No.

Mary leapt up and threw a pitcher of water over the curtain.

So, no flames tonight but just the smell, that familiar smell.

So that's the way it is, is it? What has been said cannot be unsaid. That's good, John. Did I just think of that? Anyway, never mind who thought of that. Where do we go from here? Mad, crazy? That change is still coming. I can feel it. Why did she have to say that? Shall I give her a chance? She looks sorry, her head down like that. No. Now she is looking at me only sideways. Is she looking at how easy it would be to get out of my room? She knows where the door is. She should do. She lives here. I know what I'll do: I'll feign interest in her reasoning.

'Mary, what makes you say I am mad or crazy?'

There, how reasonable am I sounding?

Mary looked up, clasping her hands together and raising them towards me.

'Oh, sir, I had not meant to call you mad or crazy. Not you, sir. It was the idea that was mad or crazy, not you, sir. I could not see how your idea could work! That is all, what with me being a real maid and all.' She stayed slightly hunched forward. She resembled a supplicant in a religious painting anxiously asking for forgiveness from the person in front of her who had the power to forgive or to damn.

Does she seriously think that there could be a different outcome now that she has started down that path?

'But, Mary, I am my ideas. This is what makes us different from the animals. God allows us to think in any way we choose. Not like the animals. They think – if their base instincts can be termed such a thing – of food, shelter and reproduction. Oh, don't look so shocked, Mary! Reproduction is natural. We do it best because we are not base creatures. We believe, or are taught to believe, that to do it without the blessing of the Church is a mortal sin. Where is the pleasure? I ask you. So, think on, Mary. The Great Creator has made us in His image or so we are told. Do you consider yourself a Christian, Mary? Man has been given the power of thought; the ability to create ideas. So, Mary, if, as you say, it is my ideas that are mad or crazy, then is it God who is mad or crazy or me, John Machele? What do you have to say to that, Mary, housemaid of these lodgings, who feels unable to accompany me for an evening of more pleasure than you have ever experienced in your life before? Pleasure and enjoyment beyond your wildest dreams in the company of people you have never dreamt yourself fit to mingle with.'

Mary looked confused; perplexed. Was she being forgiven? Had I said I understood what she had meant about the impossible position I was attempting to place her in?

'Sir, Master John, Mr Machele, you use words and arguments to leave me confused. I know what I meant but you are much cleverer than me. I am a housemaid, as you say, and I know my place, which is why I cannot go with you.' She spoke in what she felt to be a conciliatory tone, hoping to reduce the rising tension that seemed to be emanating from me and spreading to fill every corner of the room.

She continued. 'I really should be going now, sir. My mistress will be wondering what I am doing in a room alone with you for all this time.'

She started to make her way to the door when she heard a loud, metallic click. Turning her gaze fully on me, she saw that I was holding a cocked pistol. It was not pointing at her but at my own head.

'You see, Mary, my life is mine to do with what I will, and now I choose to say farewell to it but only with your permission. So, you see, I place my life in your hands, Mary.'

Mary moved cautiously towards me with her arms reaching out beseechingly. 'No, Master John, no! I cannot give you permission to do this. You are not being fair to me. Put it down, please, Master John.'

Her voice, which had begun high-pitched with a shocked tremor, lowered to a beseeching pleading as she got closer to me.

'Please, sir, please.'

'What is it, Mary? What is it to you if I live or die? Do you think you'll be blamed and lose your position? Here, Mary, take the pistol.'

I lowered the gun from my head, took the barrel in my left hand and held it out to her. She grasped it by the butt and her forefinger instinctively slipped inside the trigger guard.

'Be careful, Mary,' I cried out, in a condescending tone of mock concern. 'It is loaded. Point it away from us both or, better still, just put it down.'

Mary hesitated, uncertain as to what would be best. If she put the pistol down too hard, it might go off. If she held on to it, she could point it at me whilst she left the room to fetch her mistress.

'Have you ever cocked or uncocked a pistol, Mary? Cocking is just pulling back on the hammer so then after it clicks you just squeeze the trigger. Do you think you know how to do that, Mary? You slowly squeeze the trigger.' We both looked down at the pistol in Mary's hand, where her forefinger was only a hairbreadth away from the trigger itself.

'Uncocking is just a trifle more difficult. Concentrate, Mary, concentrate. Here is my other pistol. See, the hammer is cocked. Now copy me, Mary.'

She watched as I pulled the hammer of this pistol a little further back and eased it forward and down.

'There, Mary, be gentle but firm. You are in control of your pistol. Gently lower the hammer, making sure there is no spark from the flint. That's it, Mary. Well done.'

Mary had followed the instructions as though in a trance, mesmerised by the realisation that throughout this I had been holding another pistol.

'Why do you stare so, Mary? A gentleman never has but one pistol. They come as a pair or a brace as we call them, just like game birds. Two birds equal one brace.

Did not your mistress teach you that? Or maybe the cook? Were you never sent to order a brace of partridge or pheasant? You must have been, for I have been served game here in this house. Or are you, being a housemaid, only expected to carry out tasks within the house? Don't tremble so, Mary. We each have a pistol so we are evenly matched. You a maid and me a gentleman. And this is how it would be at the house of entertainment that you would not accompany me to tonight because you think the idea to be madness. A maid and a gentleman on even terms. So, what do you think now, sweet Mary, now we are equal?'

I moved to the bed, still holding the second pistol and caressing its barrel. I climbed onto the bed, plumped the pillows and sat upright, resting my head against the wall behind me.

Mary was still seated, whilst her eyes constantly flicked to and fro, looking at me with my pistol, looking down to the floor where her pistol now lay and measuring the distance to the door.

I called across to her from the bed, 'Mary, a cushion if you please behind my head. This wall is exceeding hard.'

At this request, Mary became a maid, a servant, once more. This was a world she understood. Wait for a legitimate instruction and carry it out.

'Yes, sir,' responded Mary, her voice still a little tremulous as she rose from her chair to do my bidding, taking the cushion from behind her back as she did so. She made her way across the room to the bed and offered the cushion to me.

I leant forward and said, 'There, Mary, there. Behind my head.'

I leant back against it as Mary held it in position. It was whilst she was still holding it that she heard the metallic click again. My pistol was cocked. She saw me place the barrel in my mouth.

Afterwards, she could not account for what happened next. It was all over in a split second, but she saw it as though in a slow dream. She still had hold of the edge of the cushion and as she jerked involuntarily away, it caught my arm, pulling the pistol from my mouth.

She had never heard a pistol discharge in a confined space before. In fact, she had never heard a pistol fired at all. The sound was deafening, the flash so bright and the smell acrid through the smoke. God, the smoke. And surely it could not be snowing?

No, she could see the wall now just above the looking glass. A large expanse of plaster was missing where the pistol ball had lodged itself. Mary slowly felt herself returning to the present. Time had seemed to be almost standing still for a short while, but reality and a touch of logic entered her world. She knew the pistol to be harmless now and she speedily removed it from my hand, and I appeared as surprised by what had happened as she was. Instinctively, she dropped it to the floor and kicked it across the room to join its twin by her chair.

Then she remembered. The pistols were identical twins yet still differed in one very important aspect. Hers was still loaded. But what to do? Could she cross the room and get out of the door before I tried to stop her? Yet again, she found herself measuring the distance to the door but realised it was not so simple this time. She had her back to me and she turned her head gradually until she could see what I was now doing. I seemed to be doing nothing at all. I was still sitting upright on the bed, staring before me and giving every appearance of being frozen in time. She knew that she would have to go to her chair to collect both pistols before running out of the door to safety. I could follow and possibly catch hold of her before she could open the door and flee the room. And there was no question of leaving the pistols there. She could not even simply scoop up just one since she wasn't certain that she could remember how to tell which one was loaded.

She turned her head again towards me and was transfixed by what she saw and heard.

'Ah, Mary,' I mused, giving every appearance of a man whose mind was far away. 'The smell, Mary. The smell. Isn't it the most wonderful thing? The smell of gunpowder. So acrid yet so sweet. And the smoke. Is it not a pitiful shame that so soon there will be no smoke and no smell remaining? Come, stay and sit beside me still.' I patted the bed to show her where I thought would be a better place for her. 'Come, just for a moment.' I moved across the bed so she could now perch on my right.

Mary could see no reason at all to do as he requested and her doubts as to the wisdom of being closer to him were manifest, but there was something about the way he spoke which she found herself unable not to cooperate with. She settled herself as comfortably as she could in her still-alarmed and nervous state. She was thinking to herself that surely she would hear the sound of feet pounding up the stairs at any moment, then she caught a glimpse of light reflecting off metal. What was he doing now?

I was holding a penknife to my throat and making sawing movements across it but without the blade coming into contact with my skin.

'Oh, Mary, Mary, Mary, do you really think you could stop me from meeting my Redeemer by my own hand and at a time and place of my own choosing? It is called free will, Mary. God gave us that to differentiate between us and the beasts of the fields. You must know that, Mary.'

All the while, the blade moved back and forth, back and forth, and Mary found herself becoming more and more fascinated and focused on its mesmeric quality.

She knew she had to speak; to say something, to do something. Where was her mistress? Where were the other servants? Surely, they must have heard something.

At last, she heard people coming up the stairs, calling out, asking if everything was all right. They were calling her name, but when she opened her mouth to reply no sound came out, or if it did it was a muffled croak that no one could have heard.

I had also heard the approaching footsteps and the calling-out. My head jerked up and I stared in the direction of the door. My right hand holding the knife rested on Mary's upper leg as the focus of my attention shifted. Mary must have felt my grip on the penknife slightly loosen. She seemed to make as though to place her hand over mine in a reassuring and understanding way, and I released the knife into her hand as she slid from the bed and ran to the door, gathering up the pistols as it burst open.

'Just what is going on in here, Mr Machele?' thundered the mistress of the house, Miss Bywater.

She was an angular – some would say a bony – woman, six feet in height, with tendrils of straw-like hair coming loose from the white cap she habitually wore. She had piercing blue-grey eyes and a pointed nose, which her guests swore could sniff out any form of trouble through a keyhole. Her gaze swiftly swept the room and took in the plaster that had shattered on the floor and the sight of me sitting on the bed with my head resting on the wall, looking for all the world as though I were dozing.

'Well, Mr Machele? And what have you done with Mary?'

Miss Bywater heard a muffled cry, seemingly from behind her.

'I'm here, Miss Bywater.'

'Where are you, girl?' Miss Bywater cried querulously.

She turned in the direction of Mary's voice and, pulling the door towards her, realised that in her haste to effect an entrance, she had pinned Mary against the wall, trapped by the door.

'What are you doing there, girl? And what are you holding? A knife and two pistols? Are they loaded?'

'Only one of them, ma'am,' replied Mary.

'So, who shot a hole in my plaster, eh, Mr Machele?' she said, challenging me to supply an immediate explanation, which was not forthcoming.

Mary then added, 'Don't forget there is a penknife as well.'

She felt her speech starting to gush.

'It's Mr Machele, Miss Bywater. I came as usual to see if there was anything he needed and before I knew it he had a pistol in his hand and was pointing it at his head and said he was going to end it all and then he gave the pistol to me asking if I knew how to use one and when I had it I looked up and he had another one in his mouth. I managed to get it off him but he shot the wall and then got out a penknife as though to cut his throat and I got that off him as well. He said I held his life in my hands and...' Mary finally ran out of breath and began shaking.

'Go downstairs, Mary, and tell Cook I said you were to have a large glass of my brandy. You are not to blame for anything that has happened here today. You're a good girl. Leave Mr Machele to me.'

Mary scuttled from the room, still clutching the pistols and the penknife, grateful to be going anywhere away from me in my present state of mind. A large glass of brandy would be most welcome as she told Cook her story. A glass of Miss Bywater's brandy. That was a rare occurrence indeed. Her mistress drew a fresh line on the bottle after every serving.

'Well, Mr Machele, I am waiting for an explanation of what happened here today. This is not the first time you have been the source of serious disquiet in my house.'

I lazily opened one eye and focused it on Miss Bywater.

'Why, Miss Bywater, what a pleasure to see you in my room. What brings you here?'

My expression was my most innocent and guileless. I knew Miss Bywater would appear eventually and was secretly quite terrified of her, as were her other guests. Innocence, misinterpretation and deliberate misunderstanding of any questions would seem to be the best approach in this situation.

That's right, John, pretend you have no knowledge of what has happened but offer to have the wall replastered even though I would deny that I had caused the damage when I discharged my pistol. That's it, John, feign ignorance, but be prepared to take the blame and make recompense. That should do it.

The lodgings were comfortable enough even if Miss Bywater was a tyrant. At least I knew that she was a person who was watching me, as did someone wherever I lodged.

'Mr Machele,' continued Miss Bywater, 'I see through you and your pretence. You know perfectly well why I am here. You know fully why Mary, a good housemaid, and the Lord knows they are hard enough to find, let alone keep, has taken your pistols and your penknife so do not pretend otherwise. Your look of innocence and overly polite expressions of surprise are wasted on me, sir. Since you came here, your behaviour has become increasingly worrying and, dare I say it, bizarre. Do not think for one minute that I will not report this latest occurrence to the payer of your lodgings, and I do not expect you will be with me for very much longer.' She paused.

I instantly changed my expression to one of contrition. I concentrated my gaze on her and spread out my arms from where I still rested my head against the wall whilst remaining on the bed in what I felt to be a gesture of conciliation. 'Miss Bywater, if I have been the cause of upset on this or any other occasion to yourself or any other member of your household then please accept my most humble and sincere apologies. I will willingly pay for the repairs to the wall. I have to be honest with you, Miss Bywater. Sometimes I do things and have no recollection of having done them but, I assure you, I mean no harm.'

That sounds well enough, John. My, the woman is a hard person. A veritable harridan. I'm sure that I'm right that she works poor Mary too hard for very little thanks. But that was a well-put-together apology, and the "no recollection" was a touch of genius. Well done, John. What will she say to that? I wonder.

'Mr Machele, that is all very well and good, but your behaviour causes concern. I tell you now, sir, that a member of my household will be watching over you through the night in case you should try to harm yourself again. Do not gainsay me, Mr Machele. This is what is going to happen.'

She turned on her heel and walked towards the door. Pausing, she added, 'Do you hear me, sir? Do you understand? Someone, a male servant, will be with you shortly.'

'Yes, Miss Bywater. Thank you for your concern,' I responded.

'Good night, Mr Machele,' she said, and left the room with the door still wide open.

I wonder who she'll send. I would wager it to be that surly brute of a groom, Jeb. What does bizarre mean?

ANOTHER PROBLEM SOLVED FOR THE PERSONAGE

February 1796

'What is the boy about, do you think, Brown? This business at his lodgings. I thought all was going well until this. Tried to shoot himself with his pistols? Threatening to cut his throat with a penknife? Shooting the plaster off the wall? And all this with a maid in his bedroom? What was she doing there anyway? As if I couldn't guess! But that's maids for you, eh, Brown, eh?'

The personage sat in what he referred to as his working chair, a carved Sheraton desk chair upholstered in fine chestnut-coloured leather. The chair and the desk before it faced Grosvenor Square, where he could take note of the various comings and goings when he tired of the correspondence awaiting his attention. He had rolled his chair on its castors back from the desk and turned it inwards to face Brown, standing in the centre of the room. He ruminatively rubbed the beringed and slightly podgy fingertips of his right hand in a circular motion on his forehead, slightly above the bridge of his nose.

Brown, in his habitual bottle-green suit, was pleasantly surprised, not only at what his master said but the way in which he said it. He knew from years of being in his service how his master was susceptible to mood swings, some of which could be quite extreme. Today, he gave every appearance of being jocular and even bordering on the familiar. There had been no explosive outburst; no expletives. The spluttering had been kept to a minimum and evidently apoplexy was not to be featured on today's bill of fare.

'Quite, sir, quite,' Brown responded, 'but if I may be permitted to say, sir, he is no longer a boy. John is now twenty years of age and fast approaching his majority.'

'Good God, man, don't you think I know that? I of all people am more than aware of that. But what's to do? What's to do? Glad to see he had a maid in his room. Do him good, eh, Brown?'

Brown cleared his throat, sensing that his master was fast approaching a – possibly unwitting – crossing of a boundary between informality and familiarity, which he believed it was essential not to cross.

'That may well be, sir. There have been concerns over the past few months regarding his behaviour and the effect it has had upon the household and the other guests, sir. I do not have the details of all the incidents to hand, but it has been reported to me by way of Mr Brooks, who, as I am sure you remember, has not been directly involved in John's lodging arrangements and asserts that John's landlady, a Miss Bywater, has described the way he has behaved on occasions as bizarre. She is also, so I am told, of the opinion that he has too much time on his hands and is likely to slip into bad habits.' He waited to see what response would be forthcoming to that.

His master looked at him with a wry grin on his face.

'Bad habits, eh? What, a bit of drinking, time at the card tables and some wenching at a house of pleasure, I don't doubt. Well, good for him, I say.'

Brown watched him closely, knowing full well that his master could, at any moment, become quite manic and that he had to have a plan of action based on everyday practicalities for him to focus on in order to divert him.

His master continued.

'I did my fair share of that when I was younger, otherwise, there wouldn't be a young John Machele, would there, eh, Brown, eh? And you did say the landlady was a MISS Bywater, did you not? A spinster, eh? But I take her point even though it was not asked for. Too much time on his hands. She's probably right. I know we have him watched, but that's only to keep an eye on him to make sure he doesn't come to any serious harm. What he needs is something to occupy him. A career of some kind. Even, perhaps, a profession, something respectable and even with responsibilities. What do you think, Brown?' He looked intently at Brown, willing him to come forth with a workable solution, which he knew was Brown's particular area of expertise.

Brown gave every appearance of a man seriously seeking the answer to a tricky problem. The reality was that he had designed what he believed to be a satisfactory solution long before he had entered the room.

'Sir, he needs a position which will allow him to use what skills he has. He knows how to use pistols and he likes the smell of gunpowder. He also has a penchant for finery and so—'

The personage interrupted him: 'So perhaps the navy. I can have a word with the Admiralty...'

'Sir, if I may be permitted to finish, sir,' said Brown. 'He also rides exceedingly well.'

The personage responded, 'Ah, so it's the army. Of course. From my personal knowledge, bizarre behaviour is more than quite acceptable. Yes, make it the army. They dress better. That will appeal to young John.'

'If I may suggest, sir. It is my understanding that the Duke of York has succeeded Sir Jeffrey Amherst as the Colonel of the 2nd Regiment of the Life Guards. You could request that he take young Machele under his wing—'

He was interrupted again; only this time there was a spluttering sound. 'No, no. That would be much too close to the family.'

'Very good, sir. I see the problem,' quickly interjected Brown. 'What about the Royal Horse Guards, The Blues, sir? If you recall, Sir Charles Lennox, the Duke of Richmond, now has the command.'

'No, no, that won't do at all,' said the personage. 'Played cards with Richmond. Lost a pretty penny to him. Was never sure how he constantly won. There's no love between us, and there was that matter of that doxy as well. No, sorry, Brown, just won't do.'

'Well, sir,' said Brown, about to suggest his chosen solution, 'there is another royal regiment, and I'm sure you believe it to be only right and proper that John joins a royal regiment, but this one is slightly removed from the household ones. The Royal North British Regiment of Dragoons.'

'That's a bit of a mouthful, Brown.'

'Yes, sir,' responded Brown. 'They are now referred to as the Royal Scots Greys. Commanded by Archibald Montgomerie, Earl of Eglinton, and I am assured that their uniforms qualify as finery.'

'Mmm. Eglinton, Eglinton. Oh yes. Scottish fellow. Isn't he a patron of that poet chap, Robert Burns? Can't make out a single word he says but then that's his affair, I suppose. Army officer as the patron of a poet. Humbug. However, this looks as though our problem is solved. Where is the regiment at the moment?' he asked.

'At their barracks in Canterbury under the command of a Major Archibald Bothwell, sir.'

'Excellent, Brown. Excellent. I shall have a word with someone in the family who I am certain will be able to inform Eglinton that he would do well to award a commission to the lad and to expect his regiment to welcome Cornet John Machele to its ranks in the near future. The commission will need authorisation, but that's an internal matter, you understand. He will be granted a commission, and not by purchase, either. Acceptable though some bizarre behaviour may be, he has to learn the rules of the army and the customs of the regiment before he gets any real responsibility. Can't have madmen running the army, eh, eh?' He guffawed loudly at some private joke and wiped his mouth with a spotted kerchief.

'Very good, sir,' acknowledged Brown. 'I shall make the necessary arrangements and ensure Mr Brooks is thoroughly aware of the way matters stand.'

BROOKS & BROWN

February 1796

George Brooks studied the note from Mr Brown once again.

> *If convenient, should be obliged if we could meet today at two o'clock at your office. Machele to join Royal Scots Greys.*
>   *Your Obedient Servant, B.*

As far as George Brooks was concerned, it was as if John Machele had been spirited away after the affair with the Naval Academy four years ago and was now to be spirited back again.

Now it was February 1796, and he simply thought of the intervening time as Machele's missing years. It was almost as if John's behaviour warranted his being looked after somewhere until someone, and he still didn't exactly know who, felt he was fit to rejoin the wider world and society.

So here he was, soon to be having the care of John Machele again, but how long would it be for this time?

He pondered the idea and the cost of Machele joining the Royal Scots Greys. Brooks knew that whatever expenditure was necessary, the bills would be met in full as soon as they were presented, which was just as well. He knew the cost of a commission. He should do. Enough of his customers' children went into the army and often requested overdraft facilities to meet the additional costs incurred. So, it was to be His Majesty's 2nd Royal North British Regiment of Dragoons, known as the Royal Scots Greys. It was one of the royal regiments and prided itself on the quality of its officers. This was largely ensured by the ability to meet the cost required to be an officer. Commissions were for sale and officers' uniforms and equipment were indeed expensive, not to mention an expectation that an officer would supply his own horse. A court dress coat was 40 guineas and a jacket 15 guineas, with other equipment comparably dear.

There was a knock on his office door, and his clerk, Dodd, announced: 'Mr Brown, sir,' and, having ushered him in, he closed the door firmly behind him.

Brooks came out from behind his desk and extended a hand in greeting, which was gripped and shaken with some warmth by Mr Brown.

'Take a seat, Brown, take a seat,' said Brooks, with a welcoming smile on his face. 'It has been too long, sir, since I last saw you. You are well, sir?'

'I am indeed well, as you see,' replied Brown, seating himself comfortably. 'Our business with young John has not necessitated our meeting like this for some time, mainly because others have had the care of him until it was felt he should live in lodgings with his own allowance. Although you continued to manage his finances, we did not see the need for you to be directly concerned with his living and social arrangements until now. We are obliged to you for acting as the conduit for the reports from John's lodgings with Miss Bywater and are most grateful indeed for agreeing to listen to her last report about the latest incident with his pistols.

He cannot stay much longer with her. Indeed, she has made that perfectly clear herself. There is no doubt in a certain personage's mind that young Machele needs to be somewhere that he feels of value and, please don't laugh, where he can dress in what he would regard as finery. He rides well, has had extensive training in swordsmanship and, despite shooting plaster off the wall at his lodgings, is actually an exceptionally good shot indeed. It is felt that in the army he will have a certain status, dress well and will live according to accepted rules and customs of the regiment.

Although by its very definition an army is a tool of war, it is, likely, somewhere that he will feel, if not exactly safe, at least secure. He will know where he fits and that, it is agreed, is the overriding need for his future.' Brown paused. He looked like a man who had needed to have his say on the matter and was relieved that in George Brooks he had found a sympathetic ear.

'My dear Brown,' said Brooks, 'I quite agree with you, sir. The signs of his troubled mind give me great concern. I may not have seen him for some four years, but I have wondered how he was managing. I felt it to be a good thing when I heard he had moved into lodgings, and I continued to make the necessary disbursements. Not too much in the way of gambling debts, which is always a good sign. No, he hasn't played footloose and fancy free with his Newmans, sir.'

'His what?' interjected Brown.

'My apologies. His Newmans. His money. The Chief Cashier of the Bank of England is one Abraham Newman, and his signature appears on all the banknotes. Hence, people often refer to them as Newmans,' he explained. He continued: 'I know the cost of fitting out a young gentleman for that regiment, and it is substantial. I assume he will be having a commission purchased?'

'Actually, no, sir. He will be awarded a commission as a cornet,' responded Brown.

'Awarded a commission? How can that be? I know the cost of a cornet's commission to be £840. How can he simply be awarded one? He must have friends in very high places indeed.'

'My dear George. I feel I may call you by your given name after all this time. John Machele does indeed have friends in high places and, unfortunately, I must refer you back to our first meeting where it was stressed that the identity of the personage, my master, would never be made known, and I'm afraid that has to remain so. I sincerely regret that this has to be the case but it does,' said Brown, tilting his head to one side with a rueful expression on his face but then adding: 'I should feel it a gesture of friendship, if I may make so bold, if you were to call me Augustus.'

'With the greatest of pleasure, sir, I mean, Augustus. Come, let us look to the future with a glass of brandy, sir, for I feel that my role in Machele's affairs is about to enter into a new phase, and there are questions which I must ask and hope that you will answer.'

George Brooks produced a bottle and a pair of elegant brandy glasses from his right-hand desk drawer and poured two exceedingly generous bumpers.

'Something the French do so well, Augustus. Best not to ask how I came by it, eh. Your health and that of John.' They clinked glasses, drank appreciatively and settled down to the business of the day.

'Now, George,' said Brown, savouring his brandy, 'I sense what your first question is going to be, bearing in mind the events of four years ago. No, you will not have to inform John of this latest choice of career for him this time.'

Brooks exhaled slowly, his relief showing visibly on his face as he relaxed further into the friendly warmth of his imported brandy, which was, in fact, a rather glorious, aged cognac.

Brooks began: 'That is a weight off my mind, Augustus. I well remember how amenable young John was to being enrolled at the Naval Academy, and he both enjoyed his time there and learnt a considerable amount. It is my belief that, at that time, he would have been more than content with a future in the Royal Navy. But there were those unfortunate incidents. That trip to Vauxhall Gardens; that was just boyish high spirits with his friends, and friends are not something John had really had before, what with the way he has been continually moved from one set of carers to another throughout his life. Showed a lot of initiative, though. That demonstration with the gunpowder was certainly dangerous, but that is John all over. He sees a different way of doing something that he believes to be better and goes ahead and does it. What there is no denying is that he can be a little impetuous and even misguided at times. But the fire. Well. We'll never really know the truth of that, but we all know the outcome. He is fascinated by the sight and smell of fire. At least he didn't set fire to Miss Bywater's house; well, not completely.' He chuckled to himself. 'There were a couple of curtains that had a good singeing. But nothing really alarming until this latest affair with the maid and his pistols.' He paused.

Brown took up the thread of the conversation: 'It was a disappointment that his time in those lodgings had to end in this way. We had placed him in more closely supervised ones before this and he did very well indeed, which is why it was thought he was ready for, what was to all intents and purposes, a fully independent situation.

As you know, George, he was still under, dare I use the word, surveillance, but in such a way that he was probably unaware of it. He was free to come and go as he pleased, and he gave every appearance of developing into a fairly mature young man. It was not only my opinion, but also that of the personage whom I have the privilege of serving, that John was learning the ways of a young gentleman of private means without greatly abusing that position.'

'Well, that is the whole point, is it not?' interrupted Brooks, his hands cradling his cognac and leaning forward.

'Young John is not so young anymore. He is twenty years of age. He will attain his majority next year and then what happens? The army may well be the answer. He does have a passion for dressing well, and he gives the appearance of being able to display a certain hauteur, which some may snigger at in one of his age but, with the trappings of a fine uniform, who knows?'

'Indeed, sir, indeed,' continued Brown, who, in turn, leant forward so the heads of both men were no more than two feet apart. 'And as I have said to you before, George, your part in John's affairs will not go unnoticed. We are obliged to you for the way you have responded to each of Miss Bywater's, shall we say, reports on John's behaviour. Tact and diplomacy every time. You are certainly a man who can calm stormy seas. And you have done it in such a way that there has never been a need to meet with Miss Bywater herself or to be directly involved with John, which may have, despite his previous liking for you, increased his sense that he was still being watched.'

'Well,' said Brooks, 'clearly, I shall be much more closely concerned with his affairs now. Do I assume that it will be my task, after he has been told of his future enlistment in the army, to make the various arrangements to facilitate such a move?'

'My dear George, I think you may enjoy your reacquaintance with John. As I said, he still holds a liking for you from four years ago. He sees you as someone who listens to what he says and makes him feel that he is involved in making decisions that affect his life. He appreciates that. And, possibly even more importantly, he regards you as a person who does his best to help him. Not only that but, for reasons I cannot fathom, he does not associate you with the people who watch him.'

'That is very nice to hear, Augustus,' responded Brooks, 'and I look forward to meeting him again as well. So, to details, Augustus. What is to happen and when?'

Brooks reached for the decanter and poured some more cognac for them both; the sweet, heady fumes filling the space between them.

'Very well,' resumed Brown, leaning back in his chair. 'It is anticipated that John will formally join the Royal Scots Greys early in March as a cornet. His commission, officially sponsored by Earl Eglinton, the colonel of the regiment, will require the signature of His Majesty. Nothing unusual about that. Standard procedure for commissions.' He added the latter point hastily, noticing a knowing expression forming on Brooks's face accompanied by slightly raised eyebrows, hoping to nip in the bud any conclusions, false or otherwise, that he may have been coming to. 'There will be the question of his uniform and other equipment to be organised. We will arrange the purchase of his mount, of course. Can't expect you to chase all over the country seeking the best piece of grey horseflesh to be found, eh?

'What I have in mind, George, assuming you can make yourself available, is that John comes to see you here the day after tomorrow at, say, eleven o'clock on his own. I don't see any need to accompany him, and it will further confirm to him that the relationship between the two of you is one that is in his best interests. One that is unencumbered by the possible interference of other people, and especially me.'

'Good idea, Augustus. Yes, man to man. He will appreciate that,' replied Brooks.

Brown continued: 'I should like you to go with him to the military tailors, Hawkes, with whom I have made an appointment on that day at twelve noon. Just time for you to have a chat first. My carriage will bring him and will remain at the service of the two of you and will return John to his lodgings at the conclusion of the day's business. Now, at the tailor's, he will be measured for his uniforms. Yes, uniforms. More than one indeed. Everyday barrack uniform, dress parade, mess and, of course, even if he may not need it for some time yet, that very expensive one, the court dress uniform. It is the very idea and sight of that outfit that John will be particularly taken with.

'The templates for uniforms are held at Hawkes and are subject to royal warrants to ensure all uniforms are uniform.' Brown allowed himself a little chuckle. 'He has already been measured for boots at his bootmaker's only a month ago, so I shall simply order more from them to the army pattern. Saddles, bridles, etc., will be handled by us, as will his regulation sabre to the new pattern, and a brace of officer's pistols will likewise be supplied. Can't have him using the same ones he shot the wall with, can we?' He chuckled again.

'Most excellent imported brandy, George,' he continued. 'How does that sound to you, eh? Oh yes. When his joining date is agreed, we would like you to accompany him to the Royal Scots Greys barracks in

Canterbury. My carriage will, of course, be made available for that purpose.'

'Very good, Augustus. I shall make the necessary arrangements here to ensure my time is free as required and shall await John's arrival the day after tomorrow at eleven of the clock. Will the various bills be presented to the bank to be met out of your funds?' Brooks asked.

'As usual, yes,' replied Brown. 'I shall, of course, ensure that adequate funds are deposited.'

'Excellent, excellent. Never doubted it, Augustus.'

Brooks rose to his feet, suddenly becoming aware that perhaps the amount of cognac consumed could be described as a little excessive for that time of day.

'I thank you for both your understanding and your hospitality, George, and I bid you good day.'

They shook hands like old friends united in a common cause. Brooks opened the office door and called: 'Dodd. Show Mr Brown to his carriage and see that I am not disturbed for the next hour.'

Brooks looked forward to an hour of contemplation about what the new future for John Machele might hold. He also felt a warm malaise coming over him as he settled himself back into his very, very comfortable and welcoming chair. 'Damned fine cognac. Damned fine,' he murmured to himself.

MOVING ON

February 1796

I knew damn well I couldn't stay much longer in those lodgings. Looking back, I can see that shooting at the wall was not really the sort of thing that any landlady should have to put up with. But I still, for the life of me, cannot understand why that maid, Mary, refused to be my partner, my guest, my equal for an evening, and maybe even a night of pleasure. Is it any wonder that I felt as though my life was worth nothing when even a mere housemaid rejects me thus?

However, life has taken another unexpected turn and for the better, I believe. I could see that that fellow Brown was a little hesitant when he broached the subject with me.

'My dear John, this is a fine to-do, don't you agree?' said Brown with a stern look on his face as he sat in the armchair in the lodgings with his two hands resting on the handle of his cane and his chin resting on them.

'Indeed, it is, Mr Brown, but a fellow can only suffer so much. The girl is a maid. A maid. Why does she think she has the right to reject an offer from me? I apologise for the damage to the wall. That was inexcusable, I know. I suppose you have come as usual to simply tell me where I am to be taken to next. I am twenty years of age now. Not a child. I am a gentleman and I want a gentleman's future. I am too old and very tired of other people always telling me what to do and where to go. Don't think that I don't know that even though I am told that where I am now at Miss Bywater's lodging house marks me as a gentleman, I am being constantly watched. And that means that people are reporting on everything I do. I am tired of it. I am tired of life if this is how things are to be forever.'

I could feel myself working up to a fine old temper. I began pacing in a most agitated manner from one side of the room to the other and back again whilst Brown's eyes followed me back and forth. He has known me so long that my actions and complaining tone no longer hold any surprises for him. He will wait until I have finished and then carry on with whatever message he has come to deliver to me. I know this.

'John, John, John,' said Brown, in what he felt to be a calming way. 'It is time to move on, as you say, but let us, together, give some thought to where that should be.'

Good Lord. Who else have I heard talk like that? I remember. It was that banker fellow, Brooks. He was the first to make me feel I was worth listening to and I was only sixteen then. Now I'm twenty and at last Brown gives the appearance of allowing me to be involved in shaping my own future. Well, well.

'I am not certain just what future I see for myself, Mr Brown. I wish to be regarded as a gentleman, but what else is there? Four years ago, I thought that my future lay in a career in the navy. I think I would have liked that then but things went wrong for me. So surely I am not to join the navy after all, am I? I don't think I want to anymore, so what else can a gentleman do?'

I looked expectantly at Brown, looking for some guidance, although, based on past experience, I sensed that a decision had already been taken. I also remembered that Mr Brooks had asked me in the past what I was good at and what I enjoyed before I learnt anyway that I was to be enrolled at the Naval Academy. Was this to be the same approach?

Brown continued. 'I can think of a very fine future for you should you be favourable to the idea, but I must ask you to think about what your interests are. What do you enjoy doing? What are you good at?'

'Well, sir…'

Almost word for word what Mr Brooks had said to me. Does Brown really think that I cannot see through his little ruse? Oh well, let us play his game and see where we finish up, shall we? Who knows, he may have something to my benefit up his sleeve, although I very much doubt it.

'Being a gentleman is in the forefront of my thinking, sir. The dress and the manners. The doors that open because of it. I could say that I enjoy shooting, but not usually at walls.'

I thought an attempt at humour would show me in a good light.

'You are aware of my skill with the sword from all the tuition I have had, and I ride exceedingly well.'

Time for another try at humour, I thought.

'Oh yes, I can drink a fair amount without falling over as well.' I gave a little chuckle at this, and even Brown raised an eyebrow, and the corner of his mouth began to twitch.

Well done, John. Well done.

Brown raised his chin from where it had been resting on his hands and said: 'What you have just described to me sounds like an officer in the army. A gentleman: an officer has to be a gentleman, John. He lives by what you currently see as manners, which in the army would be the way of living within the expectations of the regiment, which is often not just a matter of regulations but also one of tradition. As for the dress, well, an officer dresses in different uniforms according to the duties he is performing. As an officer, you would also have to be prepared for special occasions, which means another uniform for the possibility of being presented at court. That uniform can best be described as finery, John. Now, what else? Ah yes. You shoot. You're a good horseman. You are an excellent swordsman and, according to you, you can hold your liquor. This last attribute would stand you in good stead indeed.' He chuckled to himself.

So that was it, was it? I knew it all along. Someone has decided I am to join the army. The decision has already been taken regardless of what I may think. Somehow, though, I am not greatly perturbed by this. The army? Now I think about it, yes, I can think of no reason why not. I remember at the Naval Academy I met other lads like me. We liked each other. We were chums and I liked that feeling. He's looking at me in that appraising way he has. I can almost hear his thoughts. Will I go along with this idea or not? If not, then what happens next?

'Mr Brown, what a splendid idea. I would never have thought of it myself. I like the idea of finery very much. Whose idea was this really? Don't answer that. I know you can't tell me. You'll only say it was someone who takes an interest in me. So, what next?'

'Well, John, I am so pleased that you like the idea so much. I'm certain this will be a grand life for you.' The relief in his voice was clear to hear. 'It has been arranged, now that you agree, that you will join one of the "royal" regiments as befits your gentlemanly status. You will be commissioned into the Royal Scots Greys as a cornet and be stationed at their barracks at Canterbury. Now it is just a question of getting your uniforms and equipment organised as soon as we can. Oh, and a fine grey mount for you also. Do you have any plans for tomorrow, John?' he asked.

'Tomorrow? Why no, not at the moment.'

I could hear a slight stammer coming into my speech. Tomorrow? This is all very sudden. Still, better to take a decision quickly than put it off. That sounds like the army way.

'Splendid,' continued Mr Brown. 'I understand that you felt a certain closeness to the banker, Mr Brooks. Am I right?' he asked.

'Yes, indeed, sir, I did. I felt him to be a man I could trust. Is he to be involved again?'

It all began to fall into place. Brown, Brooks, a new

career. All planned. All plotted. But Mr Brooks? Yes, I would look forward to being with him again if that was the intention.

Mr Brown went on. 'My carriage will collect you tomorrow morning at ten o'clock to renew your acquaintance with Mr Brooks, whom you will meet at his bank at eleven. At twelve noon, there is an appointment with Mr Hawkes in Piccadilly, where you will be measured for your uniforms. My carriage, without me, will be at the disposal of you both until the day's business is concluded. John, I am so pleased that this meets with your approbation, so very pleased, as will be that certain personage whom I represent.' He raised himself from the chair, bowed in my direction, made as if to leave the room in one fluid movement and then paused. He walked towards me and shook my hand warmly, saying, 'Very good, John. Very good,' and, turning on his heel, he left.

TO HAWKES: MILITARY OUTFITTERS

February 1796

At half past ten on the Thursday morning, George Brooks opened his door to the outer office and called: 'Dodd. Here a moment, if you please.'

The bespectacled Dodd clambered down from his high clerk's stool at Brooks's call.

'Yes, sir?'

'At eleven o'clock, I am expecting a visit from Mr Machele. Do you remember him?'

'Yes, sir,' replied Dodd. 'He was the young person you had dealings with at the Naval Academy if I recall.'

'Quite so. Good memory, Dodd,' continued Brooks. 'Anyway, he is not so young now and will be coming to see me, as I said. Please ensure that he is shown in to me as soon as he arrives. We shall be leaving together for another appointment shortly after, and I expect to be back around the hour of two or three.'

'Very good, sir. I will show him in immediately on his

arrival and ensure the other partners are aware of your absence on the bank's business,' affirmed Dodd.

George returned to his office and mused on two matters. Dodd had proved his worth as a clerk. His competence at accounting was definitely adequate, and over the years he had begun to show a propensity for establishing a good working rapport with the customers of the bank when he had direct contact with them. He didn't fawn over them in that annoyingly obsequious way that some of the other clerks did. He presented a very professional air to them. Polite and deferential but always firm in carrying out whatever instructions he had been given regarding a particular customer. 'I think I should encourage Dodd. Give him a little more leeway and variety. See how he copes,' he mused out loud.

The other matter, of course, was John Machele. Now twenty years of age. A young gentleman. His state of mind gave cause for concern. No doubt about that. Was he serious in that attempt to take his life at his lodgings? George pondered the issues whilst at the same time acknowledging to himself that he had not seen John for four years and was not fully informed of what had happened to him during that time. It was fortunate that the reports he had been in receipt of from Miss Bywater had detailed not only his behaviour but also his appearance and demeanour, so he had a fair idea of what to expect when he arrived that morning.

His reverie was interrupted by Dodd rapping his knuckles on the door, the door opening and Dodd announcing, 'Mr Machele for you, sir.'

'My dear John,' said Brooks, moving out from behind his desk and extending a hand in greeting, which was gripped in turn, at first rather tentatively and then firmly, by them both.

'How good to see you again. Has it really been four years? My, you have grown. Oh, I do apologise. That was most rude of me.' Brooks had been taking stock of John's appearance as he entered his office. He was slightly above average height. His light brown hair was gathered at the back with a black silk ribbon. The slightly protruding eyes and the way his forehead sloped back to his hairline were as he remembered. His dress was a credit to his tailor. A rust-coloured frock coat with a canary yellow waistcoat complemented his complexion well. His buff-coloured breeches were tucked into his highly fashionable black boots. The reports were right. He did carry himself well and, whilst there were signs of hauteur, thank goodness, they were not to excess. 'Here, John. Sit yourself down.'

John sat, as requested.

Mr Brooks does not appear to have changed. Both he and his office are as I remembered them. Even the clerk who ushered me in is the same. Does everything stay the same whilst it is me who continually changes?

'Mr Brooks. A pleasure to see you again. It was unfortunate, that affair at the Naval Academy, was it not, but I was much younger then. Now it looks as though it is the army for me. Not the navy after all. I don't think the navy is really the thing for me now that a commission awaits in one of the royal regiments. No, not the navy.

Have you seen the uniform of the Royal Scots Greys. Quite magnificent. Finery indeed.'

'And talking of finery, John,' interrupted Brooks, 'let us make our way to the carriage. You have an appointment at noon in Piccadilly at that most prestigious of military outfitters, Hawkes. It's only a mile or so, but with the number of conveyances on the streets it could take a little while.'

Brooks indicated that John should lead the way, and they passed through the outer office to the waiting coach. This carried them on, with much urging of other conveyances to clear a path by the coachman, who cracked his whip repeatedly, more to the alarm of the passengers than other road users, it seemed. The sign over the shop's façade proudly announced its status as being in the forefront of military tailors, with beautifully cut examples of their work displayed in the windows.

They entered the premises to the accompaniment of a discreetly ringing bell attached to the door to announce their arrival.

'Good day, gentlemen. I am Thomas Hawkes and you are most welcome in my establishment.' Brooks gave a visible start, seemingly surprised at being welcomed by the proprietor himself, but John merely nodded to him.

'A pleasure to meet you, Mr Hawkes. I am George Brooks and this is John Machele, who is to be measured for his uniforms as a cornet in the Royal Scots Greys. I must say that I had not expected the appointment to be with you in person.'

'My dear Mr Brooks, anyone coming here by

arrangement of your Mr Brown will always warrant my personal attention,' responded Mr Hawkes.

Brooks tried hard not to look in any way surprised, but he did have cause to wonder if Hawkes was someone else who had been assured that his services would not go unnoticed.

'So,' continued Hawkes, 'as I understand it, Mr Machele is to be measured for a complete set of uniforms suitable for every occasion, from barracks duty to a possible appearance at court. Mmm. You cut a fine figure, young man, and will cut an even finer one once you have been outfitted by us.'

Brooks felt John tugging at his sleeve. 'Excuse me a moment. Yes, what is it, John?' he asked, temporarily turning his back on Mr Hawkes.

John whispered, with his hand covering his mouth, 'Is Hawkes all right? I mean, he won't measure me the way my tailor does, will he? He does take such a long time making sure my breeches fit very snuggly.'

'I'm certain it will be fine, John. Anyway, I am here,' Brooks responded reassuringly. 'So many senior officers are fitted here, and if there was anything, shall we say, odd, they would soon change tailors.'

'Mr Hawkes,' said Brooks, turning back to the tailor, 'Mr Machele is your customer and he has been admiring the uniforms on display and was wondering if he had a choice regarding what cloth his uniforms would be made of.'

'Ah, Mr Machele,' continued Hawkes. 'Come and I will show you a fine selection of materials from which you may choose. The style, the cut, the colour is dictated by royal warrant to ensure uniformity. We can't have one officer looking different from another, except by indicators of rank, can we? Now, despite this, cloths can vary in their intrinsic quality.' He led them to the far side of the shop where a selection of rolls of scarlet cloth were laid out for inspection. 'Well, Mr Machele, which of these do you prefer? And, Mr Brooks, come, see what you think.'

Brooks took each one in turn between his forefinger and thumb and inspected them closely. 'These are very fine examples indeed. Where do you get your cloth from? Do you personally visit the weavers?'

'Come, Mr Brooks. No, I do not visit each potential supplier and, no, I cannot tell you who my suppliers are. These are trade secrets, as I am sure you understand. The materials we use here are of the highest possible quality. What I can tell you is that one of my most trusted members of staff is Sam Beesley. What Sam doesn't know about the quality of cloth and what we should pay for it is not worth the knowing. If Sam says this cloth is the best and at the right price, then that is all I need to know. Reputation is all, sir.'

'Quite. Quite. I just wondered. I am a banker, as you know, and I have little or no knowledge about the world of tailoring except that I do know I have to trust my tailor. It is a relationship that often lasts longer than a marriage,' said Brooks. 'Well, John, which cloth do you feel to be the best for you?'

'I should think this one, sir,' he responded, looking from one to the other with a questioning look on his face.

'A very good choice, if I may say so, sir,' said Hawkes approvingly. 'This fine weave will suit your build perfectly. Now, let us take your measurements. If you would come with me to the measuring room.'

John looked appealingly out of the corner of his eye at Brooks. 'Come along, John,' said Brooks. 'I have never seen anyone else being measured. Lead on, Mr Hawkes.'

The measuring did not take as long as they thought it would. Mr Hawkes wielded his tape measure at an almost bewildering pace and called out numbers to an assistant who wrote them down.

'Measurements are always taken in the same order, Mr Brooks. The speed is simply a matter of years of experience. They will either then be used in their exactitude in the case of a gentleman's outfit or adapted in part to meet the appropriate regimental template. There, Mr Machele. That is complete.'

'Thank you, Mr Hawkes. Last week, I had no idea I was going to join the army, but I am liking it already. These uniforms, I just know, will make me feel the way I have always wanted to feel. They will show the world just who I am. I am John Machele, a cornet in the Royal Scots Greys. I will be saluted and called sir.'

Brooks interrupted: 'Now, John, I believe our business here is, for the time being, concluded for today.' He exchanged looks with Hawkes who, although giving mostly the appearance of the professional military outfitter, was conveying a sense of puzzlement bordering on concern as he heard John's last remarks. Brooks continued. 'My thanks, Mr Hawkes, and we shall await your notification regarding fittings at your earliest convenience. Come along, John.'

As they made for the door, Mr Hawkes added: 'It will be very soon, sir. The templates are ready to hand and you may expect my communication within a few days. My cutter will be busily marking out within the hour. Good day, gentlemen.'

Brooks and Machele got into the waiting carriage and, as John gazed wistfully at the splendid uniforms on display, they moved off.

'Well, John,' said Brooks. 'What did you think of that?'

'A most enjoyable experience, sir. Most enjoyable. I got to choose the cloth for my uniforms and Mr Hawkes complimented me on my decision. I will look just wonderful in regimentals made of the cloth of my choice. I will have to tell all my brother officers that I chose the finest cloth there is. That will impress them. Show them I am a man of inordinately good taste.'

'John, John, John,' interrupted Brooks. 'Slow down, please. This is very exciting for you, I know. And quite rightly so. If I may make a suggestion – and that is all it is, a suggestion – one of the marks of a true gentleman is that he has no need to act in a way to attempt to impress others. His style and well-mannered behaviour, as well as the cut of his clothes, announce him to be a gentleman. Fit to move comfortably in whatever company he chooses. Now, you are about to join the army, and a royal regiment at that. It will be the assumption that all officers are gentlemen. The difference between the circles you currently move in and the army is that there is a clearly defined hierarchy.

You know simply by looking at someone's uniform what their rank is, and, by the same measure, they know yours. Everybody knows where they fit within the regiment, and there are expectations of what behaviour is deemed correct and what is not. Does that mean anything to you, John?'

'Of course. I understand, sir. It is just that I am very excited. When I wear my uniform, I will wear it with pride. I also know that a cornet is the lowest rank an officer can be. I will learn the rules of behaviour and respect those of a higher rank than me and earn their respect in return. I am pleased that you have been with me today. I should like to think of you as a friend now that I am older. I remember how you listened to me four years ago and made me feel involved in a decision about my possible future for the first time ever, and I thank you for that. I feel I can trust you and that you won't betray me,' he said, fixing Brooks with a piercing stare of almost bewildering intensity.

'John,' continued Brooks, finding it hard to maintain a stare equal to that of John's. 'I know you would appreciate what I was trying to say and I am pleased to hear your response. I had no intention of causing you any upset. Friends? I should be honoured to be thought of in that way. As friends, we can be honest with each other. Say things which we would otherwise be unable to because of the constraints placed on us by the conventions of polite society. But, John, why use the word betray? Why and how could I possibly betray you?'

'Pretend I never said it, sir,' rejoined John. 'My life has not always been a happy one and I may see people who are, usually for only a short time, claiming to care for me and then who are more than happy to say goodbye to me, often for reasons I do not understand and certainly do not have explained to me. So, I am sorry for using that word, Mr Brooks. I apologise.' John finished talking and resting his head against the back of the upholstered seat of the carriage, closed his eyes until it pulled up in Chancery Lane and Brooks took his leave.

'Goodbye, Mr Brooks. I shall see you again in a few days, I trust.'

'Indeed, John. Indeed,' replied Brooks, as he re-entered the bank. Returning to a world with which he was totally familiar. One where, in the privacy of his office, he could reflect on John Machele's return to his life.

AND SO TO CANTERBURY &
THE ROYAL SCOTS GREYS

March 1796

There was a knock on George Brooks's office door. 'Come,' he called.

Dodd's bespectacled face peered around it. 'It is ten o'clock, sir, and I have been informed that Mr Machele's carriage is awaiting you outside.'

'Thank you, Dodd. As I have informed the partners, I have every intention of returning to the bank the day after tomorrow. They know that you are more than capable of handling the affairs of my particular clients and will refer matters to them should any insistent demands be made which are above your authority to meet. You know which particular clients I am referring to, do you not, Dodd?'

Dodd nodded and they shared a look between them which showed the professional trust that had built up over the intervening years.

'And, Dodd,' continued Brooks, with a twinkle in his eye, 'come in for just a moment and close the door. I have two things to say before I leave for Canterbury.'

Dodd did as he was requested, albeit a little nervously as he thought about any errors he may have made regarding a customer's account.

'Dodd, I feel it is time that the work you perform here, both in your role as a clerk and the direct assistance which you give to me, received some formal recognition. It is in my mind to offer you the position of my personal assistant. You will be known as the personal assistant to Mr Brooks. That will be official. You will also have the responsibility of supervising the other clerks and monitoring their work. You will not be expected to continue as a clerk yourself. I should like you to think this over and give me your answer on my return. It will be a position of considerable responsibility and I shall understand if you choose not to accept it. There will, of course, be a significant increase in your salary and an initial clothing allowance to reflect your new status.'

Dodd felt his jaw literally drop.

'Mr B-B-Brooks,' he stammered, 'I don't know what to say. I mean, I'm going to say yes and thank you, sir.'

'Well, Dodd, I did say there were two things, did I not? The second is this. Could you carry my bags out to the carriage? Thank you. Oh, and not a word to anyone about this until I make the announcement on my return.'

He chuckled to himself as Dodd left the office carrying the bags. Dodd looked as discomfited by pleasure as could possibly be. A young man with a secret for which he would need all of his self-discipline to keep to himself for the next few days, and he couldn't help but wonder what the look would be on the face of the clerks' team joker when he was told.

Brooks left the bank and was surprised, although he probably shouldn't have been, when he saw not one carriage but two. The first, Augustus Brown's regular one, had its door open, and John Machele, seated inside, waved at him in greeting.

'Mr Brooks, I give you good morning, sir, and what a fine morning it is too. A portent, I am sure, of what the future holds.'

'Good morning to you, John,' responded Brooks, indicating to Dodd to place the valises inside the carriage. He turned to Dodd and said, 'Not a word now; not a word.'

'Silence will be my watchword, Mr Brooks. Have a good journey, sir,' replied Dodd as he turned to re-enter the bank, his face hardly inscrutable with a smirk playing at the corners of his mouth.

'Well, John,' said Brooks, seating himself with his back to the horses and facing John. 'This is very pleasant indeed, and the other carriage?'

'All my things, Mr Brooks. Too much for Mr Brown's little carriage so it was thought best to take a second so everything arrives at the same time. Better than sending it all by regular carrier. It came as something of a surprise even to me when I realised how much an officer had to provide himself.

'All my uniforms took up the trunks on their own,' he explained, as the little convoy embarked on their journey. 'Then there was just a small selection of my personal things, including my travelling toiletries and my campaign desk, not that I should be going on campaign in the near future but it is possible.' He grinned impishly as the carriage rattled, rolled and swayed its way over the bridge across the Thames to the south bank, on its way to the road to Canterbury.

'But what else have you had to bring?' enquired Brooks, wondering if John, like so many young gentlemen, had all sorts of non-essential fripperies that he couldn't possibly do without.

'Well, it's equipment really. Nothing I don't have to have. I did take some advice from Mr Hawkes when I had my final fitting. He remarked that some junior officers took so much with them when they joined their regiment that when they were sent to serve, or go on campaign as they call it, they either had to leave most of their things behind or have their own string of pack horses or mules, which they would be responsible for purchasing and looking after.

'No, the rest is equipment. There's all the stuff for my mount. That's how officers refer to their horses. Mounts. There's the harness and the saddle, not to mention the special scabbard to hold my carbine, and there are the saddle bags and the special thing that goes behind the saddle to hold your bedroll and a waterproof cover. Really, there is no end to it. The other ranks have all this issued to them, but that is the price you have to pay for being an officer and a gentleman. The price you have to pay. I like that. Quite funny really. Anyway, there's as pretty a pair of dragoon pistols as ever you did see. Quite splendid. It's a good job I didn't have to pack my actual mount as well, isn't it? She'll be delivered and waiting for me at the barracks.' John paused, fairly breathless, his excitement at this change in his life showing in every inch of his body. His face was lit up and he was using his hands to emphasise all he was saying.

'I am so pleased that you are entering on this… may I call it an adventure, in such a positive spirit. Have you been to Canterbury before, John?' asked Brooks.

'Never. I do know something of it by story alone. It has a cathedral. Thomas a Becket was murdered there and the Archbishop of Canterbury is the head of the Church of England, or is that the king?'

'That is about all I know of the town as well, but it does have some fine inns. We are staying at the Little Inn tonight and shall be glad of the rest indeed after a long day spent in this carriage, finely equipped though it may be,' said Brooks, adjusting his body to the different motion of the carriage as it jolted onto an unpaved road at the outskirts of south-east London.

They made good time but it had still been dark for the better part of two hours when they arrived at the Little Inn. It may have been called the Little Inn, and it probably was little when it first opened its doors in the fifteenth century, but nearly four hundred years later it was far from that. As its reputation grew, so had the inn itself. What had started out as somewhere for pilgrims to rest their weary heads had, by 1796, expanded and furnished itself to a level that would have made it virtually unrecognisable to its original, often impoverished, travellers seeking a roof over their heads.

'Well, John,' said Brooks, barely suppressing a yawn and stretching to ease the muscles in his back, 'the ostlers will take care of the horses and if you need anything carried to your room, I'm sure that will be done. Just tell the lad. And then a light supper and, for me at least, to bed.'

'Very well, sir,' responded John. 'Food certainly and perhaps a cup of chocolate with some of their imported brandy. I'm certain there will no shortage of that, being close to the coast and that much nearer to France!' He looked at Brooks and gave the nearest hint of a wink.

'Not that trunk. That one,' he shouted at the harassed potboy who had been detailed to carry whatever the guests wanted upstairs in their rooms. 'And where will the rest of my baggage be stored tonight?' he asked imperiously, as though he was an English milord on his Grand Tour.

'They be kept on the baggage coach by the stables where Your Lordship can rest assured all will be safe and secure, what with the ostler and his boy sleeping there as they do,' said the potboy.

And so, after a light supper of some mutton pie and a ripe stilton, washed down with a pint of claret apiece, Brooks made his way up the stairs to his room, which overlooked the cobbled street with the impressive sight of Canterbury Cathedral in full view, providing he opened his window and leant well out. This he decided not to do for he was tired, and Canterbury in early March was cold enough to warrant a good fire in his room and a heated pan in his bed.

John played the role of the English milord for the better part of an hour before he succumbed to the call of sleep. The chocolate and the very best of the inn's imported brandy performed their task most efficiently, and he wearily and just a little unsteadily climbed the stairs to his room next to Brooks's, from which he could just detect the slightest hint of snoring.

It was nearly nine o'clock the following morning when George Brooks, at a breakfast of chops, ham, eggs and hot buttered toast with two pots of coffee, heard a sound he was unable to put a name to. It was moving along the passage and then came down the stairs, across the hall and into the dining room. It was not exactly a clanking noise but more of a jingling sound. The door opened and their stood John Machele in full court dress of the Royal Scots Greys, with his hat under his left arm, his dress sword hanging by his side and his decorative spurs affixed to his boots.

So that was the jingle I could hear, thought Brooks to himself and then said aloud, 'Well, John, what a fine figure you cut indeed. Absolutely splendid. Come sit down and have some of this excellent breakfast and, whatever you do, don't drop any egg on your finery.' He spread his hands expansively and John seated himself, with not a little difficulty because of the snug fit of his court dress trousers, on the bench opposite.

'Yes, it is rather fine, is it not? I think I look rather splendid. A real officer and a gentleman, and I have the proof of it in my satchel. Here.' And he waved an oilskin wrapper at Brooks and took out a rolled-up parchment. This is my commission saying that I am Cornet John Machele of the Royal Scots Greys and have been so since

5th March 1796, only four days ago. I must show this to my commanding officer, Major Bothwell, but it is my responsibility to keep it safe. Isn't that wonderful?'

George Brooks eyed John carefully, ready to calm him if he seemed to be verging on the uncontrollable but, to his relief, John's manner, he felt, could simply be put down to pure boyish enthusiasm.

'Well, John, I feel we should be off within the hour so that you can officially report for duty. The barracks are not far. I think you'll be impressed. They were only completed in 1795, and the first regiment to occupy them this last year was the New Romney Light Dragoons under Colonel Dering. As I said, it's not far from here, over in Northgate Street, but the size may come as something of a surprise. These barracks stretch for over half a mile. Oh, and I am sure you will be pleased to know they are named The Royal Cavalry Barracks. What do you think of that, John?' Brooks looked at John enquiringly, who was consuming a plate piled high with food as though he was uncertain when he would get to eat again or even what quality his next meal would be.

'Mmm, mmm,' replied John, his speech muffled by a mouthful of food. 'Yes, within the hour. Must hurry.'

Their miniature cavalcade came to a stop at the barracks' main gate. Seeing two unmarked and clearly civilian carriages, a sentry stepped forward, saying, 'Please state the nature of your business.'

John put his head out of the window and called, 'Cornet Machele reporting for duty.'

'Very good, sir. Just wait there a moment if you please whilst I fetch the guard commander, sir.'

John drew his head back into the carriage, saying, 'There, Mr Brooks. Already I have been called sir by a soldier on guard. I am going to like this, I know I am.'

'Steady, John, steady,' responded Brooks. 'All I will say is first impressions. Remember how important they are, John.'

Their little cautionary exchange was interrupted by a tapping on the coach door, and a face dominated by a luxuriant moustache peered in.

'Captain Rutherford, guard commander. Which one of you is Cornet Machele?' he asked, his eyes not adjusted yet to the comparative gloom of the coach's interior.

'That is me, sir, reporting for duty, sir.'

'Good. Your papers, please. Commission and reporting orders,' requested the captain.

John fumbled with the numerous fastenings of his court dress uniform jacket wishing he had kept the documents in his satchel but at last withdrew them and passed them to Captain Rutherford for his scrutiny.

'Commission correct. Good. Letter of joining instructions from Lord Eglinton. Good,' acknowledged Captain Rutherford. 'You will report to Major Bothwell and he will formally welcome you to the regiment.'

'Thank you, C-C-Captain, er, I mean, sir,' stammered John.

'Private Douglas,' barked Rutherford. 'Jump up beside the coachman and take the equipages to the regimental office.'

'Yes, sir. On my way, sir,' he replied, saluting.

It was a comparatively short distance but from the coach window John quickly became aware that his future home, the barracks, was like a small town. Numerous buildings he was able to identify as stores, stables, a smithy and blocks of what looked like large low houses, which he took to be living accommodation, not to mention the large open spaces where soldiers were carrying out various manoeuvres which he was unable to put any meaning to.

They came to a halt outside an office building where Private Douglas with great agility leapt down from the driver's box and said, 'If you'll just follow me, gentlemen.'

'Mind your spurs as you get down, John,' said Brooks, as the soldier opened the carriage door for them.

John successfully navigated his way out of the carriage and down the step until he was standing on firm ground. Private Douglas's jaw visibly dropped at the sight of the figure of John Machele in all his finery as he emerged.

'This way, sir,' said Douglas, thinking to himself: *Just wait until I tell me mates about the little tin soldier we've got here.* He led them into the office and, saluting, said to the adjutant that the glorious apparition before him was in fact Cornet Machele reporting for duty.

'Very well, Private,' he said, looking John over from head to toe and thinking to himself: *Well, well, what have we got here?* 'Find out what equipment he has brought with him and ensure it is taken to Mr Machele's quarters.'

'Yes, sir,' acknowledged Douglas. Not only did he have a little something to tell his mates about, but he could also see himself being able to spend almost all of his remaining two hours of boring guard duty on this little task.

'Just one moment, gentlemen,' said the adjutant. He knocked on the door, which the sign announced was the office of Major A. Bothwell: Commanding Officer, and, hearing a muffled response, which he knew meant he could go in, he entered the inner sanctum. Within seconds of entering the office, he emerged, saying, 'Go in, gentlemen. Major Bothwell will see you now.' He ushered them in and returned to the outer office and the pile of papers awaiting his attention.

John Machele and George Brooks approached the man seated behind a highly business-like desk. He stood up and leant forward, intending to extend a hand in welcome, when John, with a jangling of spurs, stamped himself to attention and, standing as rigid as a statue, stared at a point over Major Bothwell's left shoulder and, in a voice approaching a bellow more suited to a parade ground than an office, cried: 'Cornet Machele reporting for duty as ordered, sir.'

'Quite, quite. Welcome, Mr Machele. No need to stand on ceremony. At your ease, sir. At your ease. And you, sir, you would be?'

'George Brooks. I am, if I may put it this way, Mr Machele's man of business, and I have the care of him at this time.'

'Ah yes. Mr Brooks.' This time, the major did fully extend his hand and the two men shook firmly.

'Very well, Cornet Machele, I understand the guard commander has already seen your papers but if I could just...' He stopped talking, having clearly not expected to have to witness the sight of John wrestling with the fastenings on his court dress jacket. To cover the awkward silence that had settled whilst this feat was being performed, Major Bothwell continued: 'I see Mr Hawkes has done you proud, Mr Machele, as he has so many of the officers here, me included. Thank you, Mr Machele. Mmm. Commission. Yes. Letter of appointment from our colonel. Good. Good. All in order.

'Welcome to the regiment. Obey orders and listen and learn from anyone giving you instruction, regardless of their rank. That is all for now. Report to the adjutant in the outer office and request that he details one of your fellow cornets to show you to your quarters, and he'll explain fully what your duties will be. Dismissed.

'Oh, one other thing, Mr Machele. Court dress is exactly what the name implies and not usually expected to be worn within the barracks unless there is a specific order. You will find what the dress of the day is according to your duties posted in the Orderly Room.'

'Yes, sir. Thank you, sir.' John retrieved his commission, replaced it inside his tunic and turned to Brooks. 'Until we meet again, Mr Brooks.'

'Yes, indeed, John. Yes, indeed,' he answered, as John turned about with the usual accompaniment of the jangling of his dress spurs and left his commanding officer's presence to begin his career as an officer in the Royal Scots Greys.

BROOKS & THE MAJOR

'Well,' said Major Bothwell after John had left the office, 'so that is John Machele.'

'Indeed.' Brooks responded as noncommittally as he felt he should, not knowing what the major was likely to say next.

Bothwell continued. 'Please take a seat, Mr Brooks. A glass of something?'

'Thank you, Major,' he replied.

'Mr Brooks, I will be plain with you. Whilst I am always pleased to welcome a young man to the regiment, I admit to feeling there may be circumstances relating to Machele to which I have not been made privy. I have, as you may be aware, a letter from the colonel of our regiment, Lord Eglinton, informing me of the awarding of a commission as a cornet to this young gentleman. That raises a question in my mind. He is twenty years of age and most cornets begin their careers at around sixteen. This is, in itself, unusual, sir. What is even more out of the ordinary is the awarding of his commission. Commissions are customarily purchased. To be awarded, one comes either from an act of particular bravery on the field of battle or else denotes patronage from the very highest level; often through a general or, in this case, the colonel of a regiment. This latter is most often through a family connection. Lord Eglinton makes no mention of a personal connection whatsoever. He merely states the award of the commission and for me to await Mr Machele's reporting for duty.

It makes me somewhat curious as to who Mr Machele actually is. My curiosity is further engaged by two more points. I have received a confidential letter from a Mr Brown who informs me of these two things. Firstly, that "a certain personage", who will remain anonymous, has an interest in Mr Machele. The letter also says that my duties as his commanding officer "will not go unrecognised", and that leads me to my second point. This is that I was informed that you, Mr Brooks, would be accompanying Mr Machele and that you are authorised to disclose such information about the young gentleman as you deem necessary and within your discretion. I admit, sir, I look forward with the greatest interest to just what you feel able to disclose.'

He formed his fingers into a triangular shape as a support for his chin and fixed Brooks with an intensely questioning look. 'Oh, and as another matter of interest, I return to the subject of Mr Machele's commission. Since there is no indication of any connection between him and Lord Eglinton, then I am minded to conjecture just how high-ranking this "certain personage" is that he could request or even direct the Colonel of the Royal Scots Greys in this way. So, just who are you, Mr Brooks, and what can you tell me about Cornet John Machele?'

'I shall tell you as much as I feel able within the constraints that have been placed on me, Major Bothwell, but I must make it absolutely clear from the outset that I cannot tell you anything of which I am unaware. I have no knowledge of the identity of the "certain personage" or his relationship to John Machele. All of my communications are between myself and Mr Brown. A condition of my arrangement is that I make no attempt to identify the "certain personage". Otherwise, my role in this affair will instantly be cancelled. I may have made certain educated guesses but they are private to myself.' George Brooks leant forward in his chair and matched the stare of Major Bothwell with one of his own. 'This is what I am able to tell you, sir.'

George Brooks outlined how John Machele had entered his life four years previously in 1792. He started by saying that John had been brought up by a succession of people who had the care of him and was often moved at very little notice. He made it clear that John had never known a normal family life. Major Bothwell listened with great interest to what he was told about Machele's time at the Naval Academy and raised an incredulous eyebrow when he was told about the incident with the gunpowder, and both eyebrows shot up when he was told about the damage caused to the land-based mock-up training ship.

'There is no actual proof that John set light to it but…' Brooks spread his arms, with the palms of his hands uppermost and his own questioning look on his face. He then went on to tell the major about the arrangement of a naval sloop and its crew being detailed to construct, with the assistance of the young gentlemen at the Naval Academy, a fully working replica of the damaged training vessel as an exercise to help sailors in the Royal Navy be seen in a positive light ashore as opposed to being a drunken, womanising rabble.

'Someone, and I know you don't know who, has sufficient influence to arrange this? A fully manned ship of His Majesty's Royal Navy? Astonishing. Absolutely astonishing.' Major Bothwell seemed totally lost for words. 'It's unbelievable. This is almost beyond belief, but I don't doubt your honesty in the story you are telling me, Mr Brooks, but astonishing.'

George Brooks put his head on one side and smirked.

'Indeed, Major, indeed,' he continued, 'but that was in 1792, four years ago, and he was sixteen years of age with the high spirits that go with that. It was the first time he had lived with boys of his own age in a setting away from people who were being paid to bring him up in a pretend parenting way. And, before you ask, I am unaware of what happened to him for most of the intervening four years except to say that immediately prior to joining your regiment, sir, he was living in lodgings and gave every impression, according to the reports I received, that he was fitting well into his role as a young gentleman.' Brooks looked slightly sideways and then refocused on Major Bothwell. 'I have to stress that John is, how shall I put it, perhaps touchy might be a good word, yes, touchy about people not seeing him as a gentleman.'

Bothwell responded instantly.

'He will have no problems with that here, sir, I can

162

assure you. All the officers are gentlemen, and the few who were not born as such and have since gained a commission from the ranks are deemed to be gentlemen by their officer status.'

'I assumed as much, Major,' replied Brooks. 'I will tell you this but only in confidence. There was a spot of bother at his lodgings shortly before the decision was taken that he should join the army. The full details are not necessary. Suffice to say it involved his having decided to take a maid from his lodging house for an evening out. He had not consulted her prior to making the arrangements, and when she refused his invitation he tried to take his own life. No,' Brooks raised his hand, 'please do not interrupt me, sir.' Seeing the major on the verge of possibly raising an objection to having someone who, from what he had heard so far, would try to commit suicide over the refusal of a maid to fall in with his plans without having been asked at the outset as a cornet under his command, Brooks continued. 'It is my belief that we need to look beyond this particular incident at the lad himself. He has become aware over the years that other people have not been brought up in the manner which he has. He has no knowledge of who his parents are. Neither his mother nor his father. The people who have had the care of him, and there have been many, he knows they are paid to do so, sir. In short, sir, there are seeming to be occasions when he seriously questions exactly who he is, and with no real answers to hand, it is easy to imagine his slipping into a state of despair. There is no real harm in John that I can ascertain. He does tend to get overexcited sometimes, and in his desire to be accepted he often creates the wrong impression.' He paused.

'Ah yes,' interjected Major Bothwell. 'Like this morning, reporting for duty wearing his court dress uniform.'

'Precisely,' responded Brooks, visibly pleased at the major's insight. 'It is all part of his not really understanding where he belongs, which is why being commissioned into the Royal Scots Greys is so important to him. It is one of the royal regiments, which makes him proud in itself. What the regiment offers him is a career, a framework of rules and regulations where he knows what is expected of him and what he can expect from others. It is my earnest hope, and I believe it to be John's also, that the regiment will provide him with the family he has never known. There, sir; that is what I feel you should know about your latest cornet. I leave you my card, Major, and should be most obliged if you would keep me informed as to his progress.' Brooks stood up from his seat and placed his card on Major Bothwell's desk.

Major Bothwell came out from where he was ensconced and extended his hand to Brooks to shake. The two men looked each other in the eye for a short while until Bothwell broke the shared silence.

'I thank you for your candour, Mr Brooks, and you may rest assured that the tale you have related to me this day will not go beyond my office, and I shall be pleased to keep you informed. I do not expect you to comment, but I rather deduce from what you have said that Mr Machele has lived his whole life with people making reports about him, so he will probably make that assumption here. The difference in the army, of course, is that everybody is observed and has reports of one kind and another written about them, including myself. I shall leave instructions for your two equipages to be brought to the main gate and trust you have a good journey back to London.' Together, they left the major's inner sanctum, and Bothwell unhurriedly left the necessary instructions.

'You will have no idea where your two coachmen are at this moment, but the duty corporal will soon find them and by the time you have strolled to the main gate, they should be well on their way. If they are anything like my men, they will have found someone to offer them some alcoholic refreshment.' Major Bothwell opened the outer door and said, 'A pleasure to meet you, Mr Brooks.'

'Indeed, Major. The pleasure was mine, sir,' said Brooks, as he stood on the steps of the regimental office and gazed at the impressive main gate on the other side of the parade ground, which was still being used to teach men how to march in various formations to the barked commands of a ruddy-faced non-commissioned officer.

'Hmm,' said Brooks to himself, 'the shortest distance between two points is a straight line. I shall not walk the hypotenuse but follow the route along the other two sides of that right-angled triangle. I am not getting caught up in the middle of that lot.' He chuckled to himself as he strolled in a rather unsoldierly fashion towards the main gate, the carriages and London.

SLICING THE LEMON

'Morning, gentlemen. Today, we will be looking at the main weapon of a dragoon, whether mounted or on foot,' bellowed the sergeant major to us newly commissioned cornets.

I say he bellowed but it only sounded to us like that. To him, it probably sounded as though he was talking in a rather paternalistic way to his group of young charges, who were standing in a semi-circle holding their grey mounts by their bridles. I say his young charges, but I was not so young. All the others were around sixteen years of age, and here was me at twenty. Nobody had told me that the usual age to enter the army as a cornet was sixteen. I know I was awarded this commission. I just don't know how it came about. All the other fellows had theirs bought for them. Why couldn't I have been "bought in" as a lieutenant so I didn't have to share quarters and training with these boys?

The sergeant major continued: 'You all have hanging at your side a sabre which is the new 1796 model. It has been designed for the use of the heavy cavalry and before any of you, including our Mr Machele, reminds us that this regiment of dragoons is classified as light cavalry, I am fully aware of that fact.' He grinned at us as though pleased at being able to anticipate one of us, or rather me, making the inevitable remark. 'Your sabres are, themselves, heavy, which makes them an excellent cutting weapon. Most of your fighting will involve hacking, chopping and slashing. Your enemy, being from the Continent, prefers to thrust just the way you would expect foreigners who have been trained by poxy fencing masters to do. Fighting with a sabre has nothing to do with gentlemanly codes of conduct. It is brutal and it is deadly. There are some people who take a file to the end of the blade to make a sharper point, so if it does become necessary to thrust then its effectiveness is greatly increased. But remember, gentlemen, first and foremost, your sabre is a slashing and cutting implement, which when treated well will not only kill the enemy but prevent him from killing you.'

All were holding their sabres and inspecting its blade. They were in the presence of an experienced soldier. A man to be looked up to. Not a young, inexperienced officer whose father had paid in cash for his rank and had not seen any action as yet. No, this was a grizzled veteran. They expected him to launch into a series of tales of his experiences and what it felt like to be face to face with the enemy. Strangers to each other but seeing themselves as either the killers or the killed. He didn't tell them his stories.

What he said was: 'Marching boots, horses' harnesses jingling, sun flashing off badges and the sword blades, although don't always expect blue skies. It'll be raining and muddy, as like as not, and then the very ground beneath you will be just as dangerous as an enemy infantryman coming at you with his bayonet fixed to his musket. Mud is a terrible thing to have to fight in, gentlemen, but not today. Today, we have a demonstration of what standard of mounted swordsmanship you should aspire to. If you would all like to turn about-face, you will see Captain Rutherford on the far side of the grassed area at the internal perimeter wall of the barracks compound.'

Why can't he just say, 'Look over there'? It's just a waste of words. All we have to do is look over there. It is obvious who or what we are to look at, since there is no one else there and he is only about twenty-five yards away. Level with us at a distance of maybe ten feet is what I take to be a gallows. What on earth is that doing here? Are we also to be instructed in the correct way to hang someone?

The sergeant major continued. 'I can see you young gentlemen have observed the gallows. Now, what is that doing there? I hear you ask. You see that rope hanging down at a rough approximation of the height of a man's head? There is no man's head there but what there is affixed to that rope is, in fact, a lemon. And why is there a lemon tied to a rope on a scaffold?'

Suddenly, before anyone could attempt an answer, the sergeant major waved his sabre in the air, at which signal Captain Rutherford set spurs to his grey mount and quickly came towards us, his sabre pointing ahead of him like a small lance. Without slowing, he raised his sabre arm and as he came level with the gallows, he gave an almighty swipe of his blade and reined in beside the sergeant major.

I don't think we knew what we were expected to have taken notice of. It had all been so quick.

'Gather round, gentlemen. Captain Rutherford, if you please, sir, show the young gentlemen your blade,' said the sergeant major.

The captain lowered his sabre from the salute position for our inspection so that we could all see, and smell, the liquid on his blade. It was lemon juice. No denying it. Lemon juice. Captain Rutherford had, at full gallop, sliced an object as small as a lemon when it was hanging from a piece of rope.

'Gentlemen, I wish you good sport,' said Captain Rutherford, grinning beneath his luxuriant moustache and trotting his mount back to the stable block.

Our instructor resumed his lesson. 'That little demonstration or exercise is, believe it or not, called "slicing the lemon", and yes, it is as difficult as you imagine it to be. That is why you will not be attempting to slice the lemon, but you will be attempting to slice the turnip. I shall make it easier still for you. As you can see, the work party is hammering some wooden stakes into the ground and on top of each one will be affixed a turnip. Although the heads of most soldiers are considerably larger than a turnip, I do know from experience that slicing a turnip feels very much the same as your blade slicing the head of your enemy. And also remember that your enemy is more than likely going to be wearing his helmet, so to reach his head you have to cut through that first. Right, gentlemen, on my command, mount. Mount,' he cried, in his full parade-ground roar.

We duly mounted and spaced ourselves out in a line abreast, as though preparing to charge. Some twenty-five yards ahead and slightly to the side of each of us was a stake with a turnip mounted on it.

The sergeant major roared again: 'On the command Charge, the company will charge at the enemy known as the turnip and slice through it. Charge!'

This was exciting. This was like real war. The distance of the charge to the turnips was not long, but the horses knew a charge when in one. There were only a few of us but we did thunder. We also yelled at the top of our voices, 'Scotland forever.' No one told us to do this. It just seemed the right thing to do. I had only just finished that cry of the Scots Greys when I came upon my turnip. I slashed wildly, anticipating the shock of the impact as it spread up my arm. It never came. I had missed my turnip completely and now I was in danger of falling from my saddle. I straightened myself and reined in my horse and then wheeled it around in as tight a circle as I could and charged again at my unmarked turnip. No mistake this time. A sweeping slash, a solid impact, blade tugged free and galloped back to where the sergeant major had been waiting and observing.

'So, Mr Machele, what do you think you have achieved by that?' he enquired.

'I have charged my turnip and have destroyed it with my blade,' I replied, fully expecting the praise for my skill which I felt I fully deserved.

'Mr Machele, where are your brother cornets?'

It was then that I realised they were all formed up at the end of the line of targets.

'Mr Machele,' continued the instructor, his voice gradually rising, 'whilst it may be commendable that you succeeded in slicing your turnip at the second attempt, did you, at any time, have any awareness of where your fellows were? Don't interrupt. Congratulations on being the only one to achieve the main object of the exercise. Now, consider that reining in your horse so suddenly and wheeling it about for another attempt caused your brother officers to take avoiding action to prevent a collision with you, which, in turn, had an effect on the performance of them all. In an engagement, if you miss your first target then you carry on to the next. Keeping going forward. There will always be a next one, sir. In a charge, the enemy is in front of you. If you turn around, you will be facing your comrades and will have an enemy at your back. You will in all probability only get the chance to do this once. The enemy at your back will not believe his luck, and any luck which you may have will run out at that point. Your, shall I say, action, as far as a mounted officer was concerned, was, at the very least, unexpected by your fellow officers and in a real combat situation would be considered as dangerous to your own companions. Think on that, sir. Dismissed.'

I really don't like looking slack mouthed. This was so unfair. I am training to be a soldier. My job is to kill or be killed, and I had been publicly rebuked for what I believed a soldier should do. And this was only my first lesson in combat skills. I had done well and I knew it. Putting others in danger indeed. On the battlefield, it was every man for himself, wasn't it? All that matters is that you win, and every enemy you kill is one enemy less. And that lesson was only about attacking on horseback. What rules governed fighting on foot? I bet I can do just as well at that. I know I can fight on foot. I've had lessons from that French fellow. Can't remember his name, but I recall the fighting was mainly about thrusting and learning how to parry. He didn't like hacking and slicing when I used it against him. He thought it was not the way a gentleman fights.

It was then I remembered the turnips. There must be a pile of them somewhere. Otherwise, how could they keep putting them out for us as targets? I'd never seen them served up in the mess. Did the other ranks eat them? I'm not going to be admonished like that without redress. I'm an officer and a gentleman. I have a commission signed by His Majesty. Does the sergeant major have that? I think not, but he does hold the king's warrant.

Now, when would it be a good time to find the store of turnips? After official lights out, I should think. No one really around then apart from those on guard duty, and I'm sure they wouldn't be guarding a pile of turnips.

It has to be after midnight. All I can hear around me are the snores, grunts and farts of the other cornets in their little cubicles. It's nice that we have our own little bed spaces even if we are only separated from each other by wooden partitions. I push back my bedclothes and, as quietly as I can, get up from my cot. I'm fully dressed and I've wrapped a piece of cloth around my sabre to prevent any clinking from waking the others. No spurs, John. No spurs. Well done. Good thinking. I make my way out of the quarters and, keeping to the shadows, I move silently around the edge of the parade ground, past the stable block and then to the stores. Round the back and there they are. A great pile of turnips. I need to see them as enemy soldiers. This is the turnip army and I am going to defeat you. I draw my sabre from its scabbard, yell, 'Scotland forever' and charge them, hacking and slicing and even occasionally thrusting at any and all turnips that come within range of my dismounted one-man charge.

'Mr Machele, what on earth do you think you are doing? Are you out of your mind, sir? Put up your sabre this minute, sir, and explain yourself.' Captain Rutherford, the duty guard commander, accompanied by Cornet Hankins, a corporal and a private stood with his hands on his hips staring in bemused disbelief at the sight before him. A junior cornet in full uniform, his sabre in his grip, surrounded by chopped-up turnips.

'I've won, sir,' I said, bringing my sabre to the salute position.

'Won? Won what?' spluttered Rutherford, his mind working overtime, desperately trying to make sense of both what he saw in front of him and what he heard being said to him.

I continue, although I don't think any explanation is necessary. The evidence is here for all to see.

'I beat the turnip army, sir, did I not? And beat them well. If I knew their leader, then I would demand he surrender his sword to me.'

I watch the captain for his response and expect some sort of commendation. There is something niggling away at the back of my mind. Slowly, I begin to conclude that what I am doing and saying could possibly, but only possibly, be misinterpreted. It could be, possibly be, regarded as just a little bit out of the ordinary. Not odd but just out of the ordinary. I hastily add, 'I was so excited and full of admiration after witnessing your display of slicing the lemon this afternoon, Captain Rutherford. The slicing of the turnip, which we engaged in afterwards, was so exciting that I found it hard to sleep, sir. Perhaps I have shown an excess of zeal in this instance, but if I have, then it was in the best interests of the regiment, sir.'

Captain Rutherford responded, 'In what way do you mean, Mr Machele, for I cannot comprehend your thinking on this matter. How is this in the best interests of the regiment?'

His puzzled expression makes me doubt his ability to follow a perfectly straightforward line of thinking. He is a professional soldier. A captain in a fine regiment and yet he cannot understand what I am saying. Incredible.

'Sir, the Scots Greys do not always fight on horseback. I am a cornet in this fine regiment but have not as yet been trained in fighting on foot and feel this to be highly remiss. That is all I was doing, sir, fighting on foot.'

Cornet Hankins leant towards Captain Rutherford and whispered out of the side of his mouth, 'A word in private, sir, if I may.'

The pair turned their backs and took two paces towards the corporal and the private, who were doing their best not to burst out laughing. They held their carbines across their chests, the muscles of their cheeks twitching with a life of their own.

'Keep an eye on things here for a moment, Corporal,'

said Rutherford, as he and Hankins moved out of hearing range.

'Well, what is it, Hankins?'

Hankins looked around, making certain that they would not be overheard.

'Oh, come on, Hankins. Spit it out, man. What is it?' said Rutherford, not sure whether to start laughing or not and a little intrigued by what Hankins may want to tell him. At the same time, he was just a little annoyed at having what should have been a restful guard duty disturbed.

'Well, sir, he's a bit odd, sir. He likes his uniform, calls it his plumage. Doesn't really mix with the other cornets.'

'Yes, but what else? As a soldier, is he shaping up well?' queried the captain.

'Learns the drills well enough, sir. No better or worse than most of them. It's just that he is a bit old for having just entered as a cornet, sir. That sets him apart. I sense he is like a boy of fourteen going to school for the first time and being made to sit with the six-year-olds. He has the same level of knowledge about army life as the most junior cornet but a much more advanced knowledge of the world, sir.'

'Very well, Hankins. Are you saying he is a bad influence on the others? What are you saying?' interrupted Rutherford, who was beginning to feel that the cornet was prevaricating.

'Not really, sir. He tends to ignore them.'

'And his horsemanship?' queried the captain impatiently.

'Rather good, sir. An excellent horseman. Can't fault

him there. He spends more time with his mount than his fellows. In fact, he talks to it more than he talks to anyone else. He has been heard holding entire conversations with it. Not just the usual endearments and words of praise or encouragement that you and I would engage in, sir. He talks to it as though it understands and has opinions of its own. He pauses in what he is saying as though waiting for and then listening to its response before continuing.

'I have had it relayed to me, sir, that on one occasion he was heard making flattering remarks to it. He told his horse, a very fine mount, as I'm sure you agree, sir, that he was a very superior beast. He then waited in silence, nodded his head and then continued to explain that his reasoning was that since the horses for the troopers were supposed to be purchased at £23-10s, it stood to reason that his mount was superior in every way, including the price. He then nodded at his horse, saying, "Good point. The price paid is not always an indication that it represents good value. Well said." He planted a kiss on its muzzle and then told it that it could stand easy and followed this with the cry "Dismissed." Just thought it was time you were made aware that all is not necessarily well with Mr Machele, sir,' finished Hankins.

The pair returned to the scene of the defeat of the turnip army to see Machele, having sheathed his sabre, standing rigidly to attention and gazing into the middle distance.

'Cornet Machele,' said Captain Rutherford, eyeing him from head to toe, or where his toes were presumed to be beneath the hacked remains of the turnip army.

'You are dismissed from the site of your engagement and subsequent victory and are required to return to your quarters and your cot, sir. The report of your encounter will be conveyed formally through the usual channels. Dismissed, Cornet.' He then added: 'Corporal, Private, see that Mr Machele gets safely to his bed and then report back to the guardhouse.'

Rutherford watched as the party of three made their way back to the cornets' quarters and then turned to Hankins, his moustache quivering as he finally gave up to the ever-threatening explosion of laughter. 'He's completely mad. The man is mad. The mess will just love this. It'll cap most of the stories we hear there. Bit of a shame the corporal and private had to witness it. Just as entitled to a good laugh as we are, but we'll have to keep a watch in case it has an effect on discipline, though. Still, time for a glass or two, I feel. What about you, Hankins? Fights turnips. Listens to the opinions of his horse. Quite mad.'

'I'm with you there, sir,' replied Hankins, as he turned his gaze ruefully on the remains of the regiment's store of turnips. 'I'd better detail a party first thing in the morning to clear that mess and do whatever people do with defeated turnips. Whatever we do, I'm certain the story will be all over the barracks by then anyway.'

REGIMENTAL RUMBLINGS

Richard Jones, the Surgeon of the Royal Scots Greys, or the Second or Royal North British Dragoons, as he thought of the regiment in one of his more formal moods, breathed a sigh of relief.

It had been a particularly busy yet intensely boring and repetitive sick parade at the Canterbury barracks. A queue of twenty-two enlisted men all reporting with the same condition. Some embarrassed. Some just accepting it as a natural hazard. But all the same. The French pox. Did they call venereal disease in France the English pox? he wondered. Still, twenty-two men reporting sick and all with the same contagion was a little unusual in itself. He would have expected a fair smattering of sprains and bruises with the odd hernia thrown in for good measure, but no. Not today. Maybe tomorrow, he thought.

No reason to be all that surprised really. It was always the same old story with so many men in barracks this close to the town. Life could become quite boring. Endless drilling, cleaning, polishing, all the preparations for making the regiment into an efficient fighting machine but without the actual fighting. The only fighting many of the men saw, mostly the unmarried ones, happened in the streets of Canterbury as a by-product of the time spent in the local taverns. As was the pox.

He also wondered if there was a mathematical formula that could accurately forecast the increase in the number of prostitutes in an army town, as Canterbury was rapidly becoming, once the barracks had been established and the soldiers took up residence. He had not heard of any fights between the local whores and those who had come to Canterbury from far and wide for the easy pickings. He laughed to himself as he remembered a brawl he had witnessed involving a crowd of women when he had been stationed in another garrison town. They did not appear to fight in the same way that men did. A considerable amount of energy was spent on screaming insults at a level of obscenity which even he was unaccustomed to hearing, and he thought he had heard most things during his years as an army surgeon. His musings were interrupted by a knock at his door.

'Come in,' he called, thinking to himself that surely there wasn't yet another soldier seeking merciful relief from that irritating itch down there!

He raised his head from the daily sick parade report and was both surprised and pleased to see Captain Rutherford entering the room.

'Morning, Richard,' said Captain Rutherford.

'Ah, Edwin. Good morning. Surely not you as well?'

'Not me what, Richard?' queried Rutherford, confused.

'The pox, Edwin, the pox,' clarified Richard.

'Good Lord, no, Richard. Nothing like that.' He laughed. 'No, I wanted a word with you about something else entirely.'

'Sorry, Edwin. What seems to be the trouble?' enquired the surgeon, adopting his professional façade.

'It's not about me, Richard. There is concern about the behaviour of one of the junior officers, and I thought you could give me the wisdom of your experience.'

'Well, I can certainly listen to what you have to say and perhaps give an opinion. When you say there are concerns regarding this officer's behaviour, what has he done?' asked Richard.

'Very well, I shall tell you the reasons why he causes concern,' continued Rutherford. He seated himself before the surgeon's desk and, brushing his luxuriant moustache, he told his story.

'I don't necessarily want to make this official without having consulted you first. It's the behaviour of Cornet John Machele that I need your comments on.'

'Ah yes. Young but not so young Mr Machele,' interposed Richard, with a hint of prior knowledge in his response.

'Quite,' continued Edwin. 'You have probably heard that he arrived at the barracks to report for duty wearing full court dress, which could be excused due to his not having been informed of the correct form of dress when reporting to barracks. Unfortunately, the other ranks started to refer to him as the little tin soldier. Not within his hearing, of course, but still not good for discipline. I gave an exhibition of slicing the lemon to illustrate the desired level of skill that a mounted officer should be able to achieve. The assembled cornets were then set the same task but using turnips on posts instead. Mr Machele missed with his first attempt and wheeled his mount about and charged back the way he had come to try from that direction. The sergeant major informed him of the likely consequences of such an action if he did this on the field of battle, namely, that he would be, in effect, charging into the oncoming ranks of his own men. This meant he would be putting them and himself in immediate peril. He did not take this public rebuke and the reason for it very well.'

'But surely, Edwin, this could be put down to an excess of zeal. Besides, he has only been with us a short while and perhaps cannot be expected to have a firm grasp of all military matters,' said Richard.

'I agree. And I made that allowance at the time, but what happened later gave me more than just pause for thought. I was called to a storehouse, where I found Mr Machele in the midst of a pile of turnips that he had savagely attacked with his sabre. I asked him what on earth he thought he was doing, and he replied that he had defeated the turnip army. He was not making a joke. He was absolutely serious. I sent him off to his quarters under escort, with instructions that he was to be put to bed.'

'Oh, Edwin, that is ripe,' laughed the surgeon. 'How did you manage to keep a straight face?'

'With much difficulty, Richard. My initial reaction was one of utter disbelief at what I saw. This was compounded by Machele's report to me about this defeat of the turnip army, which he had achieved single-handedly against what he clearly regarded as a genuine foe. I kid you not,

Richard. This was not a man in his right senses. He gave no indication that his actions were in any way whatsoever out of the ordinary. I am somewhat at a loss, Richard, and I return to what I said before. Episodes like this are bad for discipline. I have no knowledge of anything that was said either to or by his escort, who, incidentally, reported that Machele retired to his cot a little tired and as though nothing out of the ordinary had happened. What I do know is that the men, and some of his fellow officers, no longer refer to him as the little tin soldier but now by the soubriquet of Turnip Machele.'

Richard Jones closed his eyes and pinched the bridge of his nose with his thumb and forefinger. Looking up, he said, 'There is real cause for concern here, Edwin, and you have done the right thing in bringing this matter to my attention. In my opinion, it brings into question Machele's suitability to be an officer, or indeed a member at any rank, of this regiment. I shall have to make this official, you realise, and I will report the concerns to Major Bothwell. In the meantime, I assume a watch will be kept on him. Is there another officer, perhaps of a rank closer to his, who could do that without Machele being aware of it?'

Rutherford thought for a while, involuntarily stroking his moustache.

'I think Cornet Hankins may be the right person for this, Richard.'

'Yes, I think so too. Thomas Hankins is a little older than the others. Not as old as Machele. Yes, a good choice, Edwin. Well, I shall leave that side of things to you then. A worrying business, Edwin; a worrying business.'

It was some three weeks later that Cornet Hankins paid a visit to the regimental surgeon to report on his observations of John Machele. It was not a responsibility he had been particularly relishing. It was not a duty as such, but with Captain Rutherford having requested he perform it as being in the best interests of the regiment, he felt that he was left with little or no choice. He had asked Captain Rutherford if he could speak candidly, and when told he could, he expressed his aversion to what he saw as spying on a fellow officer. The captain had said he fully understood that but then further explained should it be decided that Cornet Machele was, in fact, insane but remained an officer, the effect that would have on the men's morale. He then added that what may appear amusing whilst in quarters may not appear so in action. Hankins had considered this and, having seen action himself, fully accepted the captain's reasoning, and now he was reporting his observations to the regimental surgeon. He trusted he would not have to continue in this, still to him, rather distasteful task for much longer.

He knocked on the surgeon's door.

'Come,' called Richard Jones, and glanced up from his sick parade returns, glad of any diversion from the paperwork which sometimes seemed to take longer than actually treating his patients.

'Ah, Thomas. Come in, come in. Sit yourself down. I trust you have not come as a potential patient?' He looked enquiringly as Lieutenant Hankins sat himself down.

'No, Richard,' said Hankins rather hesitantly. 'Captain Rutherford, as you are no doubt aware, approached me to observe the behaviour of Cornet Machele, which he felt was giving rise to a certain level of concern. It is not a task I have been overly comfortable with. It feels a little, oh, I don't know, like betraying a trust. It is not as though we are friends as such, but he is a brother officer and—'

Richard Jones interrupted him at this point: 'Thomas, I quite understand how this task could be distasteful to you. But, as I am sure Rutherford made clear to you, this is a matter that is in the best interests of the regiment to be resolved. Should it be deemed that Machele is, in fact, insane, then this can be regarded as a medical matter so he can be retired from the regiment because of that. It will not be a disciplinary matter. He will not be discharged but retired, and the difference is significant. Should he be given a dishonourable discharge due to his behaviour, then he would lose the right to use his rank as a title and would not, in many circles, be regarded as a gentleman, which, and I hardly need tell you, Thomas, would severely restrict his admittance to society. Being retired, he retains the right to use his rank as a title.

'Having said that, desiring to be known as Cornet Machele would, at the very least, be regarded as pretentious, especially as he got older. He will also still be regarded as a gentleman. You see, Thomas, should it come to it, the task you have been performing is not only in the best interests of the regiment but also in those of Mr Machele. So, what do you have to report?' He looked speculatively as Thomas Hankins gathered his thoughts.

'Well, Richard. First of all, I have not committed this to paper, for to do so, in my opinion, would make what

I have to say an official report, and I was unsure if that was a requirement of the request. Should this be deemed necessary in the future and I am ordered to do so, then of course I will comply.'

'Come, Thomas. We have known each other for some years, have we not? Let us just talk this over, perhaps sharing some claret, which seems to have miraculously found its way here from across the sea in great quantities.' He uncorked a bottle and poured two large glasses. 'Your very good health, Thomas. Now tell me your story.'

Cornet Hankins raised his glass and sipped appreciatively. 'Well, Richard, asking me to tell my story is indeed what this may sound like. A story.' He took more of a large swallow than a sip of his claret and waited whilst Richard refilled his glass before continuing.

'John Machele talks to his mount.'

'Yes but doesn't everyone?' queried Richard.

'Indeed, they do, sir. Indeed, they do,' he agreed, nodding his head, 'but he doesn't talk to his the way you or I would talk to ours. John Machele holds actual conversations. One-sided to anyone listening, but John gives every impression that it is a regular two-sided one. He asks it questions and then responds as though pondering the horse's reply and then continues accordingly. I have it on good authority that there have been occasions when he has actually argued with the animal. Now, I have two particular examples which I shall relay to you.

'As you know from your own experience, for some parades everyone is mounted and for other ones they are not, which is usually determined by the training exercises to follow. On the first occasion, Machele marched onto the parade ground late. This was a mounted parade. In making his due apology for the lateness of his arrival and to explain why he had come on foot, he stated that his mount had insisted that today's parade was to be held on foot. Because of this, his mount had refused to attend.

'On another occasion when he was again late on parade, he gave as his reason for his late arrival as being again that his mount had again argued that the parade was to be held on foot and had initially refused to come. Machele then stated that he had to show his mount a copy of the *Daily Orders* before he would permit John to mount and attend the parade.' Thomas paused.

Richard interjected. 'And these incidents were obviously in full view of the whole assembled regiment. What happened?'

'Well. There was the sound of muffled laughter throughout the ranks on both occasions, which the NCOs had great difficulty quelling. What effect this was having on discipline, you can only imagine. Turnip Machele's appearance on parade or carrying out any of his other duties would appear to be dictated by his present relationship with his horse. I admit to having found it hard indeed not to burst out laughing, and I could tell by the way the other officers' jaw muscles were visibly twitching that I was not the only one. Machele gave every appearance of being totally unaware of the effect his words and actions were having. He believes utterly that what he says is the truth and that there is nothing odd or out of the ordinary about it.'

'Good Lord. This is extraordinary. What about how he gets along with the other officers?' asked Richard, trying hard not to laugh himself and to regard this purely as a medical matter.

'Well,' continued Hankins, trying to keep his own reaction to the telling of the tale under firm control, 'he has a respect for authority and is fully cognisant of his place within the military hierarchy and, as a rule, performs his duty in an acceptable manner but...' And here he paused again as he thought about the best words to use to place before the regimental surgeon. 'John Machele is regarded as being of exceptional good value in the junior officers' mess. Apart from always being willing to pay his way and honour his promissory notes after losing at billiards or cards, he does tell the most absolutely gripping tales about his life. He tells of girls he has known – remember, he is older than the other cornets – excursions to the Vauxhall Pleasure Gardens, some time that he spent at a Naval Academy and a reference to a mysterious fire whilst he was there. He also talks a lot about gunpowder and the smell of smoke. Often, he will tell stories of how many different places he has lived in, but never with his parents. He tells all these tales in such a way that his brother officers almost fall off their chairs with laughter. And then something changes. Someone may laughingly ask him if it is all true. One of them actually said about something John had told them that it sounded crazy. That is when his behaviour completely changes, as though someone has lit a fuse. He shouts at the other fellows that everything he says is true. What he is telling them is what it is like to be him. That he has never known his parents. Has never had a home. Has never had a family. The only people who care for him are those who get paid to do so. The change that comes over him is so dramatic that the whole atmosphere in the mess undergoes a complete change. The others begin by looking at him open-mouthed and then, as one, they all turn their gaze downwards. Machele then, without fail, storms out, and his parting words are invariably the same: "You have laughed but this is real. Ask my banker fellow." You see, Richard, he also worries his brother junior officers. They enjoy his stories but have to be so very careful what they say to him. It is as though there are forbidden words such as crazy or mad which, whilst not necessarily being directed at him, if he hears them he makes the assumption that they are, and then the way he reacts confirms what people may be thinking about him. I'm sorry if that sounds a little muddled, but the whole picture regarding John Machele is just that. Muddled.'

'Thank you, Thomas,' acknowledged the surgeon. 'Word of this simply has to go to Major Bothwell. I can only give my opinion as to what Machele's behaviour indicates, but I will say that there are clear signs of his often being out of his senses and that could make him unreliable, to say the least, in a position of any authority. I believe Rutherford has already mentioned other incidents to the major. What action he decides to take will be his decision alone. Thank you again, Thomas.'

With that, Hankins took his leave and left the surgeon's office, feeling as though a great weight had been lifted from his shoulders.

Major Bothwell looked across his desk at Regimental Surgeon Richard Jones, who was sat opposite him.

'Well, Richard,' said the major, tapping the surgeon's report with his hand, 'this is a fine state of affairs indeed, and I thank you for bringing it to my attention. I fully understand why you felt it to be appropriate to formalise matters. From the incidents with which you have become acquainted, and others of which I am already aware, I am forced to say that I concur with your diagnosis. Mr Machele is ofttimes out of his senses and may be deemed to suffer from bouts of insanity. It is a fine line that we walk, is it not, between what we may find highly amusing in someone else's behaviour and a realisation that that same behaviour can cause that person to be unreliable and unpredictable and a possible danger to themselves and others.'

Richard Jones returned the major's look and said, 'On an official level, I am stating that, in my professional opinion, John Machele may be deemed to be insane. He may not be everybody's idea of a lunatic, but then lay persons' expectations of the insane are that they act in an uncontrollable and irrational manner, which is manifestly recognisable. This is not so, sir. They measure insanity by what they see or hear about in Bethel or Bedlam as it is more popularly known. Places where people are charged money to witness the antics of those poor tortured souls who are inmates there.'

'You do not approve of this then, I take it?' queried Major Bothwell.

'Indeed, I do not, sir. Indeed, I do not. I believe that

what so many lay persons, and even some medical men, have no understanding of is that persons suffering bouts of insanity are following their own form of logic. Look at Machele. Does he not, almost without fail, present a logical explanation for his actions? I am certain you have witnessed his utter bewilderment when his explanation is denied belief. And yet to him, what he has said is the truth and it is the other person that he feels to be lacking in the ability to follow his reasoning. This then leads to his frustration and possible loss of his temper. I pity the lad in his suffering. And suffer he does. Make no mistake about that, sir. And yet, in other respects, he does have the makings of an officer but not sufficiently to outweigh his periods of insanity.

'I will be honest with you, Major, I do not know of any treatment for this disease, which is an illness even if it cannot be seen. The difficulty we are facing is that John Machele is in the army, and whilst it can be a safe place for men with all sorts of problems, it cannot be that for an officer, albeit a very junior one, whose behaviour it is not possible to predict from one day to the next. What has to be gauged, in my opinion, sir, is the level of danger he could possibly pose to other members of the regiment in the field of battle. As a medical man, I have concerns for Machele as a patient, and before you say it, sir, he is my patient in that I am responsible for the medical care of the officers and men in this regiment. I feel, with your forgiveness, sir, that your view will be that of an army man who is responsible for the discipline and morale of the regiment in its entirety.'

Richard Jones felt he had said quite enough. He had expressed his thoughts about the state of mind of Cornet John Machele and the possible effect that that could have on the other members of the regiment and also the effectiveness of it as a fighting unit. Whatever Major Bothwell decided to do about it was another matter.

'Thank you again, Richard,' said Major Bothwell. 'I must balance what is right for Machele against what is right from a military standpoint. I believe I know what I must do, but I must, at the very least, consult or inform the colonel before I take the action that I feel to be correct. Very well, Richard, leave it with me, and keep your ears to the ground if you would.'

Richard eased himself out of his chair and left the major to pursue the matter in the best way he thought fit.

Bothwell knew exactly what action needed to be taken. Under ordinary circumstances, he would have contacted the parents of one of his cornets and request that they remove their son as being medically unsuited to a career in the army. Cornet Machele's position was rather different. He was twenty years of age. There was no record of any parentage. His commission had not been purchased but had been awarded by the Colonel of the Regiment, Lord Eglinton. So, it was to Lord Eglinton that he was to write, explaining the situation and the concerns.

His suggested outcome was that Machele be retired from the regiment. This would mean, in effect, his voluntary resignation and would not carry the possible stigma associated with, to all intents and purposes, a physically fit young man being discharged on medical grounds. He could only hazard a guess as to what Lord Eglinton's reaction would be, for Bothwell sensed that Machele was not a protégé of his but that someone else had requested that he be regarded as such. Bothwell was as certain as certain can be that since Eglinton was essentially a military man, he would agree that this solution was in the best interests of the regiment.

It would probably be the better part of two or three weeks before he received a response to his report, mainly, he suspected, because certain arrangements to which he would not be made privy would need to be made to ensure that Machele's retirement was handled with discretion. Meanwhile, the army life and its routine would have to continue, with Captain Rutherford and Cornet Hankins keeping him informed.

SO, IT IS TO BE THE ROYAL NAVY

1ˢᵗ July 1796

'Brown, Brown. Ah, there you are at last,' cried Brown's exasperated employer. 'Don't hover, man. What do you think about this?' he said, waving a letter in the air.

'I really have no idea, sir,' responded Brown who, whatever he did, did not consider that he hovered. He may wait patiently in close proximity to his master, but he certainly did not hover. 'If perhaps I may be permitted?'

'What? Oh yes. Read it for yourself. It's from Eglinton, that Scots fellow.'

Brown took the missive from his master's podgy beringed fingers and quickly scanned its contents. It was just as he had feared as soon as he heard who it was from.

'Well?' queried his master. 'What to do now? What to do now?'

'Sir,' replied Brown, 'if I have a full understanding of its contents, it is this. The word from the commanding officer of the Royal Scots Greys on the recommendation of the regimental surgeon is that your protégé, John Machele, has exhibited multiple signs of insanity which it is believed should disbar him from military service. He is considered from the evidence enclosed to be a likely danger to himself and the men under him. What I am unsure of is whether Lord Eglinton is requesting permission to have John retired from the regiment or is stating that he will anyway.'

'Quite, Brown, quite. My understanding too,' said his employer. 'I think back to our conversation when it was decided that the army would be a good place for him. I believe I said something about not having madmen running the army.' He looked enquiringly at Brown.

'You did indeed, sir. Almost prophetic, if I may say so, sir.'

'You may indeed, Brown. But what to do now? He can't stay in the army, and we know what happened at his lodgings. Think, Brown. What can we do with him now?' He fixed Brown with a look that was almost pleading, willing him to come up with a creative solution to yet another, to him, unsolvable problem.

Brown thought for a moment and wondered, not for the first time, what his master would do without him to find ways around all manner of difficulties. Still, that was what he was paid for and paid very well indeed.

'Sir, I believe a speedy resolution is called for. One which will meet everyone's requirements, and what I propose, if you agree, of course, is that he should join the navy.'

'The navy!' exploded the personage. 'We tried that before and look what happened then. No, no. Think again, Brown. That will never do!'

In the pause that followed, Brown put his argument into some sort of order; sufficient to quell his employer's initial rejection of the very idea.

'Sir,' he continued, 'the affair at the Naval Academy was four years ago, and he was only sixteen years of age. He is now twenty.' Brown thought that by itemising why the navy could be appropriate and a speedy solution, he could, with comparative ease, gain his employer's acceptance of what was becoming a plan. He continued. 'The navy would mean he would be on a ship and therefore in a confined and secure place. Should the ship not be at sea, instructions may be made that he was not to be permitted ashore, thereby keeping him away from that possible temptation. He could enlist as a midshipman, which, as you are aware, sir, is not an officer as such but does still require him to be addressed as Mr or sir. He would also wear a uniform, which declares his rank. These will all appeal to him.'

'Yes, that's all very well, Brown, but what if he refuses to go?'

'I don't believe he will, sir. Although there are periods when he is out of his senses, he also has a very logical mind even if his logic is not always easily comprehended by others. He can, I believe, be accepting of the fact that the alternative may well be that he is kept somewhere else under close supervision, which is not something he would relish. In fact, he would likely resist that with all his might.'

'Very well, Brown, I can see how this just might work, but the mechanics of it. How do we contrive to make this happen?'

'Sir,' said Brown, thinking to himself that now might be the right time to bring his master's sense of importance into play and to demonstrate to him that without his valuable contribution, the plan was unworkable. 'The key to itself is your relationship with the Royal Navy, sir. I feel certain that you paying a visit in person to the Admiralty could quickly bring your influence to bear to arrange for a request to be made for a captain of a ship moored close to Canterbury, where Master John is currently in barracks, to accommodate him as a midshipman.'

'Yes, yes, I can certainly bring what influence I have to bear, Brown. Near Canterbury, eh? That will be the Nore, will it not?' The personage peered at Brown, pleased that this little piece of naval knowledge would both surprise and impress.

'Indeed, sir, I believe it is.' Brown added a touch of admiration to the tone of his reply and was rewarded by seeing a not-very-attractive smugness appear on his master's face.

'So. To the details,' continued Brown. 'You, sir, as you have indicated, will make the arrangements with the Admiralty, who I am certain will respond with all haste. Might I suggest, sir, that arrangements be made for him to join whatever ship is chosen on the 14th of this month?' He paused.

'Yes, yes. In two weeks? Yes, of course. I shall tell them the date. I'm off now. Not a moment to lose!' He moved towards the bell rope to summon a servant to bring his carriage round.

'Just one moment, sir, if you please,' quickly interposed

Brown. 'I feel I must inform you of the other arrangements that must be put in place.'

'Oh, very well. Get on with it, man.'

'Yes, sir. A reply from you to the colonel this very day agreeing that John may be retired from the Royal Scots Greys but not until, say, the 9th of July. This will give me time to arrange for myself, with some gentlemen, to escort him after retirement to suitable accommodation where he may await the news of which ship he is to join. I shall return here and the gentlemen will keep him company after I have informed him that he is to go to sea. I shall inform Mr Brooks, by letter, with time being so short, as to what has transpired and request that he make rendezvous with John on the 13th of this month and that he accompanies him to the selected ship. John trusts Brooks so his continued association is essential for this to be executed smoothly.

'John will require kitting out, of course. Can't have him joining the navy wearing an army officer's uniform, sir.' Brown was rewarded for this little piece of humour by a slight puckering of his master's prominent lips. He continued. 'I shall call on Mr Hawkes, who will have all of John's measurements and, because of the urgency, I shall take them to Mr Gieves, the naval outfitter, for him to provide the necessary uniforms for a midshipman. Perhaps, sir, you would find out from someone at the Admiralty what other sundry items and equipment will be required and instruct that they be purchased and delivered to Mr Brooks by the 12th. I shall specify that same date and destination for delivery of his uniforms.

'I must stress, sir, that to be retired from the regiment

is not the same as being dismissed. It means he can keep his rank, which I feel will be very important to him. It confirms him in his belief that he is a gentleman, sir.'

'Thank you, Brown. As usual, you have found a solution where I fear it may have taken me a trifle longer. Now, to the Admiralty. Good day. Good day.' And he swept past Brown, who bowed his head as the portly figure left on his mission.

BROWN TO BROOKS: THE LETTER

3rd July 1796

Dodd, now confirmed by George Brooks in his position as personal assistant as well as responsible for supervising the other clerks, much to the chagrin of Thompson, rapped with his knuckles on Brooks's office door and entered holding a sealed letter.

'This just came by private messenger, Mr Brooks.'

'Thank you, Dodd. Leave it on my desk, please,' he acknowledged, barely looking up as Dodd left the room.

He was used to having letters delivered by private messengers. Usually, they were requests for overdraft facilities or permission to delay a loan repayment, so this one could wait whilst he finished the correspondence with which he was engaged.

It was some thirty minutes later that he picked up the letter. There was no name of the sender and the wax seal was plain. That in itself struck him as a little unusual, for the majority of the bank's clients insisted on the wax seal bearing some form of insignia or crest to impress the recipient. He broke the seal, unfolded the sheet of paper and read:

"My Dear George…"

Who is this addressing me at the bank in this manner? he thought to himself, hastily looking to the end of the missive.

"Your humble and affectionate friend, Augustus."

'Ah, Mr Brown. What has Master John been up to now? I wonder.' He read on:

I take the liberty of writing to you instead of calling in person to appraise you of certain developments regarding John Machele and crave your support regarding the arrangements I am required to put into place.

I shall put the matter simply.

John has exhibited certain behaviours that have raised serious concerns within the regiment. It has been decided that he will be retired but not dismissed, and he may keep his rank should he wish to use it. He is not yet aware that this action is to be taken nor that a date has been decided upon. It is to be on the 9th of this month.

Two gentlemen and I will be at the barracks in Canterbury and will escort him to The Red Lion in Sittingbourne. I will then return to London whilst the two men supervise John at the inn.

Moves are afoot for him to join the Royal Navy as a midshipman. It will have been put to him that the alternative will be for him to be confined under a strict regime. He felt himself to be happy at the Naval Academy so, hopefully, he will be amenable to this.

I have been informed that he will be joining his ship, probably HMS Sandwich, at The Nore on 14th July.

What I humbly request of you, George, is that you journey to Sittingbourne and stay overnight at The Red Lion, where private rooms have been engaged for you on the 13th of this month. On the following day, 14th July, my master would consider it as being most obliging if you were to accompany John to the ship, not escort but accompany, and see him duly on board. The Sandwich *is commanded by a Captain Mosse. My master would be further gratified if you could request of Captain Mosse that John not be permitted to go ashore without the express permission of the admiral.*

Anticipating that you are willing and able to comply with this request at such very short notice, the necessary uniforms and equipment for John's transformation into a midshipman will be delivered to you on 12th July. My carriage will, of course, be made available for the entire period.

My master and I are obliged and in your debt in this matter. Apart from the business arrangement, which we share, I trust you do not feel that I am presuming upon the friendship that exists between us. As you may imagine, this matter was only brought to my master's attention on the 1st of this month, hence the urgency and lack of time to approach you in person. My request for your continued assistance with John's affairs is also made because of your relationship with him. Put in plain terms, John trusts you.

I thank you again, George, and would be most obliged if you would convey your agreement to this request by a note to the usual address.

George sat back in his chair and tried to analyse his thoughts. He had thought he would not have anything more to do on John Machele's behalf for some time yet. He had seemed so proud and happy to be joining the Royal Scots Greys. There must be quite a story behind this. Meanwhile, as far as he knew, he could afford a few days out of the bank, especially now that Dodd had assumed so much responsibility, and a trip to Kent and going aboard a ship of the Royal Navy was something to look forward to. He hoped that Augustus was proved right and that John did trust him and did not see him as someone else now who was always around to interfere with his life.

What George Brooks could not anticipate, of course, was the speed with which events precipitated by John once he had joined the navy would engage him so fully.

THE PERSONAGE HEARS OF
A COURT MARTIAL

August 1796

The man, immaculately dressed in bottle green, approached his employer knowing full well the scene that was to follow.

'Sir, Mr Brooks presents his compliments and I have to inform you of the news he has from the *Sandwich*. Sir, the particular young man, your protégé, is accused of attempting to assassinate the first lieutenant and he is to be court martialled.'

'He's done what? They're having him court martialled? But… but… he'll hang. I always said he would. Can't you stop it? Don't they know who he is?'

The man in bottle green waited, knowing it was pointless to try to explain until his master was prepared to listen to reason. Hopefully, full apoplexy would be avoided and his eyes, which were bulging out of his head, would resume their usual slightly protruding position and his shaking jowls subside with the throbbing vein in his forehead.

The spluttering continued. But the man felt able to enter into an explanation of the situation as he saw it now the initial explosion was over.

'Sir, this is no longer a private matter. A request for a court martial has been made formally by the officer, a Lieutenant James Hills, and that request has been granted by the admiral commanding at the Nore. The charges are of a most serious nature, sir. Captain Mosse was most apologetic in his communication to Mr Brooks, but whilst disobedience of orders and showing contempt could possibly be handled internally and discreetly, trying to kill the first lieutenant cannot be dealt with like that.'

'Come now; surely he can be transferred to another ship. Sent overseas? I never understood why he was on that ship in the first place. Moored in the mouth of the Thames, for God's sake. Don't tell me yet again it was to make it easier to keep an eye on him. It's not good enough. And, of course, I know they don't know who he is any more than the boy himself, but surely something can be done? What about your people?' He looked enquiringly at Brown.

'Sir, with respect, with witnesses to the lad's attack on the lieutenant, there is no way he can be found not guilty. We could suggest to him what it might be in his best interests to say in his defence but, judging by past experience, Master John will either deliberately ignore any suggestions or be as outspoken as the mood takes him on the day. But there may be another way this could be approached. Perhaps if there was a certain amount of "guidance" given to the officers sitting at the court martial implying that he is not always in full possession of his senses, then questioning could, possibly, follow that line,' he suggested encouragingly.

'You mean get them to declare him mad?' said the personage, not sure if he had fully understood what Brown was suggesting and also slowly becoming aware of the possible implications of a not guilty verdict by virtue of the lad not being in full possession of his senses.

The man in bottle green was also concerned about what steps would have to be taken regarding John Machele's entire future should the court come to this decision but decided it would be best to take one step at a time.

'You follow my thinking exactly, sir, although perhaps we should encourage the use of the word "insane", which has a more medical sound to it. With your agreement, sir, and that of the Admiralty, I feel that Admiral Buckner could be encouraged to discuss the case with his captains and plant that seed.' Brown felt this was the best solution that could be effected with the likelihood of the trial being in the next few days.

THE BOARD'S INFLUENCED DELIBERATIONS

29th August 1796

Captain Trollope began: 'Well, gentlemen, I believe there is only one conclusion we can come to, but it leaves us in a fine pickle, as I'm certain you all agree.'

The other captains looked at one another, and each seemed to be mulling over in his mind his individual inner conflict. Clearly, Machele was guilty as charged. That was indisputable, for all the evidence spoke for itself. There were only minor differences of detail which were insignificant and could not influence their final decision. The issue going through their minds was the fact that they, as a group, had had it indicated to them that a verdict of not guilty by virtue of Machele's insanity was the desired outcome. This had come from Admiral Buckner himself, but what the original source of this desire was he did not or, more likely, could not state. It was possible that even he had not been told directly.

The door to the steward's pantry opened, and the steward, on whom the lower deck depended for their information, entered with his assistant, carrying eleven glasses and half a dozen bottles of Captain Duff's best Madeira.

'Thank you, Andrews,' said Captain George Duff, who was the commanding officer of the *Glenmore*, his Scots burr still prominent despite his having been at sea since he was thirteen years of age in 1779. 'You may leave us now. No, not in your pantry. Wait outside with everyone else.'

Andrews said: 'Aye, aye, sir,' but his whole body showed his disappointment. The story of their deliberations would have cost his shipmates any number of tots of rum, and he had already been trying to work out why these exalted personages had found themselves to be in a pickle.

'Anyway,' continued Duff, turning back to the other members of the board, 'your very good health, gentlemen.' They raised their glasses.

'In my present role as president,' resumed Captain Trollope, 'let us see what the chaplain and young Machele have to say for themselves. D'you mind if I read the statements out to you?' There were nods of assent.

'Well, first the chaplain's.' He skimmed through the document. 'Just what may be expected from the chaplain. I will spare you the details. "Young man… not long in His Majesty's service… regrets his actions… only known to me for less than two months… out of character… would request mercy, etc." Nothing really personal or significantly pertinent to the case. Seems to be done as a duty, not that I question his desire for mercy, but still insufficient to warrant it, I feel.

'Now,' he went on, breaking the seal on the well-folded second piece of paper. 'Let us hear what Mr Machele has to say in his defence, although I find it most strange that he asked Captain Mosse two questions in open court yet refused the offer to give his defence there. Be that as it may, gentlemen, this is what he has written:

'To the Hon'ble President & members of this Court
Gentlemen
The charges for which I have been brought before you I am now fully sensible are of the most serious nature.

In Defence of which I can have but little to offer but as some extenuation thereof I hope the Court will take into consideration my being forced into a service I was totally unacquainted with, since which event I have conceived myself no other than a prisoner, having been Deprived of the Indulgence extended to others/such treatment in addition to the distresses of mind I have laboured under for some years past through disappointments in concerns of a private nature and other circumstances too numerous to trouble this Court with.

I humbly hope will be considered in some degree as a parturition of the charges exhibited against me, in particular that of assassination, which was totally foreign from my Heart; activated by the frenzy of the moment and agitated with the most poignant feelings could only have caused me to plunge myself into the unfortunate Dilemma in which I now appear before you.

Thus situated allow me, with a true sense of the

rashness, and violence of my conduct, Humbly to beg leave, with a Heart full of contrition, to throw myself on the Mercy of this Honourable Court.
   John Machele
   August the 29th: 1796

'So there it is, gentlemen,' continued Trollope. 'Can I take it that we are all agreed that the prisoner is guilty as charged and we have no option but to pass the ultimate sentence?' He looked at each captain in turn, all of whom gave their assent to the verdict.

'I would just like to add, although it really has no bearing on things, that I don't think Mosse came out of this very well,' interjected Captain Paget Daily. 'Whatever did he mean by saying he knew him to be a violent young man? Sorry, gentlemen, but I just felt I needed to say it.'

'Thank you, Daily. That may be said but I cannot help but feel for the man. He gave every sign of being most uncomfortable and that he wasn't so much being totally open in his answers to our questions as more being aware of what he felt he could not say in open court. He was a man under pressure, but the source of it?' so acknowledged Trollope, as he paced up and down and poured himself another glass of Madeira. 'Sorry, Duff. It's your cabin, not mine, but I trust I have your forgiveness?'

'You do and let us not stand on ceremony, especially with my steward and his ever-flapping ears having been temporarily banished.' George Duff sensed a slight easing of the almost palpable air of hesitation and uncertainty that seemed to have settled over the group.

'I believe I am not the only person here present who, for one reason or another, wishes that we did not have to pass a sentence of death on Mr Machele but, although it is our decision to take since we have no option under the Articles of War, would it be the wish of all assembled that I propose we jointly petition His Majesty for mercy in this case? We cannot do it on the grounds of insanity, but might I suggest we word it in such a way that it is based around his youth and inexperience and stress to His Majesty that this will not form part of the record of the court martial but is personal from ourselves. If made public, it could be felt by others that they too could escape death by the same means, which would be no deterrent regarding future acts of a similar nature. If we are to despatch such a letter, and I suggest it is to Mr Nepean as secretary to the Admiralty then, since we have already reached our verdict, may we not draft and sign it now whilst we are all in one place and of one mind?' continued Trollope.

'And whilst there is still some of your fine Madeira left, George,' added Captain Surridge, lightening the proceedings considerably and then continuing, 'I do not feel we should have the clerk prepare a fine copy for us to sign as this is a private recommendation and will not be contained in the court record when passing sentence.'

'It seems we have, be it unwittingly, agreed a form of wording to which we can all append our signatures,' said Captain Trollope. 'Now, who writes the fairest hand? Certainly not me, for I can barely make out what I've written only a few days later. Mansfield, you're a fine scholarly fellow, always got your nose in a book, and I've seen your notations on many a chart. Always damned easy to read.'

Charles Mansfield cut a tall figure despite his permanent stoop from years of service aboard His Majesty's ships; a necessary stoop to avoid being knocked unconscious by crashing his head against the deck beams. He had a habit of holding his head slightly to one side, which gave him a questioning look that many of his subordinates found unnerving and quite often left them searching their consciences even when they had made a perfectly normal report about the ship's course.

He made his way to what was the clerk's table, making sure he didn't spill his wine and, taking a fresh sheet of paper from the pile, commenced to write:

His Majesty's Ship Glenmore
At the Little Nore, the 29 Augt. 1796

Sir

We the members of a Court Martial who have tried Mr. John Machell a Midshipman of His Majesty's Ship Sandwich *for disobedience of orders, contempt and attempting to assassinate Lieutenant James Hills First Lieutenant of that ship when in the execution of his duty, beg you to represent to their Lordships that we unanimously recommend the said Mr. John Machell as an object for His Majesty's Mercy on account of his youth & inexperience & his not having been more than two months in His majesty's Naval Service which we take this mode of*

urgency by a private recommendation it not being
mentioned in the Sentence, in order that the penalty
incurred by crimes of such magnitude might have a
more awful effect.

We are Sir
Your very obedient and humble servants
Captains:

'Splendid job, Charles. Splendid job,' commended Trollope. 'Are we all agreed and prepared to sign this plea? Excellent. Since there are no objections, I shall sign first as president and then you may all follow suit.'

With all eleven signatures affixed, the plea was folded, a wax seal applied and the document addressed to Mr Evan Nepean, secretary to the Admiralty, and in the lower right-hand corner the words: "By Officer".

'Very well, gentlemen,' continued Trollope, 'I feel it is time to reconvene, and not only because we appear to have finished that most excellent Madeira of yours, George. Can I leave the plea letter with you? I'm certain you have a junior lieutenant who would be absolutely delighted to visit the Admiralty to deliver the letter. Just make it perfectly clear that he is to hand it to Mr Nepean in person. If he should not be available then to place it in the possession of his most senior clerk for Nepean's immediate and most urgent attention with the proviso that it is to be opened only by the secretary himself. Be a good chap, Ross, and give a shout for the clerk to announce that we are reconvening.'

THE SENTENCE IS DULY PASSED

29th August 1796

There goes my marine guard again. Stamp, stamp, salute. Another reason why I'll be glad when this is all over. An end to all that noise those lobsters make at every opportunity.

Hello, the door's opening.

'Come, Mr Machele, the court is reconvening.'

This is an officer I haven't seen before. A marine lieutenant this time. Immaculate red tunic, webbing a brilliant white and the buttons shining like little suns, even in the subdued light here.

'Very good, sir,' I acknowledged and, leaving the cubbyhole of a cabin, fell in behind the marine lieutenant, with a marine private on either side of me and a corporal bringing up the rear.

An impressive escort this time. All part of putting on a show really. They only had to ask me to return to the courtroom and I'd have gone quite willingly, but I suppose they had no way of knowing that.

So, this is it. The coterie of captains have duly considered over their wine and now it cannot be long before I have secured my victory, and they are absolutely unaware that I have manipulated this system of the navy for my own ends. It is not far to the cabin being used for my trial, and I stand before the table waiting for the captains to enter and announce my fate. I scarcely took note of the other people in the body of the court as I, how shall I describe it, processed to my position. Body of the court. What an odd expression; yet I know it to be correct. If there is a body in this court then surely it is going to be mine. I did catch a glimpse of Mr Brooks again, who half turned his head and nodded as I drew level. No words were spoken out loud. I'm not sure if that was simply customary and in keeping with the creation of an air of solemnity or if people had been told that talking was not permitted.

'The court will rise,' called a disembodied voice to the right of me.

I am already standing so this doesn't apply to me, but the noise the others make! Well. Shuffling and stamping of feet, benches being scraped on the deck. All they have to do is stand up, so why all the noise? Of the many things I won't miss, noise is near the top of my list. I can see the door to the right of the table has opened and here they come. My coterie of captains looking serious, as they should, but also several seem to be wearing half-smiles, as though they know something I don't. That can't be right, surely. Everyone must be solemn, even if they have been putting several bottles to bed. I don't like those half-smiles one little bit. The only person who is going to do any smiling here is me as I am led out to be executed.

'Court, be seated,' the same disembodied voice calls, and that shameful shuffling and scraping is repeated.

'The prisoner will stand.'

What utter nonsense. Can't he see that I am already standing? It is becoming ever clearer to me that certain things have to be said at certain times, and they will be said even if every person in the court can see that they are not necessary. The captains have all taken their seats and are, without exception, focusing their attention on me. Quite right too. I am the main attraction here. If it wasn't for me, none of these people would be here at all. So, yes, look at me. Look at me now. What is that noise? It is like a reverberating growl. Ah, it's Captain Trollope clearing his throat. What is he going to say? It looks as though whatever it is will take the form of a written statement. If I was in a position to place a wager, I would wager that there is a formally worded document for all eventualities and especially for pronouncing a sentence of death. Only the name will need to be inserted. He's starting to speak. Pay attention now, John. This is what you have worked so assiduously to hear spoken. What is he saying?

'The court, having carefully and deliberately weighed and considered the evidence produced, is of the opinion that the charges have been fully proved and that the punishment to be inflicted on him for his offences be capital. The court does therefore adjudge that you, John Machele, be hanged by the neck until you are dead at the yardarm of such of His Majesty's ships and at such time as the Right Honourable, the Lords Commissioners of the Admiralty shall think proper to direct. Take the prisoner down.'

Trollope has finished his part in this little entertainment and exchanges glances with his fellow captains, who seem to have no difficulty in engaging in eye contact with me, and their faces are not as serious and solemn as I feel the occasion warrants. They have just sentenced me to death and they are having no difficulty in looking me squarely in the eye. What sort of people are these? Do they take a man's life so often that they feel no effect on themselves?

Still, no matter. Sentence has been passed. I have got what I wanted. It does feel a trifle odd, though, now that I have been told I am to be hanged. I think uncertainty would describe my feelings. Uncertain because now that my death is nearly upon me, I have that slight doubt that comes from ignorance of what happens next. I don't mean the hanging itself. That is an action carried out according to the rules. I have read them and fully understand the procedure. A rope is reeved through a pulley at the end of a yardarm. On one end is a noose, which will be placed over my head and around my neck. I will be offered a blindfold. I am not certain if I will take one or not. Probably I will because I have this fear of heights, and it would be a shame to show that fear to the assembled ships' crews. The chaplain will say a prayer for my soul. A nominated senior officer will read out the sentence again. The marine band will have been playing the Dead Man's March *and, at a given signal, the six seamen who had hold of the other end of the rope will run, hoisting me to the point where my head will reach the pulley on the end of the yardarm. The uncertainty? That little doubt is, despite the prayer of the chaplain referring to a life ever after, another wager but one I had bet on with my life without any knowledge of what I would be or even if I would be at all after I had danced at that yardarm.*

As I am being escorted from the court, my trusted friend Mr Brooks reached out and touched my sleeve. 'It will be all right, John. We will see you through this. Have faith,' he said, as he looked me in the eye. I smiled at him but said nothing.

He does not know that I knew that everything was all right anyway. Also, behind my smile, is the welcome knowledge that, at long last, I am the master of my own fate and that never again will anyone else make any decisions on my behalf.

'No talking to the prisoner,' barked the marine lieutenant, and I was taken back to that small cabin where I had waited earlier.

Why did Mr Brooks say that to me? Of course it will be all right. I know precisely what I have done and why I have done it. Yes, it will be all right.

Just a minute. Why have I been returned to this little cabin? Surely, it was so obvious that I would be found guilty and sentenced to be hanged, so why have I not been taken directly to the deck for the final scene? Oh, John, John, John. Remember how the wording of the sentence went. It had never crossed my mind that it would not be all over today. Those buggers at the Admiralty have to decide when and where the sentence is to be carried out. What am I supposed to do until then, whenever then is. Will I be kept here? Sent back to the Sandwich *and then kept in irons again? Back to that smelly hole to contemplate the error of my ways. My ways in which there lies no error.*

'Hello, can anybody hear me? I need to go to the heads.'

Another stupid thing about the navy. Why can't they just say going to the privy? Why the heads? I know the answer because I asked the question shortly after I came on board. They said it was because it was in the head of the ship. Bloody nonsense. Plank with a hole in it hanging over the sea right up forrard. Why can't they say forward or even up the front or in the bow? That would make more sense. And why is bosun spelt boatswain? Makes no sense to me at all. Good God, I need something to go in. Bloody undignified having to ask. Don't they know who I am?

'We'll fetch you a pot, sir,' came a disembodied voice from the other side of the cabin door.

My God, it has come to this. I have to ask permission to go for a shit. I am not shitting in a pot in a cabin as tiny as this. To go to the heads, I will have to have an escort because I am a prisoner. Aren't I entitled to any privacy at all? Do they think I'll jump overboard? I've tried that before and people always stopped me. I'm so tired of people interfering in my life. Taking decisions for me. This is my decision which I have taken and nobody else can do anything about it. I have no desire to cheat the hangman or, rather in this case, the gang of seamen detailed to run me up to the yardarm where I shall dance my last dance in farewell. No, I am sentenced to be hanged, and hanged I jolly well will be.

I've only been here for half a day. It isn't really a prison cell, but then neither was that reeking place I was confined in on the Sandwich. *At least it gave the impression of being a prison cell, and it did make me feel like a prisoner. I may not have liked it but at least it was of my own doing. Steady on, John, steady on. Do you really want to go back there? Dirty, smelly place, and the only light from a lantern outside, where the sentry was,*

Anyway, nobody tells me anything. No one seems to know how long I'm to be here. It's up to those buggers at the Admiralty, and I shouldn't think they ever do anything particularly quickly. Never mind. They take as long as they take and that's a fact. But, still, confined in this tiny cabin, having to ask permission to visit the privy, sorry, the heads.

There came a knock on the door and a cry of: 'Stand away from the door.'

Stand away from the door? This cabin can't be much more than six feet long as it is, so where do I have to go to stand away from the bloody door? A marine sentry peers round the half-opened door. 'Your pot, sir,' says he, proffering the item as though it were the Holy Grail.

'I'm not shitting in a pot. I'll piss but I'll not shit. How do I know how long it'll be before someone collects it? That's what I want to know. Give me the pot and tell whoever is in charge that I have urgent need to visit the heads.'

Mmm. That seems to have done the job. He places the pot on the deck, closes the door and marches off in that noisy fashion they pride themselves on. I'll just have to wait and see now. It's up to other people again. Just when I thought that I was taking all the decisions about what happens to me then, and I have to admit it, I never thought of this.

Another knock on the door. 'I am as far away from the door as is possible,' I shouted, before their little ritual could even begin. The door opened and I was invited to follow them.

Them, yes, them! A two-man escort to see me safely to the heads and back again. Well, this is the way it is going to be but probably only for a few days. I can tolerate that, knowing what I have to look forward to – the ultimate escape from other people's plans and actions.

THE PERSONAGE AFTER THE VERDICT

'Sir, as we expected, John has been found guilty and the court had no option but to sentence him to death. The matter will be presented to His Majesty in due course for his confirmation of the sentence.'

The personage, who was seated at his escritoire, gave a good impression of an affronted bullfrog with his ballooning cheeks and replied to this information in a querulous, loudly outraged tone.

'Is there no way round this? Did no one plead on his behalf? I thought we had arranged for him to be acquitted for reasons of insanity. What went wrong?'

'Sir, the court was unable to bring forth such a verdict since none of the witnesses were willing to say he was not in his right senses at the time,' was Brown's response in a half-placatory and half-apologetic way. He knew he was in no way to blame, but his master, with his quick temper, was always liable to shoot the messenger and apologise later.

'But the ship's surgeon? The surgeon? Surely he would testify to it?' demanded the personage.

'The surgeon was not called, sir, and there was nothing to suggest that any of Master Machele's previous behaviour had been brought to his attention.'

'Not called? Not called?' His master pushed his chair back so violently that it toppled to the floor. 'Outrageous, given the evidence. We can appeal, though, can we not? But how to do it without our involvement being known? That is the question. Any suggestions, Brown?' He was pacing about the room now in a state of high dudgeon and, visibly attempting to control his emotions, he turned to Brown hopefully.

'Well, sir, speed will be of the essence in this instance. Might I suggest a collection of statements from people both on the *Sandwich* and elsewhere who can swear to having witnessed any of John's behaviour to indicate that he is not always in his right senses? Our friend Brooks can gather them all together and send them under one cover to Mr Nepean, the secretary to the Admiralty, who in turn will place them before Earl Spencer who, in his role as First Lord of the Admiralty, will bring the plea to the attention of His Majesty.'

'Good. Good. I understand the last part, but how do we arrange for the statements to be sworn? There will be people from different places. How do we get it done in time?' The personage's manner had settled into a state of only mild frustration, but he was showing his grasp of the overall strategy and seemed pleased with himself that he could focus on a possible flaw in the plan.

Brown continued, noticing how his master was now

feeling himself to be part of the solution to what had seemed something impossible to achieve initially.

'Mr Brooks can request a supporting letter from Mr Bettesworth at the Naval Academy, from where John was expelled. He should be only too willing to supply one by return of post. Easy. Now, who else do we need to look to? The Royal Scots Greys. This is where I believe, sir, you may express an interest to the colonel of the regiment. This matter has come to your attention quite by accident, of course, and you seem to have remembered something about a young cornet who exhibited such signs of insanity that he was "retired" from the regiment after only a few months. Pure coincidence, of course. Statements regarding this could be despatched post-haste direct to Mr Brooks. I'm sure the colonel can arrange this, sir.'

'Will this be enough, do you think? There must have been other people on the *Sandwich* who knew him and witnessed his, shall we say, odd behaviour, and what about that business with the pistols when he was in lodgings before he joined the Dragoons?' Although expressing doubts at the sufficiency of supporting statements, the personage was beginning to experience feelings of a slight smugness at his contributions.

'Sir, I believe we can knit this together by judicious planning and the use of a little influence being brought to bear where necessary. The potential witnesses on the *Sandwich* will need to be brought ashore to swear their affidavits, but there may be concerns that some of them may run.'

'Rubbish. Captain – what's the fellow's name? – Mosse

can instruct them to go ashore with a marine escort. Problem solved.' The personage gave every appearance of a man who was playing a major part in the discussion as he eased himself back into his chair which, to Brown's surprise, he had righted himself.

'This is where things could become a little easier, sir. The *Sandwich* is moored near Queensborough, which is an easy row away. Now it just so happens that Evan Nepean, secretary to the Admiralty, is one of the Members of Parliament for that borough and he can be requested by the Admiralty to instruct a local official who is a commissioner for oaths to witness the swearing of the affidavits and have them sent to Mr Brooks.'

'But won't that have a possibility of leading back to me? Is this Nepean to be trusted in a situation of this nature? This is rather outside his usual role, surely. I don't mean to sound disrespectful but…' Despite his exalted position, the personage was clearly not privy to a great deal of the wheels within wheels that eased the smooth running of the ship of state.

'Sir, Mr Nepean can be trusted implicitly in a matter such as this. In his earlier career in His Majesty's service, he was responsible for certain secret operations within the Aliens Office. In effect, he "ran" counter-espionage operatives, where the breaking of the code of secrecy was literally a matter of life and death. He will not need to know more than is absolutely necessary. In fact, with his previous experience, he will not want to know more than is absolutely necessary, sir.'

'Very good, Brown. I shall have a word with the

colonel and then pay a visit to the Admiralty, where I shall mention the action we would like Admiral Buckner to take in instructing Captain Mosse to arrange for the additional witnesses to go ashore. What happens after that I leave in your more-than-capable hands, Brown. Speed is of the essence. Call my carriage; I have people to see.'

With that, he rose from his chair a lot more gently than previously and gazed out of the window in a pose which he felt demonstrated that he was a man who could take decisions. A man of action. The reality was that he was a man who, because of his familial connections and title, could have doors opened for him upon which others might have to knock in vain.

JOHN

1st September 1796

What day is it now? Must be 1st September. How much longer do I have to wait? Nobody seems to know anything or, if they do, then they aren't telling me. At least I'm being fed properly. None of that basic muck like the foremast jacks have to eat. I more than made my share of the messing subs on the Sandwich, *so I suppose that counts for something here on the* Glenmore.

Hello, noisy footsteps, well, marching really, now what? No knocking on the door today. It just opens.

A marine lieutenant called out, 'Mr Machele, on your feet. Gather anything personal and come with us.'

Not really a request but an order. Shame about having to stand up, though. I was just enjoying a rest almost at full stretch on the narrow bunk. Well, maybe this is it. Must make certain my necktie is neat. How is the rest of me? Smart enough, I suppose, for what is to come. Oh, blast. I still have that blemish on my breeches. Still, if what I have heard is true, there will be more than this little stain on them after the deed is done.

I march off with my escort. I'm getting quite good at marching now. Not as good as if I'd stayed in the army or if I'd joined the marines but good enough. Only a few minutes more and I'll see the crew lined up in divisions and the execution party in place.

Where is everybody?

'Over the side, Mr Machele, if you please, and into the boat,' ordered the officer in charge.

I did. I went over the side and sat in the stern sheets, with marines on either side of me and facing the oarsmen.

'Give way,' bellowed the coxswain.

'Where are we going?' I asked suspiciously.

'Taking you back to the *Sandwich*,' came the reply.

'But why?'

'Mr Machele, to put it plainly, sailors don't like to have men under sentence of death on their ship. It's a superstition.'

'But why should the sailors on the *Sandwich* be any less superstitious?'

I countered that speedily. Proud of this piece of undeniable logic. Hmm, let him answer that if he can.

'They probably aren't, Mr Machele,' the marine lieutenant responded, 'but the *Sandwich* is the ship you joined and in whose muster book you are entered. It was also on that ship that your crime was committed. And, anyway, the bulk of your possessions are on board, and you may want to give some thought as to how they should be disposed of after your, ahem, departure from this life.' He looked away, clearly embarrassed by this latter statement.

The man's embarrassed. Felt it wasn't quite the done

thing for a gentleman, even if he is only a marine officer, to remind a condemned man of what his future holds.

'Up you go, Mr Machele.'

Was it really only July when I last clambered up the towering side of the ship? When I became Midshipman Machele? Such a short time ago. Looking down, I can see the boat I arrived in already on its way back to the Glenmore, *and just above the main deck's bulwark I can catch a glimpse of the marines' headgear as they wait to become my new escort.*

Right, John, remember your manners. You are now setting foot on another one of His Majesty's ships. Turning to face aft, I touch the brim of my hat in salute. Now what's going to happen? Not that stinking hole again? Please, not that. I am a gentleman and deserve, and expect, to be treated as one. It's not a large escort, so they obviously don't think that I'm dangerous. Three marines and a lieutenant.

'Follow me, Mr Machele, At my command, if you please,' said the lieutenant, resplendent in his scarlet tunic. The two marines moved into position; one on either side of me whilst the third, who I can see now is a corporal, took up his place behind me.

'Prisoner and escort forward,' called the lieutenant.

The marines are well rehearsed and on the command instantly start to move. Honestly, they are like a machine. Once they are told to move then they move. Just like the Royal Scots Greys, moving as though there is nothing in front of them to stop them, and just as noisy as well. Stamp, stamp. That's all very well on the land but on a ship this shows scant regard for those on the deck below them. They are stamping on somebody else's ceiling. That is just plain bad manners. Something has hit me in the back. It's that bloody marine corporal behind me. I haven't moved fast enough for him. Should I administer a rebuke? Not really sure I am in a position to do that. After all, I am a prisoner under sentence of death. Act the part, John, act the part. But where are we going? Only one deck down and a row of cabin doors, one of which is open.

'In here, if you please, sir,' said the marine lieutenant, indicating that I should enter. 'You will find your dunnage has already been moved here from the midshipmen's berth so at least you have a change of clothing. Might I suggest your working rig would be the appropriate dress for your period of confinement? Food and refreshment will be brought to you, and should you have sufficient funds, you may order any extras from the mess servant when he comes. There is a chamber pot there for you. Should you wish to use the heads proper, then you will be escorted there and back.

'There will be a sentinel outside this door both day and night who has instructions not to engage with you in conversation but will communicate any request to myself, and I will, in turn, pass that request to the person best placed to deal with it.'

Having said that without seeming to draw breath, he pulled the door closed and turned a key in the lock.

How I didn't burst out laughing, I will never know. The lieutenant's little speech had been delivered in that mechanical, singsong way, so popular with soldiers and marines. Everything done by rote. Never looking the person being addressed in the eye but looking either over their head or slightly to one side. Not sure how they do that. I never mastered it when I was in the army. I always looked people straight in their eyes as a gentleman should, although when I was admonished for this on many occasions, I always responded in the same way, even to my commanding officer, Major Bothwell. I would invariably say that not looking in the eye was the mark of a scoundrel and not that of an officer and a gentleman. I had been told, sometimes very sternly, that this was the army way of doing things and that, therefore, it was the way that I, John Machele, should do it. I reported several men, corporals and privates, for what I considered to be disrespectful behaviour for not looking me in the eye when addressing me. No one was ever punished, and it was always me who was reprimanded. I never understood why, and I took my reprimands badly. I am still certain that I was right. How else could you know if someone was telling the truth and not making deceitful excuses?

Still, what's my new accommodation like? Mmm. A bit larger than the last one. There's room to dress quite comfortably. No idea whose cabin this usually is. No personal effects at all, but why would there be? It's now the condemned cell, but for how long? It would be most amusing if I am in Lieutenant Hills's quarters. I almost feel a little sorry for him in an odd sort of way. Wrong place, wrong time; that's all. It could have been any officer really, but let's face it, John, he might have been an officer but he was certainly no gentleman, as you proved. Well done, John.

As much as I like to look elegant, and elegant was the way that my friend, that banker fellow Brooks, described me

*in my midshipman's uniform, I do have to admit that I feel
more comfortable in my workaday rig.*

*So, it appears that no one is supposed to talk to me whilst
I'm imprisoned. Seems a bit harsh but then what they don't
know is that maybe I don't want to talk to anybody anyway.
That means that this is my decision really. I'll just stay here,
send out for whatever I need, be escorted to the heads and
wait for the time to pass until those buggers at the Admiralty
decide on a date. I won't be bored. Too much to think about,
haven't you, John? Let someone else worry about whatever
there is to worry about.*

JOHN

4th September 1796

There was a knocking and the usual cry of 'Stand away from the door.' I did as requested, glad of the extra space this cabin afforded.

The marine lieutenant squeezed himself into the cabin. 'Mr Machele, you will pack your things and be ready to leave in fifteen minutes,' he instructed.

Gosh. Is it today? My execution? No, not possible. Executions are done, or is it performed, at eight o'clock in the morning. I can't remember what time that is according to the navy. Eight bells, I think, but the name of the watch? Probably Morning, but I don't know, and I've just heard three bells so it must be thirty minutes past the hour of nine in the morning. Got it. This watch is the Forenoon. Well done again.

'Should I dress in uniform and where are we going?' I asked.

'Workaday rig will be the right thing for your journey,' he replied.

'Journey? Where am I going?' I queried.

'Moving you ashore to Queensborough, Mr Machele, and before you ask, it is for the same reason as your last move. Having you here is unsettling for the men. Fifteen minutes, Mr Machele.' He turned and left the cabin.

Really, this is becoming like the rest of my life. Just get settled and someone interferes. I get moved on. So, just being here is enough to unsettle the people, is it? Now, John, there's a power you never knew you had. How interesting! Right, get packing. What a great thing a sea chest is. All my life in one box.

The marine lieutenant poked his head around the door. No knock this time.

'Time to go, Mr Machele. Don't worry about your dunnage. It'll be brought to the boat and then delivered to where you are going next. Prisoner and escort, move out.' The barked word of command set us on our way, with me almost going at the same pace. Now I could see other people. Members of the crew of the *Sandwich* watching me as I disappeared over the bulwark into the waiting boat.

'Give way together,' shouted the coxswain after the bowman had shoved us off from the side of the ship and the rowers had settled their oars into their rowlocks.

It's quite a long pull to Queensborough, but the first thing I notice is the smell. It is low tide and small fishing boats are leaning at various angles, supported by the glutinous mud. It is mainly from this mud that the smell is being exuded. It is the scent of rotting fish mixed with that of human waste. From what I can work out, the main occupation here is the gathering of oysters, although there are any number of men in naval attire. Queensborough is a part of that conglomeration of naval dockyards, rope factories, foundries and the plethora of ancillary trades needed to keep His Majesty's ships afloat and in fighting trim.

Why are jetty steps always covered in weed? It makes them so slippery that anyone could fall down and injure themselves. Surely this is a job for someone. I would lay good money as a wager that if such a person was employed, he would be given an appropriate title, such as weed clearer. He could use that title to get work in one of the houses of the gentry. Different weeds, but he would have the title.

Oh, well done, John. Standing on the quay watching my chest being hauled up and not a slip from anyone. The boat pulls away with my escort on it back to the Sandwich, *so what happens next?*

'Mr Machele, come with us, please.' The speaker was a florid-faced marine officer with an empty sleeve where his left arm should have been.

We moved off at the usual command, accompanied by a corporal and two privates, with a further two carrying my sea chest.

'Here we are, Mr Machele. This is where you are to be held. Same rules as on board. Escort to the heads or privy as it may be called ashore; food and drink supplied or send out for what you want and no talking to anyone, sir.'

Well, this is a fine-looking place, I must say, and fairly new. I like the pillars at the front. Very nice indeed.

'What is this place?'

'Queensborough town hall, sir. Recently remodelled, as I understand it. There's cells over on one side, which is where you will be. A large space where the market is held takes up the rest of the ground floor. Upstairs is the court, where other, civilian, prisoners are taken from their cells to be tried and sentenced. In we go, sir.' He led the way, with the escort following behind.

'Here you are, Mr Machele. Home sweet home, if you'll excuse my humour. In you go, sir. A lot more spacious than your last accommodation, I'll wager, but then, usually, there would be four prisoners in this cell. Here's your dunnage and I'll leave you to settle in. The turnkey will be along sometime to see if you require anything. Good day, Mr Machele,' he said, almost jauntily, as he turned about in that noisy way of theirs and marched off whilst the one remaining marine, set to watch over me, closed the door and turned the key.

For a place of confinement, this is quite all right. Quite all right indeed, and it's all mine. My bed, my desk, my chamber pot, my dunnage. All my things around me. This is all mine. So much better than the other two little cabins, and I can send out for whatever I want. Eat, drink and be merry is the order of the day, John, for tomorrow I die. Do I? When do I? Why doesn't anybody know, and if they do know then why won't they tell me? I will need time to prepare. I must get my best uniform out of my chest and remove any wrinkles. And that stain. Oh, that stain. Perhaps I can arrange for a local woman to give the whole outfit a thorough clean. Yes, that's what I'll do. Good thinking, John.

Can I see anything outside? There's only a small, barred window, too high up for me to reach but it does allow real light in, not just a glimmer from a lantern. And there is the grill in the top of the door I can look out of onto the corridor I came in through. Fancy, this cell usually holding four people. Still, as an officer and a gentleman, or maybe not quite an officer as far as the navy is concerned, it is only right that I should have a cell to myself, or is it the custom for condemned men?

How shall I use my time? Reading my seamanship manuals would be good. There are puzzles in them about navigation, and I like a good puzzle. Lots of the other middies used to roll their eyes when the ship's master set them navigation problems. It always boiled down to the same thing in the end. Did you know your trigonometry or didn't you? And as for shooting the sun with a sextant, well, some of the places they thought the ship to be! Yarmouth, Isle of Wight, even Dover. Very odd indeed, considering that we were moored at the Little Nore and never moved. They only had to remember their readings and use them time and time again. Just plain duffers, most of them. Same thing in the army. Half the cornets couldn't do their arithmetic, let alone trigonometry. They could just about read a map but nothing else. It was a good job they were in the dragoons and not the artillery. How to calculate trajectories? Most had no idea. Still, to become lieutenants, it was mainly a matter of money, not brains. As long as they could afford it and there was a vacancy, everything would be fine.

Do you know, I still have no idea what Brooks meant when he said that everything would be all right. What an odd thing to say to a chap who has just been sentenced to death, but then he doesn't know that that was what I wanted. Surely if a gentleman and a friend was to say anything, it should be an expression of sadness or sorrow that things had come to such a state. But not it will be all right, John. Strange but he probably thought it would give me good cheer and help me to face my fate.

Talking about fate, I must see if I am to be feted – oh, very good, John, very good indeed – with an excellent supper. Oysters should be no problem here and then perhaps a steak pie and a pint of claret, I think. Must order my breakfast at the same time, I think. Can't risk being presented with whatever slop will be served to the ordinary prisoners. Mutton chops and a few eggs. Some coffee. Must have coffee.

JOHN

5ᵗʰ September 1796

It's very nice the way the sun slants in through that high window in the morning. Today is the 5ᵗʰ of September, and that was a fine supper and an equally fine breakfast today delivered by a very fair maid from the local inn. All in all, everything here is very fine indeed.

Hello, there's a fair bit of chattering in the corridor. I wonder what is going on. If I position myself just to the side of the grill in the door and the sentry is not blocking my line of sight, I can have a view towards the front entrance and see if it's more prisoners or people going upstairs. I know they must be marines or soldiers because of the noise they make even when they think they are walking normally. No prisoners then. A marine has gone up the stairs. Who is this following him? I know this fellow. He was on the Sandwich. *He pulled me by my coat-tails when I tried to jump overboard. What's his name? Empsell. That's it. What's he doing here? Just a minute. I know this next fellow as well. He's off the* Sandwich *too. A quartermaster. Hockless. I remember him. I offered him good money to let me go overboard but he refused. Whatever is going on here? Well, I never. Here comes that marine who took my pistol off me and then refused to run me through with his cutlass even though I asked him to. Never found out his name, but I don't think that's important.*

Not another marine still? Oh yes, John Exon. Another so-called sentinel who stopped me from ending my life. I knew he wanted to hurt me, and not only that, he tried to rob me as well. I don't remember what happened next, but I believe I retired to my bed.

Here comes someone else I know. That's Midshipman Gregg. My friend George. Left the Sandwich *for the* Hound. *I counted him a friend, but even he tried to stop me going overboard. What sort of friend is that?*

But why are they all here? I know. There is a court upstairs. Has there been some trouble involving all of them? Maybe they are all prisoners as well. They are being escorted by a party of marines. Are they all under arrest? Will they end up in the cells down here? Surely not unless the civil authorities are accusing them of something that has occurred here in town. How odd.

I think they are on the move. I can hear that characteristic tramping noise as the escort comes down the stairs with the others following. How long were they all up there? Not more than an hour, it seems. Are they coming my way? No. Straight down the stairs and out into the street. I could always ask my sentry what they were all doing here, but that would be a waste of time. I've already been told that the sentries, regardless of which one it is, will only engage with me in matters of routine affecting my incarceration.

PREPARING THE APPEAL

6th September 1796

It was a quarter to twelve noon on 6th September 1796 when there was a discreet knock on George Brooks's office door. His personal assistant, the round-faced bespectacled Christopher Dodd, entered, carrying in his hand a wax-sealed packet.

'Just arrived by special courier, sir. For you personally, sir. From Mr Stamp of Queensborough,' said Dodd, handing the packet to Mr Brooks.

'Thank you, Dodd. That'll be all. No, wait a moment. I shall want you to deliver a message for me.'

Brooks pulled a sheet of paper from a pile on his left, freshened the ink on his pen and wrote: "Depositions arrived. Please come as soon as is convenient so that we may consider their value for the appeal. Your Humble and Obedient Servant, George Brooks."

He folded the note carefully, affixed his seal and addressed it to Mr B. Green c/o Brooks Club. He looked up at Dodd and said, 'You know where Brooks Club is?'

'Yes, sir, in St James's,' replied Dodd, thinking to himself what a pleasant change a walk in the warm September air would make from copying out account details and supervising the clerks in the office.

'Good,' responded Mr Brooks. 'Take this note there and hand it to the porter. When you get back, and don't dawdle, be ready later to ensure that when Mr Brown calls he is to be shown into my office immediately. Do you understand? Immediately. Off you go and come straight back. Those clerks copying the accounts still need supervising.'

'Yes, sir. Understood, sir,' said Dodd, hastening out of the door and only just remembering to shut it behind him.

Using his ivory-handled paper knife, Brooks carefully broke the wax seal on the packet and extracted several sheets of paper. Each one was a sworn deposition signed at the bottom as being witnessed by the deputy mayor and commissioner for oaths at Queensborough, Mr Stamp. Brooks smiled to himself. Sworn before someone called Stamp. He wondered playfully if this Mr Stamp had given his "stamp" of approval to the depositions.

George Brooks had not been totally convinced that the plan of action to make a, hopefully, successful plea for mercy would make the progress it clearly had already. The first step had been completed. All these depositions from men serving on the *Sandwich*. Admiral Buckner had indeed been induced by a person or persons unknown to, in turn, "persuade" Captain Mosse to order the necessary arrangements. Now, how many were there? Six. Splendid but what did they actually say? He skimmed over the writing just to get a feel for their contents.

Mmm. There is so much more here than came out at the trial. Surely John's behaviour indicates that if he was not actually insane, then he was, at the very least, a most unhappy and troubled young man. I feel sad for him and will have to search my conscience about the part I have played, albeit unwittingly, in creating this situation. He gave no sign at all that he was resistant to the idea of joining the Royal Navy.

John had been his usual polite self. I saw him preening himself in his new midshipman's uniform. I know he said to me that he thought it rather plain but then, after the one he wore in the Royal Scots Greys with all its lace and braid, anything would look plain. I thought he looked very smart and I used the word "elegant", which he seemed very pleased with indeed. I am still somewhat nonplussed as to how his uniform was got so speedily for him and from an excellent tailor as the cut and fit proved. And then there was the question of all the other clothing and equipment required. I saw the list of what a midshipman should have when he joined his ship. It was extensive to say the least: "Two uniforms, a short blue jacket with uniform buttons and waistcoat and breeches, three dozen shirts, three dozen pairs of stockings, two formal hats and two round ones..." I was told hats are liable to be lost overboard! "...pocket handkerchiefs, night caps, wash basins, wash balls, brushes, combs, etc." Also recommended was a list of required textbooks, navigational instruments, mathematical tables... The Mariner's New Calendar, *the latest* Nautical Almanac, *slate and pencils, pens, ink powder and paper and books in which to keep his log and journal. Mr Brown had told me that acquiring the uniforms and the other necessaries required had not presented the sort of problem I might think. Apparently, or so I was able to deduce, the family of Mr Brown's master had had experience of equipping a young midshipman some years before. Anyway, no concern of mine.*

He returned to his correspondence, scribbling notes on the various requests to be permitted to extend loan periods, to have the amounts loaned increased, and the usual heated queries regarding why a customer's promissory note had not been honoured. On completion, he rang the handbell on his desk to summon a clerk. He gave the small pile to him.

'I've appended notes regarding the replies as usual. Compose the appropriate letters and pass them to Dodd before the close of business today. Thank you.' Brooks dismissed the clerk with a nod of his head. *Close of business*, he thought to himself. That would be the close of the bank's regular business, but Machele's business was rather different. True, it was, on the one hand the bank's business but on the other it was unlike any business he had ever been involved in before. Brooks admitted to himself that initially he had grave misgivings about agreeing to Mr Brown's request back in 1792, before what he liked to refer to as "Machele's missing years". He had, during the affair of the Naval Academy, both begun to get a liking for John Machele and for the type of work which his involvement with him had generated, being so different from his everyday life as a banker.

His musings were interrupted by a tap on his office

door and in answer to his call of 'Come in,' Dodd opened the door wide and said, 'Mr Brown, sir, as requested.'

'Thank you, Dodd. We are not to be disturbed under any, and I mean any, circumstances.'

He stood and moved out from behind his desk, extending his hand to Mr Brown and they shook almost as old friends or, in this situation, as well-intentioned conspirators.

'Well, George. Here I am and most anxious to see the depositions,' said Augustus Brown, seating himself in the leather-padded wooden chair which had previously been occupied by so many of the bank's customers. Some bringing cash, some wanting cash, and others checking the state of their stocks held by the bank. Brown rested his hands on the silver top of his cane and waited for Brooks to speak.

'Some claret whilst I tell you many stories that I have today become the recipient of?'

'With pleasure, George, and do not delay for much longer what you have to tell me,' replied Brown, quite visibly impatient.

George Brooks continued, holding the six affidavits in his hand.

'These tell quite a story and serve our purpose well. It seems that the court was so determined to simply hear evidence to prove the charges true that although they did ask the witnesses if they felt John to be in his senses, their questions were much too narrow and did not allow the full story to unfold. With your permission, sir, I will go through them one by one, often in my own words to make easier the understanding of the way the witnesses describe events. I defy you, sir, to not be certain of our plea's success. I may not be able to invent stories and turn them into books like that fellow Richardson, but I can certainly tell a good story from a bad one. That's what comes of being in my position when clients propose all sorts of unlikely happenstances with events coloured by their use of language as simple obfuscation. I see through them, sir, and they appear angry, ashamed, saddened and then amazed as I repeat to them their story but in my own words. Almost invariably, I see the whole gamut of emotions move across their faces as I conclude by saying, "Well, sir, is this what you are asking me to believe?" Oh, the looks on their faces as the realisation that I have seen through their attempted ruses and that my own words, mark you, my own words, defy them to deny the fallaciousness of the argument they have just put to me.' Brooks could see Brown beginning to fidget in his chair and gazing longingly at the sheets of paper held in Brooks's hand, so near and yet so far.

'George, please, sir, if we may proceed with the depositions either in your words or theirs. I have no doubt as to your abilities to describe the events contained therein so, please, sir.' His voice was edged by his growing impatience.

'My apologies, sir, my apologies. I believe my excitement after having read these documents has overridden the fact that you have not had the advantage that I have. So, please do not stand on ceremony but help yourself to the claret as you will. We will not be disturbed and there are no clerks with their ears to the keyhole.'

He felt that the insertion of a little humour would go some way to easing Brown's growing frustration and impatience as he placed the depositions in what he felt to be a logical sequence. He rose from his chair and began to pace backwards and forwards behind his desk, as though giving a performance on a stage.

'Only the first one is from a witness who gave evidence at the court martial, and that is James Hockless, a quartermaster. He saw John on the evening of the 20th of August standing on the gangway and asked him to go down into the waist of the ship. John said he wanted to go to the head – that's what seamen call the lavatory or closet – and he pushed the door to it open. Hockless followed him and before he could stop him, he had one leg on the privy seat and the other on the rail. The heads are very basic, being only a seat with a hole in it jutting out over the ship's side and a rail to hold on to. Seeing that John was attempting to jump overboard, he grabbed hold of his coat-tails or, as Hockless puts it, "the skirts of his jacket", and pulled him back onto the deck. What happened next is quite clear and best told in Hockless's own words:

"'Mr Machele then offered me a guinea to let him go overboard but I made him answer if he wanted to give me two hundred he should not go. He then offered me three guineas but to no purpose."

'Again, according to Hockless, there was a scuffle and he and another quartermaster managed eventually to get him to the gunroom, which is where the midshipmen berth. John kept repeating that he was going to jump overboard and actually attempted two or three times to climb out of the starboard porthole or window. Hockless says that they were not able to persuade him to stop, so he sent word to Captain Mosse, who ordered him to bed and set a marine to stand over him. Now, I know he does not say that John is insane, but would someone in their right senses try not only to jump overboard several times but also offer money to someone trying to stop him? Mind you, since he was not likely to have that money about his person, then how would Hockless have been able to claim his reward?'

'Quite, George,' said Brown. 'How indeed? John's behaviour is certainly most odd. He must have been very unhappy to try to throw himself off the ship. Do others confirm this story?'

Brooks resumed, fluttering the papers in the air.

'They do, sir, they do. James Empsell, another member of the crew of the *Sandwich*, saw John trying to get out of a stern porthole. At the request of the ship's clerk, he went to the quarterdeck to ask the officer of the watch, Lieutenant Johnson, for permission to place the covers over the portholes but this was refused. Ventilation is not always very good at the best of times and, as we are aware, this has been a very hot summer. Anyway, the portholes were left uncovered but a guard was set to watch over John, as we know.'

'George,' interjected Brown, 'this is all very interesting and you do tell a good tale but only about a young man who is so anxious to leave the navy that he is willing to jump overboard. This is a fairly common thing, surely. Sailors desert in this manner all the time. That is why, as I understand it, guard boats are rowed around Royal Navy ships when in sight of land. Does anyone swear they felt him to be exhibiting signs of insanity, because they certainly did not say so at the trial?' Brown emphasised the last statement by blowing loudly through his pursed lips and raised his gaze to meet Brooks's eyes.

'Indeed, they do, sir. Patience, if you please. Evidence for our cause is crystal clear from now on.'

He paused for dramatic effect and, leaning over, he handed a sheet of paper to Brown, who snatched it from him.

'There, sir, read this for yourself. The statement of the ship's clerk. The beginning of the use of words to form our appeal.'

Brown lifted his reading glasses from where they nestled on their gold chain in his waistcoat pocket and gave his full attention to the document.

I Henry Dobson (Ship's Clerk) of His Majesty's ship Sandwich *maketh oath and sayeth that on the night of the 20th August last when in my cabbin in the Gunroom James Empelle came to me in great agitation and informed me that Mr machell was attempting to go overboard out of the Stern Port and on my going out of my Cabbin into the Gunroom the Centinel who was placed near him had discovered his intention and caused him to desist – and as he seemed to have a propensity to go overboard by frequently going to the different Ports of the Gunroom and as there could be nothing to engage his attention at a late hour of the night, it created an alarm – And James Lynn a Seaman who is an Attendant in the Gunroom went on the Quarter deck to report the same and to be allowed to lower the Ports – but so that was not allowed, he brought his bedding into the Gunroom and laid near Mr machell in order to prevent any violence he might offer to the Centinel at a late hour of the Night when no one was near him. He then walked about the Gunroom for some time much disturbed in his mind and it neared not before midnight he was composed when he retired to his bed.*

Sworn before Mr Stamp Deputy Mayor at Queensborough
5th Sept 1796

'But this is exactly what we want,' said Brown, his face breaking into a broad grin. 'The key here is where he says, "He then walked about the Gunroom for some time disturbed in his mind." Although, reflecting on my first reading, I feel it not to be sufficient on its own. Is there more like this?' he said, looking at George Brooks, who, by now, had resumed his place behind his desk.

'There is not only more but, dare I say it, even better to come.' Brooks said this as in the manner of a man who was the proud possessor of a much-valued treasure. He took Dobson's deposition from Brown's hand and replaced it with that of William Green. 'See what you make of this, my dear Augustus.'

Brown read on:

I William Green a Marine says and will make oath that on the night of the 20th or 21st of August I was centinel over Mr Machell about the Hour of 8 O Clock.

He came up to me and presented a pistol to my Head on which I took him by the right arm and pushed him down on his back. In which struggle I cut His lip with a Cutlass & while he was in that position the Pistol was taken from Him while he was struggling with me. He frequently importuned me to run my cutlass through him & even endeavoured to aggravate me to do it. By presenting his naked Breast to me & using every means to provoke me to it & even opened his Mouth to have the Cutlass run into it & on my letting him at Liberty He forced himself on the cutlass but to prevent any ill consequences thinking he certainly was not in his senses I turned it away from Him & it was with great Difficulty we Quieted Him.

Sworn before Mr Stamp Deputy Mayor at Queensborough
5th Sept 1796

'Good Lord. You said earlier that you wished you could tell a story like that Fielding fellow. I have to say I enjoyed very much his *Tom Jones*, but this marine has set out a tale of action quite like the best of his. John creeping up and putting a pistol to the man's head. Where on earth did he get it from? He was under guard, for goodness' sake. Trying to force the marine to kill him? Does he have a genuine death wish? It sounds as though he is out of his mind and out of control. I thank Marine Green for his self-control in what must have been a most unfortunate and unprovoked situation, where his own life was being threatened. His words are clear: "He certainly was not in his senses."

'I am possessed of two feelings at the present time, sir,' continued Brown, gazing across the desk at George Brooks, who was, if anything, looking rather pleased with himself, as if the original plan had been his. 'I have a sense of pleasure or, rather, considered satisfaction, that evidence is building for a successful plea of insanity but also a feeling of great sadness that John seems to hate the very act of being alive. It upsets me that I had no sense of his state of mind despite having known him all his life.'

George Brooks took a moment to carefully compose his response.

'I think, sir, that you are not alone in having those feelings. I too feel a sense of a responsibility perhaps not fully discharged. I have carried out my various tasks as required but have, I am certain, not allowed myself to gain a fuller understanding of young John's inner self. Although my contact with him has been mainly of a practical one, I do have to admit a degree of affection for him. He has a manner about him that makes it hard to peer beneath the veneer of being simply a polite, well-educated young man. It is what he wants us to see and all he permits us to see.' He cleared his throat and continued. 'Let us concentrate on his appeal first, and perhaps when that has been completed we can look to providing a brighter future for him. Here is an account from another marine, John Exon, which shows John again attempting to throw himself overboard and, sir, take careful note of what this man says at the end of his deposition and come to your own conclusion.'

Re: 20th August 1796

I John Exon Marine who was Sentinel over Mr Machele at half past nine o'clock that evening maketh oath and sayeth that he attempted to go out of the larboard stern ports but just as he had got his foot on the sill of the port I took hold of his coat when he reply 'Why do you stop me – do you mean to Hurt me?' To which I made no answer. He then shortly after made another attempt by getting into the Gunroom Cabin in which there is a Port and was fastening the door where I prevented him by putting the Cutlass between the door and the door post and on my opening the door I found him taking out the sash of the port and he then desisted and went into the Gunroom with me. He was then still for half an hour and then I accompanied him up to the roundhouse and when there he fastened the door inside. I, thinking him a long time called on him but he made no answer. I then forced the door open by breaking the iron staple on which Mr Machele asked me if I was going to rob him in his own house. He then came out of the roundhouse and went below and on getting on the Lower Gun Deck he fell down in a fit and it was with Difficulty six men could hold him and in the course of an hour he had three of those fits. He then went to bed in a languid state.

Queensborough
5 Sept 1796
Stamp Deputy Mayor

'We've got it, sir, we've got it,' exclaimed Brown, rising from his chair in his excitement. 'This last statement is worth its weight in gold on its own. It's what we needed. It's medical. He's sick. He repeatedly "fitted" and went into a "languid state". This marine is not a doctor, but he swears on oath that this is what he observed. And the ship's surgeon? Where was he? Was he not called at any time?'

'He most certainly was not called at the court martial,' responded Brooks. 'I thought that odd at the time, especially as the witnesses were repeatedly asked whether or not they felt John to be in his senses. And that's not all,' continued Brooks, joining the man in the bottle-green suit on his feet and holding aloft the remaining sheet of paper.

'This is from George Gregg, a midshipman currently on the *Hound*, who was with John on the *Sandwich*. He testifies that on the 1st of August prior to these events, John tried to climb down the ship's side and from there drop into the water. He swears it took him and two quartermasters to get him back on deck and then to his cot, where he was kept under guard. You see that was only around two weeks after he first went on board. Nobody mentioned this, but it is obvious that the incidents referred to at the trial weren't isolated ones.'

They both resumed their seats, and the claret passed between them. Brooks began.

'We have sufficient to plead for His Majesty's mercy, and there are still more depositions to come. Do you feel we should wait for them or send what we have now?' Brooks looked across at Brown and awaited his reply.

'I feel we should send this right away for two reasons.'

Brown put his hands together and rested the tips of his index fingers against his upper lip before answering.

'Firstly, we are agreed that we have very strong evidence sworn to under oath by these witnesses that John was not in his right senses both from his actions and the evidence of his fitting. Secondly, valuable though they may prove to be, the awaited depositions are just that. Awaited. A covering letter with the depositions from you to Mr Nepean at the Admiralty is called for. I shall leave the wording to you, but I do feel you should give the impression that you have the care of John and that you should give your address as your house in Green Street, Grosvenor Square, rather than that of your bank.'

He stood up, placed his reading glasses back in his waistcoat pocket, drained the rest of his claret and, smiling in a very satisfied manner, he shook George's hand and on opening the office door turned to face him once more saying, 'Very good claret, very good indeed. When the other depositions arrive, please inform me. I am most keen to know what they have to say. Good day, good day.'

He left the bank by the door held open by Dodd, who appeared to have taken this duty upon himself.

Dodd went to his desk gathering up the letters and took them into Mr Brooks. 'It has passed the hour of five, Mr Brooks, and the accounts are copied. If you could just sign these letters, I shall have them taken to the post. Thank you, sir, and I bid you good night.'

George Brooks, seated at his desk, selected a fresh sheet of unheaded paper, thought for a moment, and remembering it would not be delivered until the following day felt it best to date it as such since it was to go by hand, the hand of Dodd, that is, he thought wryly as he wrote:

Green Street
Grosvenor Square
Sept 7 1796

Sir

   Mr John Machele, a young man under age who has been under my care and whom I sent on board the Sandwich *without his consent, being now under sentence of Death I beg the favour of you to lay the enclosed Depositions before their Lordships in hopes that if they shall be satisfied of his having been insane they will in consideration thereof and of his youth and ignorance of the Rules and Laws of the Navy grant him a pardon; He had not been in*

the Navy quite six weeks before the affair happened
for which he is sentenced to be put to death.

> *I am Sir*
> *Your most faithful*
> *Hmle Servt*
> *Geo. Brooks*
> *TO: Evan Nepean Esq*

NOON

8th September 1796

George Brooks sat at his desk checking the accounts that needed his attention, but his mind was elsewhere. His involvement in the affairs of John Machele was taking up far more of his time than he had anticipated. Should this have been purely of a commercial nature, he was well aware that his partners at the bank would be pressing him to negotiate an increase in the five per cent fee because of the additional work and time that he was having to devote to it. He had acquainted them with the essentials of the matter and hinted that there was considerably more to the arrangement than was set down in the written agreement. He hinted at power and patronage and matters involving what he referred to as personages who, he was assured, would be giving him, and therefore the bank, recognition sometime in the future.

He pulled his timepiece from his waistcoat pocket. Nearly twelve noon. If it was possible to gaze lovingly at a piece of engineering in miniature, he did it now despite his frustration at not yet having received the other depositions. This was one of those very rare occasions when he wished his exquisitely crafted Breguet would lie about the speed with which time was passing.

Mmm, he thought to himself, *we may be at war with France, but some things they do better than most, not to mention their wine.* He was brought back to the business of banking when there was a knock on his office door. 'Come,' he called.

The door opened a short way and the bespectacled face of Dodd peered around it.

'Sir, I was coming to you five minutes ago when a package I knew you were awaiting was delivered by special courier. I was on my way to you when two other packets arrived in as many minutes.'

'Come in. Come in. Bring them here,' barked Brooks.

Dodd opened the door fully and, clutching the packets in his left hand and holding them aloft, he fairly strode across the carpeted office floor with a broad grin on his face and handed them ceremoniously to Brooks, who had his own hand outstretched in his eagerness to see what was contained within them.

'Should I wait whilst you pen a message for me to take with all dispatch to Mr Green at Brooks Club, sir?' asked Dodd, conveying to Brooks his understanding of the likely sequence of events.

'Indeed, you should, Dodd. You anticipate me well in this but remember also your place in this business is that of personal assistant and not of an equal partner. You will only know what I allow you to know. Is that clear?' Brooks looked up from his desk to see a rather chastened Dodd in front of him.

'Yes, sir,' replied Dodd, feeling the sense of excitement that he had been enjoying so much leave him and the fact that he was a personal assistant with still some clerk's duties to perform return to him.

Brooks pulled the usual sheet of unheaded paper to the centre of his desk and wrote: "Three packages of depositions to hand. Am at the bank and await the pleasure of your company at your earliest convenience." Brooks folded the note, sealed it and inscribed the usual address. Handing the note to Dodd, he said, 'Here you are, Dodd. Don't look so glum and be back within the hour.'

Brooks had a half-smile on his face as he spoke and Dodd responded with a grave nod of his head and replied, 'Yes, sir, and thank you, sir.'

Dodd scuttled out of the office in such a way that his progress to the main entrance of the bank and out to Chancery Lane was taken note of by the ordinary clerks, any one of whom would have welcomed this opportunity as a diversion from the interminable totting-up of columns of figures. 'Doddy done all right for himself, ain't he? More out of the bank than in,' said Thompson, the office joker, to the appreciative sniggers of the other clerks.

In his office, George Brooks spread the entire contents of the three packages over his desktop. All the papers relating to the more direct business of the bank had been temporarily banished to a pile on the floor. As each deposition revealed its information to him, his feeling of excitement steadily grew. He was beginning to feel positively elated. The affair of John Machele's appeal had quite taken him over in a way which discussing the various investment options open to the bank's customers had not for several years. Investments and the calculations related to low risk, low return or high risk, high return paled into insignificance beside this. This was a real life-or-death situation. The worst thing that could happen to one of the bank's customers was that they could lose some money. True, this could harm the bank's reputation, but they did their best to safeguard this by insisting that customers attest, in writing, that they were making this investment against the bank's advice. It didn't stop the bank from charging their regular commission, however, but that was business.

Brooks's desk, which measured some five feet by half that amount, made a fine space to display the depositions to their best advantage. There were five in all centred on the desktop framed by the wood and the leather inlay. He rubbed his hands with glee as his gaze passed over them. He had anticipated a sense of anti-climax, which might strike him when he realised that they did not meet his purpose, but no. Each and every one supported their case to its uttermost limit. There were no questions or challenges that could be raised or made as far as he could tell in the short time he had had to peruse them.

There were three from officers of the Royal Scots Greys dated 5th September. Particular statements seemed to leap off the pages at him.

Cornet Hankins said: "Mr Machele showed many very strong symptoms of insanity before he left the regiment."

Richard Jones, regimental surgeon, states that John Machele: "...did for some time before he left the aforementioned regiment show repeated symptoms of insanity."

The commanding officer, Major Bothwell, confirmed that the surgeon had made him aware of his feelings and observations when he said: "Mr J. Machele, late cornet in said regiment at that time, showed symptoms of insanity."

George Brooks looked particularly at the deposition from Mary Chandler, a maid at John's lodgings the previous February, and was reminded of the incident he was informed of where John seemed to have attempted to commit suicide. It was the detail in the maid's statement which brought home to him just how terrifying an experience it must have been for her. As an example of his state of mind at the time, it was most graphic evidence indeed.

And then he smiled to himself as he read the deposition from John Bettesworth, the proprietor of the Naval Academy John attended for a while some four years ago. Bettesworth stated: "During that time the conduct and manner of him, the said John Machell, were such that I verily believed him to have been deranged in his mind and on that account I was obliged to expel him."

George Brooks thought to himself, *Was it really four years ago that the incident with the fire happened? My first encounter and involvement in the affairs of John Machele? Oh yes. What a coincidence. Wasn't it Lieutenant Hills who was responsible for the constructing of the new shore-based training ship at the academy after Machele had, allegedly, destroyed the original one by burning it to the ground, and now John is sentenced to death for attempting to assassinate the very same Lieutenant Hills without either being aware of their previous connection. Fate is a strange thing indeed,* he mused.

Bringing himself back to the present, he noticed the dates on the various documents. The ones from the regiment were dated 5th September. Quick work indeed for them to have reached the bank by today from Canterbury. Then he saw the date on the one from Mary Chandler; 7th September, which was only yesterday. And finally, almost unbelievably, John Bettesworth must have been up early indeed, for his deposition was dated 8th September. That was today. But, still, a messenger had only to come from Chelsea to Chancery Lane.

His musings about the strange ways of fate and the almost unprecedented promptness of the swearing and delivery of these, the second precious cargo of affidavits, were interrupted by a knock on his door which, as was becoming the norm, was half opened just far enough for Dodd's bespectacled face to peer around and announce, 'Mr Brown for you, sir.'

Brown gently but firmly pushed Dodd aside and entered Brooks's office and closed the door after him.

'Come in. Come in,' said Brooks, before he realised he could be misinterpreted since Brown was already in and approaching the desk with his right hand outstretched towards George Brooks. Brooks wasn't sure whether he was being offered the hand to shake or was being asked to place the depositions in it. He decided on the former, it seeming to be the polite thing to do. He was also remembering how, at their previous meeting, he had made Brown rather impatient.

'Well, sir,' said Brown. 'What have we? Are these they?'

Brooks spread his arms expansively.

'Indeed, they are, sir. Indeed, they are, and surely they will speed the granting of a pardon. I leave you time to peruse each of these in turn as you will. The speed with which they reached this office was highly commendable, as indeed was yours, sir. Dodd was only sent to the club at just after twelve noon, and it is scarcely a quarter of three now. We should be able to despatch these to the Admiralty, with your consent, of course, by the end of the day. A cup of chocolate, sir, whilst you read?'

'That would be most welcome, sir,' replied Brown, looking hungrily at the papers laid out on Brooks's desk.

'Excellent,' said Brooks. 'Here, have my seat at the desk and I shall leave you for a while and arrange the chocolate.'

Leaving his office, he caught the myopic eye of Dodd and said, 'Another errand for you, Dodd. Take yourself off to the coffee shop, the Baptist's Head at number 77, and bring back two cups of chocolate for Mr Brown and myself.'

'Yes, sir. Right away, sir,' said Dodd, as he grabbed his hat and left by the bank's main door.

'And just what do you think you're grinning at, Thompson?' said Brooks, focusing on the self-appointed office joker. 'Not enough to do? You may think Dodd is being treated differently to you, but he is only running messages. He still has his usual tasks to complete, unless you would like to do them for him. And need I remind you that having been here for over five years; he is senior to you and is my personal assistant. So, head down, Thompson. Head down.'

With that, Brooks turned his back and returned to his office. Thompson, very wisely, only exchanged winks with his fellow clerks and made no comment whatsoever.

'So, Augustus, what do you think?' asked Brooks, as he entered the office. 'No, no. Stay where you are. I don't think I have ever sat where the clients sit. It'll make a change. I can pretend that you are me, and see my office in a different light. The chocolate should not be long. What do you think, Augustus? Do you concur?' Brooks raised his eyebrows, encouraging a positive response.

'My dear George,' responded Brown from behind the desk, 'wonderful stuff. We could not ask for better. We already had no doubt that Mr Bettesworth would make a statement of this nature, especially following the rather special arrangement which was so favourable to him and his academy. And the depositions from the officers of the Royal Scots Greys are of special note since not only have three persons commented on John's insanity but one of these is a medical man. The regimental surgeon himself. But, and I remember the account of this incident myself, the sworn statement of Miss Bywater's maid, Mary Chandler, paints a picture of John's behaviour that is sufficient to raise alarms in the most sanguine of us.' He picked Mary's sworn statement up off the desk, stood up and read out loud:

In the month of February last when he lodged in the House of her mistress says his conduct was so extravagant inconsistent and unruly that she believes he must have been deranged in his Mind

And she remembers one night in particular during the time he lodged at her Mistress's House. Mr Machele had by him a brace of pistols which this Respondent has since been informed were loaded to the top and threatened to shoot himself and even went so far as to place the muzzle of the pistol in his Mouth for that purpose which – she verily believed he would have effected had she not so rested the pistol out of his hand and taken them away. And she says after the pistols were removed Mr Machele attempted to destroy himself with his Pen knife but was prevented from so doing by this Despondent she having got the knife away from him which she now has in her possession. And she herself and the rest of her Mistress's family were kept up the whole night watching in order to prevent Mr Machele destroying himself. And further says the General Conduct of Mr Machele during the whole of his Time residing in her mistress's house was such that she was fearful of his committing some act or other that would endanger either his own life or that of some other person.

Sworn before me this 7th day of September 1796
John Collick

There was a rattling noise at the office door and Dodd opened it, desperately trying not to spill the two cups of chocolate precariously propped against each other on a tray scarcely large enough for the job. What he saw as he came in nearly upset not only the tray but also his equilibrium. Brown and Brooks were looking at each other victoriously in a tableau that would easily have featured in a public performance in a place of entertainment. Mr Brown was behind Mr Brooks's desk waving a piece of paper in the air, whilst Mr Brooks had both arms aloft and was grinning like a schoolboy.

'Thank you, Dodd. Thank you. Just a little celebration, as you can see. Here, give me the tray. Mmm. Extra cinnamon. Excellent. Well done, Dodd. Now off you go.'

Dodd left the office and returned to his desk. He certainly wasn't going to share what he had seen with the clerks and definitely not with Thompson. He had seen two gentlemen looking very pleased with themselves indeed, and one of them was his employer whom no one in the office had ever seen grinning and waving his arms like that.

JOHN

12ᵗʰ September 1796

I must get my linen washed. It's all very well to have a jug of water and a bowl to wash in, but that's for me to treat my body with respect.

It's not a bad body. I have been told by men, as well as women, that I cut a fine figure. Much of that is due to my tailor but it doesn't matter how well your clothes are cut, there is a limit as to how flattering the tailor's cut can be. No, I have a fine body, which is why clothes sit so well on me. Mr Brooks has told me how elegant I look, and he is a friend and a gentleman, is he not?

Oh, come on, John, what was it you were thinking about that was so important? Linen. That's it. Linen. I must get my linen washed. I don't know how long I will have to wait here but I must have a regular woman. Yes, you'd like that, wouldn't you, John? A regular woman. Would that be permitted? Best to assume it wouldn't, to avoid any disappointment. No, get someone to find a regular washerwoman and make sure she knows how to properly clean my best uniform and, for God's sake, pay particular attention to that stain on my breeches. Mustn't forget that.

When that fine girl comes with my supper, I can ask her who can perform this service for me. Good idea, John. The sentinel can't come out with his usual cry of 'No talking to the prisoner' when I am allowed to send out for whatever I need. I wonder if she would provide me with some special services. Worth a try. I've nothing to lose, but how to go about it? She wouldn't be allowed in my cell without the guard watching every move. Maybe he would like that. Maybe she would as well. Maybe I would. Hold on, John. Hold on. Have you ever performed with an audience? What if you just can't manage it? Think how humiliated you would feel. All right, all right, I mustn't get too excited. Food, washing, clean best uniform and that's it. Well done, John.

I know what I should have done. Yes, you always do afterwards, don't you? Maybe, but because I don't know how long those buggers at the Admiralty will take to decide on the date and place of my hanging, perhaps I should have marked the days I have been here. Isn't that what prisoners do? Scratch marks on the wall? I can't see any marks like that here, but then this town hall as it is now is quite new. I could have kept a journal, of course, or even written a book.

Written a book, John? What about? Your life? What makes you think anyone would be interested in that? Even you are so fed up with your life that you've come up with this plan to ensure someone ends it for you. Yes, and have I not done it very well indeed? All my own doing and nothing and no one to ruin it for me. My plan. My life. My death. No more interference from anyone ever again.

That's good, John. Well done.

HIS MAJESTY: WEYMOUTH

12th September 1796

King George III sighed visibly as he saw the latest bundle of letters awaiting his attention, and especially so as his eyes alighted on one small pile in particular with a covering message from Earl Spencer.

His Majesty muttered more to himself than to his ever-attentive private secretary: 'I was expecting this. I just cannot get away from what may loosely be described as family matters even – or possibly especially – on my yachting holiday here in Weymouth. Oh well, best see what Spencer has sent, I suppose. I don't have to tell you that you have not heard anything I may have just said, and I don't require an answer to that, either.' This aside to his secretary, who feigned utter disinterest.

'*Admiralty, 11 September, 1796*

Earl Spencer has the honour of laying before your Majesty the proceedings of a Court Martial held upon a midshipman of the Sandwich *for an attempt to stab the First Lieutenant of that ship, together with a letter from the members of the Court to the Board of Admiralty requesting that he may, in consideration of the circumstances therein mentioned, be recommended to your Majesty's mercy, and several papers transmitted to Mr Nepean by a friend of the midshipman in question, including several statements which seem to prove that this unfortunate young man is at times afflicted with fits of insanity. Earl Spencer therefore humbly submits to your Majesty whether it might not be proper that your Majesty's royal mercy should be extended to him, and he is informed that should this be the event his friends will immediately take proper measures for securing him.*

'Yes, that seems reasonable enough. I see all this reportage has come from third parties, so no accusation of undue influence or an excess of misplaced patronage can be brought to bear. Good. I see that young Nepean has had a hand in this. Good fellow, that. Should do well. Well, having seen these supporting affidavits, it does seem that my duty is clear. Not only that, but it would be even if the circumstances were not as they are. Clearly, I shall invoke my right to the power of clemency and grant this poor lad our pardon. Just let me check back again. Good. No mention of any family connection. Clever to have made the appeal through this chap, George Brooks. I wonder whose idea that was. Probably Brown, as usual. He's the brains in that household.'

He glanced up and was pleased to see his secretary still maintaining a look of utter disinterest whilst awaiting the inevitable request for him to transcribe the letter, which he knew to be forthcoming.

'*Weymouth, 12 September*

I have received this morning the box containing the proceedings of a Court Martial on a midshipman of the Sandwich *for an attempt to stab the first Lieutenant of that ship; but as it appears so clearly that the unhappy man is at times afflicted with fits of insanity I approve of his being pardoned, provided his friends will properly confine him, that he may not do mischief to others.*

'And, of course, a covering note to Earl Spencer with the usual request that he conveys my wishes and notification of the pardon to the commanding admiral.'

A wish that was subsequently carried out in a letter to Admiral Buckner dated the following day in which he stated that His Majesty:

…was pleased in consideration of the proof which had been laid before him of the state of mind of the said Mr John Machell to extend His mercy to him and to signify to us His Royal Pleasure that he should be pardoned; You are therefore hereby required and directed so caused His Majesty's most

gracious pardon to be made known to the said Mr John Mashele delivering him into the Charge of his Friends who have engaged to take proper care of him and giving him such admonitions as you shall judge necessary and proper on the occasion.

Given on 13th September 1796

CAUSE FOR CELEBRATION

14th September 1796

At the sound of an unfamiliar knock on the door to his office, George Brooks looked up from his correspondence. It wasn't Dodd's usual tap followed immediately by his opening the door without being told, as was his accepted manner as Mr Brooks's personal assistant.

'Come in,' he called, expecting one of the clerks with some piece of routine banking business requiring his signature.

The door opened and Augustus Brown, as elegantly resplendent as usual in his bottle-green suit, stood there with a grin that seemed to have spread until it filled his entire face.

'George, George. We did it. We did it. It's here!' He came fully into the office, waving a piece of paper in the air.

'My dear Augustus. What a most pleasant surprise. Come in, sir, come in. Take a seat. Now, what's all this?' said Brooks, greeting his friend warmly.

'I'm not so certain I can sit yet. Found it hard enough

to sit down in the carriage coming over here. It's the pardon, George. It's been granted.'

'So, John is reprieved?' he queried, making certain he had heard all right.

'Better than reprieved, George. He has been pardoned. If he was reprieved, that would only stop him from being hanged. A pardon means he will be free to go.'

'So, no other lesser punishment?'

'Absolutely. He will be free to go. Have to leave the navy, of course!'

'Of course!' echoed Brooks. 'But this is wonderful news, my friend. It may be before luncheon but maybe just a little brandy to drink to John's health?'

'And why not indeed,' responded Brown, settling himself comfortably in the chair opposite Brooks's desk.

George brought out his imported brandy and poured them both a drink.

'It seems a shame to have glasses of this size and not fill them.' He laughed as he passed Augustus a glass filled to the brim. 'Here is to John. May he be free and secure in the knowledge that when he is in need, he does have people who care about him and will do all in their power to make things right for him. To John.'

'To John,' said Brown, as they touched glasses and sipped appreciatively at their brandy. 'Really, George, you must tell me where you obtain this fine cognac, for this is no mere brandy.'

'My dear Augustus, I fear I cannot actually tell you my source, for reasons which I am sure you understand. It is known to only a very few persons. You are perfectly correct in your assumption. This is of the very finest, and hard to obtain indeed. What you are drinking here is a Gautier Cognac 1762, and I have two bottles. The other is in my cellar at my house, but how long I will be able to resist the temptation I don't know. However, tell me what you desire, be it bottles or possibly even a keg, and if it can be arranged then it shall be yours. Now, you cannot just walk in here full of excited congratulations and not tell me more.' He looked at Brown expectantly as they both settled themselves even more comfortably in their seats.

'Well, George,' began Augustus, 'you know all about the affidavits and the testimonies swearing to John's insanity, which you sent to Evan Nepean at the Admiralty, and how convinced we both were that a pardon was not too much to hope for. Mr Nepean immediately on receipt of your two packages with their enclosures presented them to Lord Spencer. Without going into details, which you know I am unable to disclose, Spencer, with considerable alacrity, enclosed your communications in the box of matters which required His Majesty's attention and which was despatched to him that very day.' He paused for another sip of his cognac and then continued. 'So that was on the 11th of September. Spencer affixed a covering letter precising the contents of our appeal to draw His Majesty's attention to what appeared to be an appeal of merit. This, with the other papers of state, was couriered to His Majesty in Weymouth, where he was having a yachting holiday. His Majesty replied to Spencer on the 11th and 12th respectively, and these are copies of those letters which I shall leave for you to peruse at your leisure, for you now know their worthy contents. There, George. What do you think of that, eh? And I have a copy of the letter that Spencer sent to Admiral Buckner. Here, let me read you the pertinent part:

'*...the minutes of the proceedings were placed before the King by Earl Spencer who was "pleased in consideration of the proof which had been laid before him of the state of mind of the said Mr John Machell(?) to extend His mercy to him and to signify to us His Royal Pleasure that he should be pardoned; You are therefore hereby required and directed so caused His Majesty's most gracious pardon to be made known to the said Mr John Mashele(?) delivering him into the Charge of his Friends who have engaged to take proper care of him and giving him such admonitions as you shall judge necessary and proper on the occasion."*

'Now, George, I have been informed that John will be called before Admiral Buckner on the *Sandwich* on the 16th of this month, the day after tomorrow. Note it says, "*delivering him into the charge of his friends*", and what are we if not his friends, eh, George, eh?' Brown looked speculatively at George Brooks to see if he had followed his, as yet unexpressed, thought.

George looked up, his face slightly flushed from the pre-luncheon cognac which was having quite an effect, it having been some time since he had breakfasted.

'Augustus, I have a mind to anticipate you, sir. We

are his friends. John has particularly requested that we consider ourselves to be such. I believe, sir, and please correct me if I misunderstand your meaning, that you are suggesting that we both go to see John being pardoned and then, I assume, you will have certain arrangements in place for his future care.'

'Exactly, George. Exactly. It is short notice, I know, but are you able to leave with me tomorrow, stay the night ready for the big day on the 16th? I have to say I have engaged the two gentlemen who oversaw John's retirement from the army to ensure his smooth delivery. He did not seem to mind their company then, so at least they will be known to him. John has a way of adapting to sudden changes in his life, and this rather unexpected and dramatic one should come easier than most when he realises his life is to be spared. No longer will he be facing the awful prospect of being hanged.'

George Brooks leant halfway across his desk and, fixing his friend with a rather watery look, said, 'Delighted to accompany you, Augustus. What is the point of being a partner in a bank if a fellow can't be absent on a customer's business – and John is a valued customer – for a few days? Anyway, I have a most efficient personal assistant in young Dodd, who will take care of everything until I return.'

'Very well, George. Good,' responded Brown, his speech becoming just a little slurred. 'The two gentlemen are leaving today by a separate conveyance and will meet us there, so we will have two carriages available for the return journey. My carriage will bring you back on your own whilst my little party go to an as-yet-undisclosed destination. So, tomorrow at, say, ten of the clock here?'

'Ten of the clock it shall be, Augustus.' George stepped around the corner of his desk, only banging his hip slightly as he did so. The two men shook hands and George escorted Augustus, fairly slowly and carefully, through the outer office and said farewell to him at the main entrance.

'Until the morrow, Augustus. I can hardly wait until we see the look on John's face as he is pardoned, and the pleasure it will give him knowing the efforts his friends have gone to on his behalf.' George stood and watched whilst Augustus's coachman assisted him up the folding step into his carriage and then turned to give Dodd his instructions for the next few days. 'Oh yes,' he mused. 'The look that will be on John's face.'

JOHN

15th September 1796

My best uniform does look awfully smart hanging there. Not a blemish on it. How did she ever get that mark out? Why do I have a feeling that it may not fit quite as well as it used to? How old is it? Surely no more than two months. You see, John, that's the problem with you. You don't keep track of the days. But why should I? I will be told when my time has come. I have no need to do anything about it. Be told it's time to go. Put on my uniform and that's it. Yes, John. Put on your uniform. You think you cut a fine figure but take a good look at yourself now. You send out for so much food and wine that you may well wonder if your uniform still fits. Can't you see, John? Those breeches will be so tight now. Yes, but I have a waistcoat and that will cover the fastening at my waist, which I can always leave unbuttoned. And why shouldn't I eat what I want? It's not my fault I get so little exercise.

Will you miss anything, John? Not really. I liked it in the Scots Greys, but other people thought I didn't quite fit in. Really miss my mount, though. I had better and more intelligent conversations with her than with those chinless oddities in the mess. I'd like to see Vauxhall Gardens again. See the way all those lights were lit. So clever and I loved the smell. I've always liked the smell of oil, smoke and gunpowder. I should have been in the artillery. Not such a fine uniform, though, but the smells. If I had been on a ship going to sea to fight the French, it would have been different. But no. A bloody guardship. What's the point of having ninety guns with nothing to shoot at? And it flew an admiral's flag. Which reminds me. How much longer before I know?

That coterie of captains didn't take too long, so what is the problem with their bloody Lordships? I'll wager that they, whoever they are, are a bunch of old crusties with snuff-stained waistcoats. So old that a group of them would be called an artefact of admirals. Oh, excellent, John. That really is awfully good indeed.

Oh dear. Here we go again. Stamp. Stamp. Surely it isn't time to change the guard again. That crashing noise as those marine fellows come to a halt. So bloody noisy. Hello, the key's turning in the lock. I'm not ready for any more food yet. This is all a bit confusing. I'll have to send it back. Tell her to come at the usual time. What did I order? Doesn't matter. I quite like surprises.

'Stand to attention with an officer present.'

What? An officer present. Gosh, so there is. And that corporal had to draw my attention to it. A navy officer. A lieutenant. Never seen him before. I suppose I should, at the very least, acknowledge him.

'Good afternoon, sir,' I said, in what I felt to be a

welcoming voice. 'To what do I owe the pleasure? A glass of claret with you? Not the best but quite palatable.'

I nearly added, 'Have you come far?' but stopped myself when I saw he was giving me one of those looks which people tended to when they felt there was something not quite right about me.

'Mr Midshipman John Machele, I have been instructed to inform you that you are requested and required to attend Admiral Buckner on HMS *Sandwich* tomorrow, the 16th of September 1796 at four bells in the forenoon watch. You will be escorted from here at two bells. Best uniform.' He touched the brim of his hat as he turned to the door, saying: 'Good day, sir.' And before I could say anything more, he had gone and the door to my cell was locked once more.

So, tomorrow I see the admiral. No hanging tomorrow then but definitely the morning after. Today then is the 15th of September. What a lot of very good meals I have had here. I know what I have not heard here. Those bells. Well, there are bells but only the usual town hall's clock ones, not the bells like we have in the navy. Did I just say we? I think I meant they. Well, John, tomorrow morning at nine of the clock, you leave here. Will you have to leave the top of your breeches undone?

BROOKS & BROWN AT THE RED LION INN

15th September 1796

To an observer in the parlour of the Red Lion Inn at Sittingbourne that evening of 15th September 1796, there would have been an air of conviviality emanating from the two gentlemen snuggly ensconced in a private booth comprised of two high-backed settles, well cushioned, with a table between. The remains of a most satisfactory supper, serving dishes, plates and cutlery were waiting to be removed, as were the two empty claret bottles. The cheese and a fine crusted port, however, were not for removing. Two balloon glasses and a decanter of brandy were, as yet, untouched.

An observer, if he had nothing better to do, or was not sufficiently interested in his companion's limited conversation, may have been tempted to consider who these two gentlemen were and what business had brought them to this place.

It was this sense of conviviality that brightened the atmosphere of the Red Lion's parlour, usually a room reserved for quieter, contemplative after-dinner discussion.

An observer might be tempted to regard them, as their talk grew in volume by the time the port and cheese was being attacked with some vigour, possibly surprisingly when the size of the previous instalments of their supper was taken into consideration, in the way of being like two schoolboys playing truant. They were clearly two friends who were extremely comfortable in each other's company and had that sense of a shared secret of a most wonderful surprise for another friend of theirs.

An observer would easily be able to overhear, without being accused of that most impolite of things, eavesdropping, rather more than mere snippets of their conversation, although, being ignorant of the overall context, could only hazard a guess as to their true business.

'A splendid supper, George. Always pleasantly surprises me how well the cooks in these places serve up such good fare,' said the man in the bottle-green suit, remembering just in time to bring his hand to his mouth to cover the fact that a large belch was seriously threatening to erupt.

'Indeed, Augustus, indeed,' responded George Brooks, soberly and elegantly dressed as was befitting his position as a partner in a well-established banking house. 'Just as well after a day in a coach, eh, what?' His speech was not as sober as his dress, and his reply managed to convey that he was probably ready to enter into a fairly expansive mood. He continued. 'Mark you, there are some hostelries that are just not up to the mark, but then you, and undoubtedly your master,' he touched the side of his nose in acknowledgement that no further information as to who Augustus Brown's master was would be forthcoming, 'would certainly not be expected to tolerate them.'

'Quite, George, quite. Now, another piece of this excellent stilton to go with the port, and I sense the brandy will more than come up to expectations. Best not to even speculate on its origins. Well, its origins maybe, but not how it came to be in the innkeeper's cellar, eh!' They both shared a knowing chuckle at this.

'So, tomorrow, Augustus. The big day and an early start. Coach and boat to the *Sandwich* at the Little Nore. Quite a day, my friend. Quite a day.' George Brooks hiccupped as he reached for the brandy and poured, perhaps unwisely, large measures for them both.

'To John.'

'To John.' Their glasses touched and the toast was done.

'Those other two men? They'll be up in time with clear heads in the morning?' queried Brooks, wondering to himself what he will feel like having to get out of bed to the sound of cocks crowing but, somehow, not caring.

'Come, George,' replied Augustus Brown. 'They are professionals. The same ones. I'm certain you must have seen them with John when you took over his care again only a few months ago. They know their job, and they know how much they are being paid to carry it out. That will mean that John will know who they are and what their presence means. It all depends on John's mood whether or not he permits himself to be willingly escorted in a peaceful manner by them. You know what his moods can be like, George.'

'But surely he will be overjoyed tomorrow. Royal pardon. Dismissed from the navy but then, in reality, it wasn't his choice to join in the first place. Can I ask you something that has been on my mind, Augustus?'

'But of course, George, as long as it does not pertain to my master.' Augustus Brown sounded as though he was about to giggle at what was now a continuing joke between them.

'Did you have any idea that he was so unhappy that he would try to take his own life?'

'Good heavens, no, George. Of course not. Having those little bouts of what people see as very odd behaviour didn't, to me at least, indicate his desire to end it all. Even that incident at his lodgings with that maid could be ascribed to something akin to a boyish sulk. There was clear cause and effect, George. He made a plan but failed to involve the other party concerned. That was all. He couldn't understand why the maid wasn't willing to do what he wanted. I think, and it is only what I think and not what I know with any certainty, John was, in his mind, doing something to the maid that had been done to him all his life. Someone else making the decisions. He did have a choice about joining the navy. Either that or to be closely supervised by our two gentlemen for as long as was deemed necessary. The navy looked best, and you did tell him how elegant he looked in his midshipman's uniform. That meant a lot to him, George.'

'Thank you, Augustus,' rejoined George Brooks, 'but to be so unhappy as to attempt to take his own life. But enough of this or I fear I shall become philosophical and somewhat maudlin. Here, your glass, sir.' George refilled their glasses, only spilling a tiny bit of the brandy on the table in the course of the strangely difficult manoeuvre.

'So,' continued the man in the bottle-green suit, 'when we, all four of us, board the *Sandwich*, we will be shown to Admiral Buckner's quarters. The first, outer, cabin is used as the office for his flag lieutenant and secretary. The second cabin is his office as commander of this fleet at the Nore. This is where he will receive John and go through the regulation procedure. We will be in the next cabin. The grand cabin, with its full expanse of windows spanning the entire stern of the ship. We will be able to hear everything as it happens. At the conclusion, when John has been told he has been pardoned and is discharged from the navy into the care of his friends, that is the signal for us to emerge and see the pleasure on his face and receive his thanks for all that his friends have done for him.'

'And isn't that just what friends are for?' slurred George Brooks, raising his glass again in another toast.

'To friendship.'

'To friendship.'

The glasses did rather more than lightly touch this time, and each man inspected his own, found it sound and drained it dry, relishing both the taste and the pleasing, warming sensation inside before, with arms linked, they lurched towards the stairs and bed.

An observer, still seated in the parlour of the Red Lion Inn, would not have been much the wiser about who these gentlemen were or what their business might be. The snatches of conversation overheard made little or no sense to him whatsoever. Something about someone called John, a meeting with an admiral, a pardon and an early start the following day. None of his business at all, but it would have given him pleasure to see the two gentlemen enjoying each other's company, but he wouldn't like to feel the way they probably would after just a few hours' sleep! But, perhaps, since they were so excited about whatever the day would hold, perhaps, just perhaps, that pleasurable anticipation would be sufficient to compensate for the evening's excesses.

JOHN

16th September 1796

What's that? Someone unlocking the door already? What o'clock is it? Surely not time to leave. I haven't washed or shaved; certainly not dressed. Don't know why I even mention that. I haven't shaved 'cos someone comes and does that for me. Can't be trusted not to try and cheat the hangman, can I? Little do they know, let alone understand. Anyway, it's not the hangman but hangmen. All right, John, you really don't need to correct yourself. It's only you who's listening.

But it is early. I know it is but I have slept so well because I am now so close to getting what I want.

'Prisoner, stand away from the door.'

Ah yes, the familiar cry of my personal sentry. They all look the same to me, and they certainly all roar out their commands in the same way. Do they have roaring instruction and roaring drill like they do for marching or how to use their muskets? I wonder. Where is my best uniform? Good. Still hanging on the wall where I left it. Oh, it's breakfast time. Well, a little earlier than usual, so they must know that today is the last time they will have to prepare any meals for me. I like this serving girl. It's nearly always her who delivers my food. I don't even know her name. I asked her once, but that brute of a marine did his usual roaring thing about no talking to the prisoner and that was that. I could say thank you to her, but she couldn't say anything back. Just bob me a curtsy. I have a half sovereign somewhere. Ah, found it.

'Here you are, my dear. For all your trouble.'

My God, she looks at me like a startled creature but seeing the half sovereign glittering, she takes it and, yes, bobs me a curtsy in thanks.

She's gone now and so to eat. What joys do I have here? Beef steak and half a dozen eggs and fresh coffee. Food fit for a king indeed. Don't spill any, John. No, it's all right, I'm still in my nightshirt. Wonder what else I'll get to eat on the Sandwich. *I'll be there for luncheon and dinner, and I wonder if I'll get breakfast before they hang me. Be a shame not to. I'm beginning to think my favourite meal of the day is breakfast. Must give some thought as to what to have for that very special meal.*

Here comes the barber now. Usual fellow and also not permitted to talk to me except in connection with his work.

'Now, Mr Machele, you're not going to make this difficult for me, are you?' he asks, as he has every time he has shaved me.

'Not in the least. Carry on.'

What do some prisoners do that makes him ask that? The quick jerk of their neck as the blade touches their throat. I suppose, if done properly, it might be an easier death for some than doing that dance in mid-air but what a mess. No, not your way, John. You have your plan, and you are jolly well going to stick to it.

He's finished already. That was quick, and no blood. Well done. Couldn't see the admiral with blood on my collar. Not the done thing at all, eh, John?

I need to go to the jakes. Don't have to call it the heads ashore, but maybe the privy would be more polite. There'll be no satisfying splash, though, because the prison only has an old earth closet. Luckily, whoever the sentry is on duty takes me there, so I never have to wait. I have to close the door simply for privacy, but it does keep the smell in, and it's not just my smell, either. Anyway, that's done, so back to the cell and a wash-down. I trust the water in the jug is fresh. Yesterday, I found a dead fly in it. Could have been a bluebottle. Yes, fresh water. Good.

I must look smart for the admiral. It's only good manners after all. There is no excuse for letting standards slip. For the approaching biggest day of my life, I insist on people remembering what a fine figure I cut. Ooh. This is what I was afraid of. If I fasten my breeches at the top, I just won't be able to breathe, and as for bowing, well. Impossible. Why would you need to bow, John? You are meeting Admiral Buckner in his official capacity. This is not a highlight of the social calendar. Stand to attention before him with your hat under your arm. Under your left arm, silly. Does your waistcoat cover where you couldn't do up the fastening? I know you don't have a mirror. Do it by touch. Yes, that's just fine. They, whoever they are, forbid the use of mirrors in case a prisoner tries to take his own life with a broken shard. I told someone that I wouldn't do that but they didn't believe me. I even told them, although I now know I shouldn't have, that I had no intention of dying from loss of blood and anticipated my death being by loss of breath with quiet confidence. It was just another one of those times when I was looked at as though I was completely mad. You see, I'm used to that now. That doesn't matter. What matters is if someone actually calls me mad or crazy or even, the ultimate, insane.

I can hear that noisy tramp, tramp, tramp, tramp coming down the passage. This must be my escort. I've checked the fit of my waistcoat over my beautifully white breeches. What a wonderful job that washerwoman did. I can't even see where that stain, spot, blemish, call it what you will, was. My best coat fits so well. Another thank you if I was in a position to tender it, but the thought is the thing, isn't it? So, thank you, Mr Gieves. I might not have a mirror, but I can tell by the touch that everything is as it should be. I am as certain as certain can be that if that fellow, my friend Mr Brooks, could see me now, he would be the first to say how elegant I looked.

'Prisoner, fall in with escort.'

I know the owner of that commanding roar. Well, when I say know, I mean I recognise him. It's that marine officer with one arm. It was a good job he lost his left arm; otherwise, he wouldn't be able to salute properly, and they do a lot of saluting in the marines. I fall in with my escort. Another very odd expression. Fall in and fall out. I've never seen anyone fall over, but maybe they only do that when they're drunk or dead. Here we go. A one-armed lieutenant, a sergeant, a corporal and three privates. All for me. But I can't wait to board the Sandwich, *see the admiral and rest up until tomorrow.*

March, march. Tramp, tramp. That great crashing noise as the party halts at those slippery jetty steps. The one-armed lieutenant of marines salutes the Royal Navy lieutenant waiting with a contingent of marines under the direct command of a sergeant in the boat to take me to the Sandwich. *Come on now, John, you climbed up these steps without mishap, so surely you can go down them without too much difficulty. Yes, indeed I can. Everybody is watching me, but there'll be nothing to see apart from an elegant and immaculately presented midshipman making his way, unperturbed, to the waiting boat and an appointment with his admiral. No mirth at the misfortune of another today, my friends. There I sit in the stern sheets with my boat cloak over my breeches. I will not have a single blemish to my apparel today.*

The *Sandwich* looms above as we pull alongside. 'Up oars,' cries the coxswain, and the bowman hooks us on and pulls the boat snuggly against the ship's side.

I know what I have to do now. It's a skill and hopefully I can execute it without falling between the boat and the ship's side. That's it. Stand on the boat's gunwale, difficult enough in itself, and don't leap until the boat is lifted to the crest of a wave, be it fairly small or not. That's it. Now. Leap. Catch hold. Excellently done, John. Scramble up the side and onto the deck. A few drops of water on my shoes but that is nothing. Turn to the quarterdeck and touch the brim of my hat in the modern manner of saluting.

Now for the admiral. But first my escort, of course.

Stamp, stamp. Here they are. Marine lieutenant, a corporal and two privates all rather splendidly presented. It's that scarlet and white and those gleaming buttons. I know they haven't spent all that time for my benefit. They are going to be with me when I face Admiral Buckner. It is all show. They are very good at ceremonial. Are they better than the Scots Greys? Not really but then the Greys have so much more space to rehearse in, not being confined to the deck of a ship. What a shame that I am not in scarlet and white also, but I am, for a short time more only, a midshipman, and I look elegant in my best uniform, as my friend Mr Brooks has assured me. I know this drill nearly as well as my escort by now, so there really is no need for the roaring-out of orders, but it has to be done. No roaring means that nothing can happen. Do they all roar at home with their wives and children? Here we go then. Lieutenant in front, me between the two privates and the corporal bringing up the rear. It is only a few paces to the door leading to the admiral's domain. Eleven I counted before we were roared to a halt in front of the sentry posted there. We were obviously expected, because he saluted the officer, knocked on the door and then it was his turn to roar.

'Prisoner and escort to see the admiral.' The door was opened from the inside and we were ushered in by the flag lieutenant.

Another one of those odd naval terms. When I first heard the title flag lieutenant, I thought his job must be to supervise what flags were being flown but no. He is a lieutenant, yes. But an admiral flies his flag from whatever ship he bases himself on, so that becomes the flagship. The flag lieutenant is what in the army would be referred to as an aide de camp. He is the admiral's personal lieutenant, who has no formal position within the ship's hierarchy of officers. I am beginning to surprise myself at the knowledge I have gained about naval matters in my short time aboard the Sandwich.

So, this is the outer office where Flags and the admiral's secretary wait to do their admiral's bidding.

THE BETRAYAL OF JOHN MACHELE

16th September 1796

'Wait here whilst I inform the admiral,' said Flags, who knocked at the door to the rear of the office and entered the inner sanctum towards the stern without waiting for permission.

In the distance, I hear the ship's bell ring four times. How punctual we are. Well done, everyone. Time for one last check on how I look. No mirror, of course, but best to check by eye and hand. All seems to be in order. Waistcoat covers the top of my breeches, so the admiral will not be aware of the struggle I had trying to fasten my waistband. A quick glance further down. Oh no, no, no! What is that on my knee? It looks like a patch of green slime. How did that get there? I was so careful. I'm tempted to try to rub it off. Don't do it, John, don't do it or it will smear all over the place. Stay calm, John. There is nothing you can do about it now. The admiral will have seen a lot worse. After all, this is a ship. But what to do, John? What to do? Show the admiral that you are, at the very least, still a gentleman and make your due apology. That's the right thing to do.

'You may go in now,' said Flags. No roaring, but then he is navy and not marines.

So, this is the real inner sanctum. Could be Mr Brooks's office in his bank except for the creaking of the ship's timbers and the slight movement of the deck as the ship rides the mild swell at the Nore.

The figure behind the desk must be the admiral. He is almost hidden by the paperwork which his secretary, in civilian clothes, is tidying into piles. Surely this isn't the admiral's full-dress uniform. It looks old and rather faded and the gold bullion epaulettes decidedly tarnished. He could have made an effort at least. I did. Yes, you did, John, but then this day is more important to you than to the admiral.

I haven't heard any stamping or roaring, but here I am only a few feet from Admiral Buckner, with my escort slightly to left and right behind me. Now would be the right time, John. Say it.

'It's my breeches, sir,' I blurted out.

'What?' querulously responded the admiral, looking up and wondering if his ears had deceived him.

'My breeches, sir. They have a new blemish on them, so I am apologising for appearing before you in this state. I intend no offence, sir.'

There, I've said it in just the way a gentleman should.

The admiral's face was turning a shade of puce.

'What are you blathering about, boy? Stand to attention, be quiet and only speak when spoken to. Do you understand, Mr Machele?'

'Oh yes, sir. Be quiet, sir. Aye, aye, sir.'

That was a good touch, John. Navy for yes is aye, aye. Another one of their strange little ways. It's a private language really. Still, listen up, John. Hear what he has to say and then you can go back to planning your last, special, meal. Whatever is happening now? The admiral's secretary is handing him two sheets of paper and indicating the order that they are to be read in, before returning to a separate desk to the right of the admiral from where I am standing.

'Mr Machele.' Admiral Buckner began reading from the first sheet.

'*At a Court Martial held on board HMS* Glenmore *on 29th August 1796 you were found guilty of the following: Disobedience of orders, Contemptuous behaviour and attempting to take the life of the First Lieutenant of HMS* Sandwich *by stabbing him. In consequence of this…*

'And I quote.

'*The Court do therefore adjudge the said John Machele to be hanged by the neck until he is dead at the yardarm of such of His Majesty's Ships and at such time as the Right Hon, the Lords Commissioners of the Admiralty shall think proper to direct, etc.*'

Admiral Buckner paused.

Now he is looking me straight in the eye. None of that focusing somewhere over my head or just to the right or left of me for him. Oh no. He clearly believes, as I do, that a gentleman should always look a person in the eye.

'It would appear, Mr Machele, that you have some very good friends, some of whom are in very high places indeed.' He cleared his throat and began to read from the second sheet.

'I have received a letter dated the 13th of September 1796 informing me of His Majesty King George's action on having your case brought before him and again I quote:

'In consequence of this His Majesty was pleased in consideration of the proof which had been laid before him of the state of mind of the said Mr John Machele to extend His mercy to him and to signify to us His Royal Pleasure that he should be pardoned; You are therefore hereby required and directed that His Majesty's most gracious pardon be made known to the said Mr John Machele delivering him into the Charge of his Friends who have engaged to take proper care of him and giving him such admonitions as you shall judge necessary and proper on the occasion.

'These are the instructions conveyed to me following the granting of a royal pardon by His Majesty King George. Mr Machele, you are, as of this minute, dismissed from the Royal Navy into the care of your friends. You may go.'

What is he talking about? I'm not to be hanged. What friends are these? They've done it to me again. When will my life be truly my own to do with what I wish? Next year,

John, next year. Ah yes, my majority. I can do what I want then and no one can stop me. But it's waiting again. Why do I have to wait?

The cabin door to the left of the admiral's desk is opening. What is this? There are four figures coming in. Who the hell are they? I know those two big men. They've escorted me before. So that's it, eh. I'm to be taken away and I have a sense that I will be told that it is for my own good. What do they know about what's for my own good? Who is that third person? Oh yes. I might have known. Mr Brown. Always there carrying out someone else's instructions. What to do now, John? Go to the admiral, John. Tell him it's all a terrible mistake. Tell him they must let me be hanged. It was a promise. All the members of that coterie of captains are gentlemen, so they are honour bound to see that their word is kept. Go on, John, step forward.

'Admiral Buckner, sir. I demand to be hanged. I have been sentenced and that sentence has to be carried out.'

'Restrain the prisoner,' bellowed the admiral. 'No, belay that. Machele is no longer a serving member of the navy. This is now a civilian matter so, as required by His Majesty, his friends have the responsibility of him. Good day, gentlemen.'

The admiral turned his attention to the papers on his desk and gave the impression that, as far as he was concerned, the proceedings were at an end. He was not as oblivious to the developing scene before him as he made out. He was aware of a sight that he would remember for some time. Indeed, he would relate the tale at many an occasion over brandy with friends. He could see a man who had been granted a royal pardon screaming that he had been found guilty of attempted murder, sentenced to be hanged and damn well demanding that the sentence be carried out.

Those two big fellows. What are their names? They'll be the ones to restrain me if I need restraining. Who decides that now that I'm a civilian? No one can stop me from cursing the navy, the king and that Mr Brown, who I almost think of as a friend of sorts. Certainly, more than just an acquaintance. Those marines are looking very unsure of themselves now. They don't know what to do because no one is roaring at them. What is that expression on their faces? Horrified disbelief describes it quite well, I think. They are powerless to intervene unless the safety of the ship is threatened, and I don't bear a grudge against the ship. All they have to do is see that I leave the Sandwich *with my so-called friends. Nothing else. The two big fellows are quite close to me now, but they seem to know that I don't need to be physically controlled by them. I'm not going to attack anyone. Why should I? I did that before and look where that's got me. Ah yes. Mr Brown over there by the door. What's he waiting for?*

'Mr Brown, sir. Always acting on someone else's behalf, aren't you? Telling me there is a personage who has my best interests at heart. Well, who is he? What is he to me or me to him? Damn him and damn you.'

I can feel myself raising my voice and it feels good. This is the first time I have felt able to tell people what I really feel. What I really think about them. This Mr Brown in particular, who represents my past, my present situation and everything which is beyond my control. I am in control of what is happening now in this cabin and I will not be gainsaid.

'I will not be moved from one place to another all my life simply because of somebody I have never met; or have I met him and not been told who he is? Am I truly a Machele regardless of how it is spelt? Why do you think I have worked so hard to be hanged, eh, Mr Brown, whoever or whatever you may be? Go on. Answer me that if you can.'

Everyone in the cabin was aware of the spittle spraying indiscriminately from John Machele's full lips, and his already protuberant eyes appeared to be expanding even more until they seemed, literally, to be threatening to pop out of his head.

'Who do you think you are, Brown? You are merely somebody's servant. You do what you are told. That is your job of work. Your station in life. I, sir, however, am a gentleman.'

'Good heavens,' cried Admiral Buckner. 'The lad is positively mad.'

'You see, Brown. You know who my parents are, or at least one of them. Don't deny it, sir. But you can't tell me, can you? Does madness run in my unknown family? You've gone behind my back again. Acted on instructions. Worked on the royal pardon without consulting me. I saw some people I know going into the guildhall where I was being held. Now I know why they were there. Evidence, sir. Evidence that you thought was for me and a pardon, but really evidence against me because I never wanted a pardon at all. I want this all to end. I demand to be hanged.'

In the emotionally charged atmosphere of the cabin, Augustus Brown, who had not uttered a word up until now and had been as shocked as everybody else at this display, turned to the fourth figure, who was as horrified as him, and said, 'George. My carriage is yours. The ship's crew will see you safely ashore and we shall meet again very soon.'

'Christ. Mr Brooks is here as well,' exploded John. 'So, you have betrayed me after all. You who said you were now deemed to be my friend.' The tears were glistening in his eyes as he spoke.

'M-my dear John,' protested Brooks, his utter disbelief in what he was hearing causing him to develop a slight stammer, 'but I have saved your life. You were to be hanged. What else could a friend do?'

'You could have left me to my fate, which I was in control of. Now I am condemned to live my life because of you.'

The tears now ran down his cheeks, and even more spittle sprayed from his lips as he put pure venom into his words.

'You have betrayed me, George Brooks. You are no gentleman, and I no longer consider you my friend.'

He turned to where Augustus Brown and the two escorting gentlemen were standing, still open-mouthed.

'I am John Machele and I give you the care of me.'

POSTSCRIPT

Another Carer or Another Career?

On 4th November 1796, Edward Smith-Stanley, Earl of Derby and Lord Lieutenant of Lancashire wrote from his address in Grosvenor Square, Westminster, to His Grace William Cavendish-Bentinck, 3rd Duke of Portland, the home secretary.

In this letter he enclosed a list of names to be placed before His Majesty King George III for approval as deputy lieutenants of Lancashire.

Within this extensive list is one John Machell (Machele).

THE CAPTAIN'S TALE

So much had changed since what Captain Mosse simply thought of as that "Machele affair" on board HMS *Sandwich* in 1796, and he still, almost five years later, wondered at how his fortunes had changed in the intervening years.

At the time of the "Machele affair" he had been the captain of the *Sandwich* and felt that his seagoing career was at an end. He had been in command since 8th February 1793 and saw little hope of being posted elsewhere soon. If that was where his lifetime at sea was to end, then would he only be remembered as commanding a receiving ship moored at the mouth of the Thames?

He thought back over the years from when he joined his first ship, HMS *Burford*, on 6th August 1757 as a captain's servant. He was eleven years old. He'd worked his way up through the ranks from his lowly start as an embryo officer to his present position over the years. Nothing spectacular but a variety of ships and as much "battle action" as could be expected at that time. It was late in 1758 that he transferred as a master's mate onto the *Lizard* for nearly five years, seeing service on the American and West Indies stations during which time for a while he was a prisoner of war. The years 1763–1771 saw him as part of the Channel Fleet on board a series of ships including the *Hussar, Tweed, Yarmouth* and *Bellona*. From there, he'd gone to the East Indies on HMS *Northumberland* as a midshipman even though he had passed his examination for lieutenant in 1765. He finally gained his promotion to lieutenant on 4th October 1771 and for the next four years served as a lieutenant on the *Swallow, Orford* and *Buckingham*. He had returned to the North American Station under Lord Howe in 1776 as a lieutenant on board HMS *Juno*. He did not enjoy remembering what happened to the *Juno* only two years later. The only way the ship could avoid the ignominy of being captured was by being scuttled. He always thought of this as a sad end to a ship with such a history.

He remembered joining the *Eagle* for a short period and when ashore in March 1780 he married his wife, Ann. He was not to be at home with her for long before he was posted in October that year first to the *Alfred* and then to the *Vengeance* in the West Indies. He thought how lucky he was not to have fallen prey to the fevers in those islands, which claimed so many sailors at that time. In April 1782, he rejoined Lord Howe as his first lieutenant on HMS *Victory*. The 15th of June 1782 was a date he would always remember. He was promoted to commander, that first all-important step towards a full captaincy, and was in command of the *Pluto*, of eight guns, at the relief of the Siege of Gibraltar until the following year, when he was given command of the *Wasp*, of fourteen guns, until September 1790.

CAPTAIN MOSSE AND
JOHN MACHELE

The 21st of September 1790; now there is another date to treasure forever. I was made captain and given command of the forty-four-gun *Assurance*. At last, after all those years serving in His Majesty's Navy, I was made post. I was on the captains' list. There is every possibility that I will hoist my flag before I retire.

It was on 8th February 1793 that I was given the command of a ninety-gun ship, the *Sandwich*. Not quite what I had hoped for, but a ninety-gun ship nonetheless and the flagship of Vice Admiral Buckner. It was in August of 1796 that the "Machele affair" occurred, and at the time I knew that things would probably change for me, as they did for Lieutenant Hills.

On 13th July 1796, I had a conversation with Admiral Buckner in *Sandwich's* great cabin. It touched on many things, mainly to do with possible fleet deployments, the usual challenges around manning and provisions. I was able to assure him that I had, in James Hills, a most able and conscientious first lieutenant, whom I trusted implicitly in all affairs of the day-to-day running of the ship, including being able to assess the level of morale amongst the people.

'Never doubted it, Mosse, never doubted it. Always regarded you and Hills as a safe pair of hands,' said the admiral, 'which is why I wanted to have a word with you about another matter.'

'Yes, sir?' I wondered where this seemingly casual remark was heading; clearly not to a reprimand, but you can never be sure when commanding officers want to have a word.

'Now, and this is strictly between us, you understand, I have been approached through certain channels to find a suitable berth, with some urgency, for a midshipman, and I thought, rather I hoped, that you could provide it. I can't make this an order, you see.' For an admiral addressing a captain under his command, he gave the appearance of someone not comfortable in making it a request and not an order.

'Well, sir, always glad to have an extra pair of hands; especially someone with seagoing experience. He'll be a welcome addition to the middies' mess. If he's coming on your recommendation, then of course he can have a berth on the *Sandwich*.'

Why should I have objected? Men were hard enough to come by, and there weren't many middies who would voluntarily join a receiving ship on harbour duties when there were frigates galore in the Channel Fleet.

Admiral Buckner made some prolonged throat-clearing noises and turned his back to the windows of the large stern gallery, leaving him facing me but with the sun now behind him, so he was silhouetted and it was not possible for me to see any expressions on his face. What I could see were the movements of his hands, alternating between being extended to his front to clasped behind his back.

'Thank you, James. I knew I could rely on you in this matter. There are, however, one or two things I have to tell you. His name is John Machele and he is about twenty years of age but – and from your point of view, probably a big but – he has no seagoing experience that I have been informed of. I am, though, reliably informed that he did attend a naval academy when he was sixteen but for how long I haven't been told.'

'But, sir,' I interrupted, 'joining the Royal Navy as a middie when he's twenty years old without having been to sea before—'

'I know, James, I know. All I can add is that this request, although it felt as if it had the power of a command when it was made of me, comes from a personage who wishes to remain anonymous. Suffice to say, John Machele comes recommended, and this is all you can say if you are ever asked. The recommendation did not come from me, and it is imperative that you understand that, regardless of anything that may happen in the future.'

'Very good, sir,' I replied, with a slightly puzzled tone to my voice; but then if a request that felt like a command to an admiral was then referred to a captain to execute, heaven only knew how high it had originated, and I was in no position to demur. 'If that is all, sir,' I said, turning to the door.

'Quite, quite. Ah, Machele should be coming aboard tomorrow, the 14th July. He'll be accompanied by a friend, who may have additional requests. Please make sure these are met, providing they don't interfere with the day-to-day running of the ship. Thank you. Good day.'

So that was it. My new, rather old, midshipman would come on board tomorrow, and I was to see that any additional instructions, for that is what they would be, even if disguised as requests, were instigated. As the captain of this ship, I was even less impressed that I was expected to obey any and all requests from this friend, of whom I knew nothing, who would be, effectively, delivering this inexperienced young man, Midshipman John Machele, foisted on me and into my care.

I tried to put any thoughts about this additional middie to one side and settled down to attend, with my secretary, to that bane of every captain's life: the paperwork. The purser's accounts had to be signed by me, and I thanked the Almighty that he at least appeared honest or was sufficiently skilled at keeping his books in such a way that they balanced with few, if any, noticeable discrepancies. The boatswain's tallying was always a challenging task and took far longer than should have been necessary, but he was excellent as a boatswain and they were not easy to come by. The problem was that he seemed to be the only person who could decipher his letters and numbers. We had come to an arrangement long ago that he would prepare his list of stores and then meet with me and my secretary, who would compile the necessary returns from his near hieroglyphics to satisfy the requirements of the clerks at the Admiralty.

It was at four bells in the afternoon watch the following day, the 14th July, when the knock came on my door.

'Come,' I barked.

'P-p-please, sir. The officer of the watch sends his c-compliments and to tell you a small boat has come alongside with two persons requesting permission to come aboard, sir,' stammered the young midshipman. He looked to be barely thirteen years of age, and his voice, which was beginning to break, had caused the message to be pitched in a random fashion ranging from a high squeak to a guttural growl without anything in between.

'Thank you, Mr Barnard. My compliments to the officer of the watch and ask him to allow the persons on board and I shall receive them on the quarterdeck myself.'

So, he had arrived as arranged, accompanied by a friend who was to present me with any requests which, as had been made perfectly clear to me, I was to accede to. I was not in the best of humours, and I had toyed with the idea of greeting the newcomers in the full majesty of my dress uniform to make a statement in no uncertain terms that I was in command of this ship. But, no; damn it. Why should I even consider dressing up and putting on a show for these two people? One was to be a midshipman and the other, a friend, was merely a companion or even an escort. Either way, he was a civilian who was effectively delivering a person in his temporary charge whose duty would be over once he had passed on any particular requests to me. He was probably a servant in someone's household.

The two persons were waiting for me on the quarterdeck. The potential midshipman standing still, giving no indication that he was in the slightest bit interested in his new surroundings that heralded the start of a naval career. His "friend", however, was gazing around as if utterly enthralled by this world within a world and seemed eager to engage the officer of the watch in conversation.

Mr Barnard squeaked to the officer of the watch, 'The captain, sir.'

'Sir,' said the lieutenant. 'Sir, may I present Midshipman John Machele and Mr George Brooks. Captain Mosse, gentlemen.'

'Thank you, Lieutenant. You may return to your duties.'

I turned to the pair before me. The two were as different as chalk is to cheese. Machele did, at least, look like a midshipman. He was of slightly above average height and had light brown hair drawn back and fastened at his collar with a black ribbon. His eyes had a slight protuberance about them, and his forehead sloped backwards to his hairline. His build suggested to me that there were signs that unless he had regular exercise and avoided drinking alcohol to excess, he was likely to run to fat. Not much chance of that as a midshipman on any ship under my command. Yet he did look like a midshipman. He had been kitted out well. The navy-blue uniform coat, the white waistcoat, white knee breeches, stockings and buckled shoes. Good. But it was the way he didn't look around at his new surroundings, as though they had nothing to do with him. He fixed his gaze on me in what I felt to be a petulant manner. I could have been wrong of course but…

'Mr Machele, welcome on board the *Sandwich*. As you

heard, I am Captain Mosse, your commanding officer. Obey orders and learn your duties and you will do well. Lieutenant Johnson, see that our latest snotty, Mr Machele, is entered on the ship's books, and Mr Barnard, please then take Mr Machele to the midshipmen's mess and settle him in. Thank you. Carry on.'

The three of them left the quarterdeck and I turned my attention to Mr George Brooks. He was a tall man with a confident air. He certainly did not look or hold himself as a servant would. He had dark hair greying at the temples, aquiline features and piercing blue eyes. His dress was sober but not sombre, with a very well-cut black coat of fine wool which offset his dark blue silk cravat very well. I judged him to be a man to be reckoned with.

'Mr Brooks,' I said, 'I have no knowledge of your position in this affair, only that you have accompanied Mr Machele to my ship as a friend and that you may have particular requests to make to me, which I will do my utmost to comply with.'

'Thank you, sir. First, allow me to present you my card. As you see, I am a partner in a firm of bankers, and I have the care of John Machele under agreed terms on behalf of a certain personage who shall remain anonymous even to myself. I receive communications regarding any business concerning Machele through a third party. All very odd but that is the way of this arrangement. The only request that I have been asked to make of you as his commanding officer is that he is not allowed to go ashore. He is to be kept on board this ship unless a further request is made to the contrary. I trust you feel able to accede to this, sir. I have it on the highest authority… please forget I said that. It was most improper and indiscreet of me, sir. Suffice to say, your service will not go unnoticed.'

'My dear Mr Brooks,' I was sure he could sense the relief in my voice that that was all I was being requested to do, 'this will not cause a problem for me. I shall make the appropriate orders known to that effect. There is nothing unusual about members of the crew of one of His Majesty's ships not going ashore, often for months at a time.'

'I am obliged to you, Captain Mosse. John's sea chest is already on board, and he is fully kitted out to meet the requirements of a midshipman. I would ask that you communicate on his progress every so often by letter to my private address in Green Street, Grosvenor Square, and in the event of a matter of some urgency, please inform me by messenger. I shall, of course, reimburse you any expenses so incurred. Thank you again for your consideration in this matter. I wish you good day, sir.'

'And good day to you, sir,' I said, and watched as he manoeuvred himself quite expertly over the side and into the waiting small boat.

Although the request made of me was, to my way of thinking, an easy thing to follow through, I did wonder why he was not to be allowed to go ashore. After all, he was a volunteer, wasn't he?

The events of the next six weeks changed everything.

I don't know why I was feeling so apprehensive about giving evidence at John Machele's court martial. I had been a witness at several and had also been a member of the board of captains many times. It was always a solemn occasion, with officers wearing their full-dress uniforms and others in their best rigs. There was just something different about this one. I couldn't quite put a name to it. It was, now I think back on it, more theatrical. Yes, that's the word, more theatrical, as though I was performing a part in a play in which everyone else had rehearsed apart from me. To be frank, or really honest with myself, I felt embarrassed. Embarrassed by the likely questions from the court, which I felt unable to answer as fully as I would have liked to.

The first few questions were concerned with identifying the knife used by Machele when he attacked Lieutenant Hills. As far as I was able, I said that I believed it to be the one. The questioning of me was then taken on by the captains sitting as the board, and I was asked if I was aware of the details of the events of the 19th and 23rd August, which led to the charges now being heard.

I was able to freely describe the events that I had witnessed firstly on 19th August. I told the court that the officer of the watch had come to my cabin saying that Mr Hills, the first lieutenant, begged that I come on deck. I was able to tell, quite openly and honestly, about the scene I witnessed. I informed the court that the only words I could use to describe Mr Machele's behaviour towards Mr Hills was that he was both contemptuous and disobedient.

'Mr Machele,' I ordered, 'consider yourself under arrest. Go to your berth.' His initial reaction was to do nothing. 'Did you hear me, sir? Get below.' And he went.

He didn't answer me at all but as he went, he said to Lieutenant Hills, 'You'll remember you collared me.'

I interpreted this to mean he would hold a grudge which he would avenge, given the opportunity, but because he never actually said as much, I could not swear to the court of his intention of any future action. At the time of my intervention I was absolutely astounded, nay, flabbergasted, that I as the captain had had to repeat my order to Mr Machele. That in itself warranted a punishment of some kind. It was not as though his behaviour and attitude had been carried out in isolation. There had been witnesses, both officers and other crew members. Word would soon spread amongst the people, who would be waiting to see what action would be taken.

I was brought back to the present by the court raising the subject of Machele's state of mind with me for the first time.

'Captain Mosse, did you then think he was perfectly sober or in a state of insanity?'

I was again able to answer, quite fully, this question since, to me, the events had, for a short time at least, been seen by myself as threatening behaviour towards Lieutenant Hills and something bordering on insubordination towards myself as his commanding officer.

'Sir, from his conduct, I should rather have supposed he had either been drinking or had worked himself into so violent a passion as to forget the subordination due to his superiors,' I responded.

I felt that I had given an accurate reflection of my thinking about the incident and had been able to avoid expressing my doubts about Machele's sanity, which had been growing in my mind since his early days on the *Sandwich*.

The court then questioned me about the events of the 21st of August, which were firmly ingrained in my memory. It had been Lieutenant Hills himself who reported to me that Mr Machele had assaulted him. When I went with him to the steerage, I had seen Machele being guarded by a boatswain's mate and some others. Even in my presence, he continued to be very agitated and, although not actually physically attacking Mr Hills, he repeated his accusations that Mr Hills had collared him.

Having described the scene to the court, I continued. 'Mr Machele added that he [Lieutenant Hills] had deprived him of or detained his property, alluding, as I afterwards understood, to a pair of pistols seized from him. Hearing and seeing the prisoner behaving in such an outrageous way, I ordered him to be confined in irons.'

I waited for the court to question me as to why the prisoner ever had a pair of pistols. They weren't from the ship's armoury, so he must have brought them on board in his dunnage. Lieutenant Hills, having previously experienced first-hand the volatile nature of Machele, was perfectly within his rights to confiscate them. Why would any midshipman need his own brace of pistols, let alone a middie subject to such erratic behaviour? Surely, if someone had supervised what was being packed to join the ship, the pistols would have been found and removed then?

A new question now cut through my thoughts.

'Captain Mosse, how long was the prisoner under your command?'

'Two or three months,' I replied.

Why did I say that? It was a matter of record that he only came on board on the 14th July, which was only just six weeks ago. There was no way I could correct what I had just said. If I did or if my statement was openly challenged then, at best, I would look a fool. What sort of commanding officer wouldn't know how long one of his midshipmen had served under him, especially when he should be only too aware that that would be one of the questions asked? I could feel a flush of embarrassment rising above my collar and hoped it was not seen. I was so relieved when the next question was:

'How long has he been in the King's Naval Service?'

This I could answer without any risk of challenge or my words being misinterpreted.

'I believe only during the time he has been on the *Sandwich*, sir.'

'And can you tell the court if the Articles of War were read in his presence?'

'Yes, sir, they were read several times whilst he was on board and I believe present.'

In my mind, I was thinking it would have been almost unheard of for any member of a Royal Navy's ship's crew not to be aware of the contents of the Articles of War, since it was ordained that they should be read to the assembled ship's company sometimes even at the expense of a Sunday church service.

'Captain Mosse, did you ever know him during the time he was under your command to be insane?'

There it was again. A question to me about Machele's

sanity. It was beginning to feel as though the court wanted somebody, or maybe just me as his captain, and hence somebody whose word would carry more weight, to tell them he thought Machele's behaviour clearly indicated that he was mad. Did the court want to declare him not guilty by virtue of his being insane? How to answer this?

'I can't say I did, gentlemen, but from his comments and actions, I always understood him to be a violent young man.'

I could feel the flush spreading higher as I realised the implications of what I had just said. Why did I not simply say, *I can't say I did*? I had now admitted knowledge of his possibly dangerous behaviour and his propensity to outbursts of physical violence. If this was confined to the middies' mess then, unless things got really out of hand, they would be left to sort things out for themselves. If I was fully cognisant of Machele being "a violent young man", then why had I not discussed with my first lieutenant what steps needed to be taken? I could almost hear the captains prepare to question me as to why no apparent disciplinary action had already been taken.

'Captain Mosse, do you know his age?'

What sort of question was that? This was almost as though they were questioning whether or not I actually knew anything about John Machele.

'I understand him to be twenty or twenty-one,' I replied. This was followed immediately by asking me if he was a volunteer or if he had been pressed into service. Another odd question, I thought. This was again a matter of record as entered in the ship's muster list. I thought it best to describe to the court how Machele had arrived at the ship on 14th July in order to leave no doubt.

'He came down in a *post-chaise* as a volunteer with a friend who introduced him to me. They came over from Sheerness in a very small boat. John Machele was recommended to me and I received him on the quarterdeck.'

As I said the words, I could feel the next two questions being formed: Who recommended him? Why would you, as the captain, receive him on your quarterdeck? Surely the officer of the watch could be responsible for this?

The next question came.

'Did he ask to go on shore again?'

'No,' I replied.

'Did he ever go on shore again?'

'Not that I know,' I answered.

Much to my surprise, Mr Machele requested permission to question me. Now what? I thought.

'Did I not once or twice ask your permission to go on shore?' he asked.

'I believe you may have asked me once for leave to go ashore, and I told you that I would not let you go.'

The way Machele's eyes seemed to bore into mine was full of challenge, as if daring me to disclose information in the heat of the moment, which I felt, in all honour, I both should not and could not do.

'Captain Mosse, sir, when you went into town, did you leave instructions with the officer of the watch that I was not under any circumstances to be allowed ashore?'

'Yes, I did leave that instruction as this was the

instruction regarding you that I received from your friend who brought you to the ship.'

Again, I felt embarrassment because I had admitted to the court that I, as the commanding officer of one of His Majesty's ships of war, had accepted instructions from a civilian telling me that I was not to allow one of my own midshipmen on my own ship to be allowed ashore. Surely this would be exposed as a weakness on my part by the board. I waited for their almost incredulous follow-up questions; expressed with quizzical looks and underlying smirks between each other. Questions like: Do you always follow instructions from civilians about how to run your ship, Captain Mosse? I knew I could not answer a question like that without either bringing my ability to command into question or breaking the terms of the understanding regarding Machele's "recommendation" or even the possible origins of the decision to send him to sea in the first place.

I waited.

'Captain Mosse, thank you,' said the president of the court. 'I don't think there are any more questions. Gentlemen? No? You may stand down.'

No more questions. So much unanswered. If I had been a member of the board, I would have had several questions to ask. All I could do was tuck my hat under my arm, bow to the court and take my leave, an embarrassed but very relieved man.

It was after Machele was sentenced and the other cases had been heard that I was taken aside by Captain Knight, who had been one of the officers sitting in the court martial that day. What he had to say to me only heightened my feelings about the strangeness of the whole Machele affair. He said that he had stared a great deal at Machele throughout the hearing and found it quite disturbing that Machele simply stared back at him with a discomforting smirk on his face. What troubled Knight was that he had a feeling that he knew him from somewhere, which he felt to be impossible. It was only after the court had risen that his memory was jogged. Machele reminded him of a midshipman he had had under his command some years before. He said he knew exactly what I meant when I had replied that Admiral Buckner had recommended Machele to me, without it being made explicit. If an admiral made a recommendation then a captain would certainly follow it. It may not be an order but... Knight confided in me that the physical likeness between Mr Machele and this other midshipman was quite remarkable, although with the passage of time it was possible he was not remembering with as much clarity as he thought he was. But still... When was it? Was it '82, '83? Yes, that was it. He had been commanding the *Barfleur*, a ninety-eight, and it had been "recommended" by Sir Samuel Hood that he take on board a particular young midshipman and take responsibility for his naval education. The rather odd condition put before him was that regardless of anything else, he was to be treated the same as any other midshipman. Captain Knight then confided in me that that condition had proved almost impossible to meet when the new middie came aboard and he was revealed to be a prince of the blood. Knight added that he could not help but recognise the strong resemblance of that midshipman to the one who had just been sentenced to death.

Captain Knight finished our exchange saying, 'Sorry to tell you what has been going through my mind all day, but I felt I had to confide in you. It was the similarities not only in the physical resemblance but the way the whole thing was arranged. Still, thank you, sir, for listening. It was all a long time ago, so banish that thought. Banish that thought.'

This wasn't my last court martial experience. I well remember the following year, 1797, acting as the prosecutor at the courts martial of the Nore mutineers and in particular the execution by hanging of Robert Parker, their leader. They were difficult times and revolution was rife. I agreed with so many of our seamen's demands, as did many officers. They were badly paid; the food wasn't always fit to eat and the fact that it was common for whole ships' crews to be simply transferred to other ships when reaching England without any leave was generally agreed to be pernicious. But mutiny was mutiny, and there had to be some show of power and authority to deter others once most of the demands had been met. Memories of the *Sandwich* were not always good ones.

In October 1797, I commanded the *Brakel*, of fifty-four guns, and in June 1798 transferred to command the *Veteran*, of sixty-four guns. These were real promotions, especially since I thought my career would end in a long period of boredom as the captain of a receiving ship. My rise has continued. Now I find myself the captain of the seventy-four-gun *Monarch*, moored in Copenhagen under the overall command of Horatio Nelson. The date is 2nd April 1801. The lull before the storm. I still wonder about the truth behind the "Machele affair".

Captain Mosse was killed in action at the Battle of Copenhagen the following day.

BUT WHY DID HE TRY TO KILL ME?

Commander James Hills was musing about two things.

Why had Midshipman John Machele tried to kill him?

And why was he now Commander Hills, appointed to the captaincy of a newly built armed yacht?

He had been a lieutenant since 1778, very nearly nineteen years. His career had followed a predictable pattern for an officer without any perceptible patronage, and although he still hoped for that promotion to the lofty heights of a post captain, he had begun to feel that that may well never happen.

He had had commands before of ships of less than twenty-four guns, which was usual for lieutenants. In 1782, he had commanded the fourteen-gun cutter *Mutine*, a ship captured from the French, and the following year had command of another cutter, the *Betsy*. That had lasted nearly three years and he remembered the sense of freedom that had given him. He wondered at the time if he would continue to enjoy that freedom, and in 1786, he was appointed to the *Pilot*, a fourteen-gun brig which was the *Pilote* before being captured from the French.

He had served his time as a lieutenant on bigger ships in his years at sea. In 1780, he had been second lieutenant on the *Assurance,* a forty-four-gun fifth-rate frigate, for nearly two years, and it was his experience there that led to his series of independent commands which had lasted well-nigh nine years. He knew full well that his years of relative independence would have to come to an end, and he couldn't help but wonder how he would adapt to life as just another lieutenant on a larger man o'war.

He found out in 1791 when he was appointed second lieutenant on the *Dictator,* a sixty-four-gun second rate, and then after less than two years was transferred to command the *Atalanta,* another fourteen-gun sloop, until 1794, when he was appointed to the *Robust,* a seventy-four-gun third rate, and subsequently in 1795 he was appointed first lieutenant on the *Sandwich,* a ninety-eight-gun second-rate ship, which from 1780 had been converted into a floating battery to protect the Thames and had then been on harbour duties since 1790.

James Hills wasn't sure at the time whether to be pleased or not about that posting. It would look good on his service record. He had progressed logically from one position to another. He had proven himself capable of command numerous times and, to the best of his knowledge, he had not fallen foul of any senior officer during his career. On the *Sandwich*, he was the first lieutenant, which meant effectively he was solely responsible for the day-to-day running of a ninety-eight-gun ship even though she was unfit for seagoing duties and was designated a "receiving ship" and moored permanently in the Thames. She did, however, act as the flagship of Vice Admiral Charles Buckner, the commanding officer at the Nore.

LIEUTENANT HILLS AND JOHN MACHELE

It had been late afternoon on 16th February 1797, a grey wintry day with a choppy sea and a cold northerly wind blowing, causing white-capped waves to break harmlessly against the bow of the *Sandwich*, when my attention was caught by a small figure approaching; one of the duty midshipmen holding his hat on with one hand whilst attempting to salute with the other.

'Admiral Buckner presents his compliments, sir, and would like to see you at your convenience,' squeaked the midshipman.

'Very good,' I acknowledged.

At my convenience indeed! When an admiral said, 'At your convenience,' it really meant immediately, or the admiral would want to know the reason why.

I made my way below to the great cabin, which was being used by Admiral Buckner as his office, made myself known to the marine sentry on duty and knocked. The admiral's secretary opened the door, with a smug grin lighting up his usually rather dour expression, and ushered me through to the admiral who, instead of merely looking up from whatever he was engaged on, came out from behind his paper-strewn desk to greet me.

'Ah, Hills. Come in, come in. Take a seat. A glass of Madeira for you, sir?'

Good Lord, this was an unexpectedly fine welcome indeed, so obviously not a reprimand or even a mild rebuke.

'Yes, p-p-please, sir, that would be most welcome,' I stammered.

'Well now, Mr Hills, how long is it you've been a lieutenant now? Nineteen years, I believe?' The admiral went on, 'You've a good record; several commands under your belt, and it is felt you handled yourself very well over that affair last year with that midshipman and the court martial. An odd affair that but never mind. All over now. What.'

'Yes, indeed, sir. Thank you, sir. Yes, nineteen years as a lieutenant.'

Admiral Buckner took his place again behind his desk and shuffled through his papers. Having found what he was looking for, he turned his gaze to me and said, 'Now, I have a task for you. There is a newly built yacht that has to be fully fitted out, and I think you are the right man for the job, Commander Hills, so what do you say, eh?'

Did I hear him correctly? Was it a slip of the tongue? If so, it was a particularly cruel one even if it was unintentional.

'That's correct. Commander Hills. I have here your commission and your orders to proceed to your new command as soon as is convenient. Congratulations, Commander.'

Never had a title and a glass of Madeira been sweeter. After nineteen years, I was at last a commander. I couldn't see any logic in being promoted to carry out a fairly routine task, but nobody would hear any complaint from me. This was the next step to being promoted to captain, which would put me on a list where seniority meant eventually flying my flag as an admiral. But I still wondered; why promote me to the rank of commander to oversee the fitting-out of an eight-gun yacht? By no stretch of the imagination was it a post requiring the appointment of a commander. Still, at least I was now a commander and would be addressed legitimately as Captain.

Thinking back, I realised I had had previous experience much akin to the fitting-out of a new ship. It was 1792 when I was commanding the twenty-four-gun sloop *Atalanta*. That was a very different undertaking to my expected duty of escorting convoys.

I had received the usual oilskin package with the Admiralty's fouled anchor wax seal, and I felt the initial thrill of the unknown contents that all officers experienced. Which convoy? What station? A cruise or attached to a squadron? I broke the seal and read the usual preamble: "You are requested and required," etc., etc. I skimmed over the rest of the preliminaries with their threats of dire consequences should I be deemed to have failed in my duties and came to the specific orders themselves. I read them once and thought I must have misunderstood. No, I was right the first time. I was to take my ship up the Thames

and moor her as near as I safely could to the naval academy
of a Mr Bettesworth. There had been a fire there that had
destroyed a mock-up of a sailing ship which was used to
familiarise the young gentlemen preparing to join the
Royal Navy as midshipmen with rigging and sail handling.
My task was to reconstruct this vessel to Mr Bettesworth's
specifications, using such members of my crew as was
necessary. I was also to involve students at the academy
in any ways deemed advantageous to their education,
training and completion of the work. Authority for the
issuing of materials and supplies was enclosed, and a copy
of this had been despatched to the captain of the dockyard
with a direct order from their Lordships that there was to
be no delay. The construction of the training vessel was
to ascertain the viability of constructing similar pieces of
training equipment for the Royal Navy's future use.

I would never have guessed I would receive such an
order. So, no long voyage but what looked like an easy few
weeks moored off Chelsea. It would be something different
for my crew, and they would have the chance to work
together on something they had never done before. The
carpenter's crew would be really excited at the prospect,
not to mention the sailmakers. I had only two questions,
and I certainly wouldn't be voicing them aloud. What was
the story behind the fire and how many of my people were
likely to run?

And now it was April 1801, off the coast of Denmark,
and I was the captain of a twenty-two-gun sloop, the
Albion, and had been since May 1798, and still with the
rank of commander.

The fitting-out of His Majesty's yacht *Mary*, of eight guns, had been a much more protracted affair than I had expected. I had sworn her into commission when I came on board on Saturday, 18th February 1797, moored off Deptford and stayed with her until 9th September of that year, when the command was transferred and the yacht's company was "turned over" into HM bomb vessel *Explosion*. There was plenty to occupy everyone initially. The *Mary* was moved and moored alongside the Deptford sheer hulk, where they made the initial laying-out of the rigging. A welcome addition was the arrival of three warrant officers and twenty men from his previous ship, the *Sandwich*, to assist with the fitting-out. Even though I had only been away from my old ship less than a week, it was good to be working with men I had known previously. In only a matter of days, I was able to get in boatswains and carpenters and warrant officers' stores, and soon had the rigging and tops over the masthead, and by Thursday, 23rd February they had the topmast up and the yards across.

Then the supplies began coming in. I was a little surprised at the variety and amounts coming on board. When fully fitted out, were they then to be sent on a mission of which I had no knowledge yet? In one day, we received, as the log states: "…2 barrels Gunpowder, 1000 Musquet and 1000 Pistol cartridges and other Gunners' stores. Received 8 casks of beer, 6 bags of bread, cask of pork and ditto Beef, 1 Firkin butter and 18 Water Casks." All this together with the anchors, cables and a new pinnace.

The ship moved, under a pilot, to Sheerness, taking nearly three days being towed by a dockyard boat. More supplies and completing fitting-out followed. Again, I thought the yacht must be getting ready for a mission involving a considerable time at sea, as the log recorded on Tuesday, 11th April: "Bread 2240lbs, Pork 25 Double Pieces, Peas 5 Bushels, Oatmeal 6 Bushels, Butter 204lbs and Cheese 294lbs."

Where were they going? The men from the *Sandwich* had left the *Mary* and I was working in her crew, most of whom I had not known before. It was a continuing round of exercising the people in sail-handling and gunnery, ensuring everyone knew their right place and role in every situation they were likely to encounter. It was also very much in my mind that every manoeuvre would be watched by all the other ships in the Thames estuary, and I certainly did not intend to be the subject of any admonishing signals fluttering up a flagship's halliards. The "mission" that I had envisaged never materialised. It seemed to me that my role after fitting-out was completed until the 19th September of that year was that of a messenger boy. The yacht spent the time mainly carrying orders from the Admiralty and the flagship up and down the Thames from Sheerness to Greenhithe, the Little Nore, Deptford and Greenwich, always at the beck and call of anyone with the necessary authority to summon them. I had to admit it; I was getting bored and frustrated. Surely this was not a job for a commander. I was quite right, for I left the ship at the same time as the rest of the people were "turned over" to the *Explosion*. I found myself, a newly promoted commander, without a ship to command. I was "on the beach" on half pay with plenty of time to brood on the events surrounding my altercations with John Machele. Always this niggling thought kept going through my mind: why did he try to kill me?

I knew I should not allow this affair to dominate my thinking, but I was certain that there was a link between the court martial and my subsequent promotion, which meant I left the *Sandwich*. I also knew that if I allowed myself to think and think about possible links which may not even exist, I would start to imagine all manner of things. The priority now was to get another ship. The thing about being promoted to the rank of commander was that positions for lieutenants were now out of my reach. Such was the price I had to pay. I was now one of many commissioned naval officers without any patronage haunting the halls of the Admiralty hoping to get a ship. Finally, a letter arrived at my lodgings bearing the familiar anchor seal. Yes, this was it. "You are requested and required..." I read on eagerly, feeling my heart racing in my chest "...His Majesty's Sloop *Albion*..." At last, a command fit for a commander. The *Albion* of twenty-two guns was mine, and I brought her into commission under my command on 19th May 1798.

No longer was I a messenger boy but I was being used as part of the protection of England's coasts. I patrolled mostly the east coast from the Great Nore to Yarmouth, Whitby and as far north as Leith in Scotland, watching for French men o'war and privateers with every chance of gaining some prize money.

May 1800 until now, the beginning of the spring

of 1801, found us on escort duty escorting convoys of merchant ships to and from the Baltic ports. There was always pressure during escort duty. With the large numbers of merchant ships, there were always many captains who were also the owners or part-owners. My problems were mainly ones of communication and understanding the difference between what I considered to be an order to be obeyed and the interpretation put on it by some other captains. I found myself chivvying up ships who did not seem able or willing to keep in close company with the main body of the convoy. A basic rule for a safe convoy meant sailing at the speed of the slowest member and ensuring that they kept close station with each other. Each dawn was a time for anxiously searching the area and counting the number of ships still in sight. I always gave clear instructions regarding course, speed and signal lights, but it was an unusual first light of day that saw the complete convoy more or less on station, which at least meant avoiding having to seek out any missing ships and delaying the convoy whilst this was done.

The *Albion* had her twenty-two guns, which were quite sufficient to ward off any privateer, but if faced by two or more marauding enemy ships, privateers or regular navy and she was heavily outgunned, then I would need to take the decision to order the convoy to scatter. This worked on the principle that if the enemy had to make choices about which ship to pursue, the odds were in favour of the majority getting away.

It was nearly five years since the incidents involving Midshipman John Machele, but the whole affair still rankled with me. I like things to be tidy. I insist on everything about my ships being smart, clean and always prepared for any occurrence and especially a snap inspection. There had not, so I thought, been a satisfactory ending to the John Machele affair. Machele had been found guilty; there could never have been any doubt about the verdict. But I felt incensed about what had happened next. Granted a royal pardon within days and then spirited away, never to be seen on this ship again?

What was that all about?

Even the muster list of the *Sandwich* gave contradictory information. I knew because I had checked. In the overall muster list for May to August, listing all the ship's company on 17th July and 9th August 1796, John Machele was entered as Crew No. 74; entered in the books, 14th July 1796, as a volunteer, aged twenty. He was immediately rated AB until 25th August, when he was to be made a midshipman. The column headed "Place and Country Where Born" was left blank. I thought that very odd. Even stranger was the entry in a separate muster list specific to July 1796.

Machele's Crew No. was given as 51. He had no rank whatsoever by his name, but it did record that he joined the ship at Sheerness on 14th July 1796. What I found exceptionally difficult to understand was that John Machele had the letter "D" by his name, indicating that he had been discharged. The date given was 14th August 1796, which was before the incidents that had led to the court martial and nearly two weeks before the court martial itself.

I still don't know why he tried to kill me. There had been no reason to believe that the evening of 19th August would be any different from any other and certainly not that a train of events would culminate in a court martial, a sentence of death, a royal pardon and, I am thoroughly convinced, in some strange way account for my promotion. I've been over the events in my mind time after time, but I still cannot find neither rhyme nor reason for it. In my role as first lieutenant, I saw someone with Mr Graham, the midshipman of the watch and, asking who was with him, was told it was Mr Machele. He had no business there and was possibly distracting Mr Graham from his duties on watch, so I asked George Milner, a master's mate, to order him off poop deck. Then what had seemed a simple matter suddenly escalated. Machele ignored the request and carried on as before without a word. I then ordered him off the poop directly. I couldn't believe what happened next. It was so outrageous that I doubted my senses. I had given him a direct order, which he initially ignored, and then when I said to him that it was my positive order that he leave the poop deck immediately, his response was: 'No, I shan't go down for you,' and then he added, 'Do you intend to collar me, sir?' This was blatant disobedience of an order and left me with no choice but to send for Captain Mosse, who repeated the command. He sent for the ship's corporal and had Machele escorted to the quarterdeck and then to his berth, under arrest.

As he passed me, Machele said: 'You have collared me. Damn your eyes. I'll not forget you. You'll repent this. You are no gentleman.'

Quite rightly, Machele was kept under guard in the midshipmen's berth whilst we discussed the best course of action to be taken. I did not see any problem with this. To me, there were only two possible solutions. It could be handled within the ship as an internal disciplinary matter, with Machele being made to kiss the gunner's daughter. This would settle the matter to the satisfaction of all except, possibly, Machele himself. He would have found the experience of being bent over a cannon whilst he was caned on his bare buttocks humiliating. It would have been a punishment more suited to a child than a twenty-year-old embryo officer and would demonstrate just what would happen if he disobeyed orders. I also thought to myself that if it had been one of the people who had behaved in that manner then there would not have been any discussion. A grating would have been rigged, the crew summoned to witness punishment and at least a dozen lashes with the cat-o'-nine-tails administered. The other course of action was to charge Machele with disobeying an order and request a court martial.

I thought back to the afternoon of 20th August 1796 when one of the other midshipmen reported to me that he believed Machele to have in his possession a brace of pistols and that he was talking in a generally threatening manner. I ordered a search of his berth and, sure enough, a brace of pistols was found in his sea chest by the ship's corporal acting on my orders. It was another confrontation with him.

'Mr Machele, are these your pistols, sir?' I asked.

He made no reply but stared me full in the face.

'I take it you brought them on board with you. You are under arrest anyway, so you cannot, as a prisoner, have in your possession pistols, so they are to be confiscated. Do you understand, Mr Machele?'

He still made no reply and just continued to stare at me in such a way that made me feel most uncomfortable. It was a threatening display of dumb insolence, and it was being witnessed by all present.

I reported to Captain Mosse what had just occurred and presented him with the confiscated pistols and asked him what we should do now.

'Leave it with me. Leave it with me, Mr Hills. We'll talk tomorrow. There are other considerations here which I cannot, at this time, allow you to be privy to, sir. Damn fine pistols. Leave it with me.'

'Very good, sir,' I said, and left his cabin feeling utterly perplexed. Here was a midshipman who had blatantly disobeyed an order and acted with contempt towards the ship's first lieutenant, and the captain was prevaricating. What was happening? What didn't I know? Why wasn't I to be made privy to whatever it was Captain Mosse either wouldn't or couldn't tell me?

Something was niggling away at the back of my mind. What was it? My thoughts went back four years to my time commanding the *Atalanta*. The reconstructing of the mock-up training vessel at the Naval Academy. Didn't Mr Bettesworth mention he thought one of his students, a John Machele, had started the fire? He hastily asked me to forget what he had just said, and I thought it a matter of little consequence at the time. But surely?

SOURCES

National Archives
ADM 36/11619: Muster List: HMS *Sandwich.*
ADM 1/5336: Transcript of Court Martial.
HO 42/39/61: Folio(s) 137A–139: Letter from the Earl of
   Derby.
WO 12/510: Muster Roll: 2nd Royal North British Regiment
   of Dragoons.

Caird Library: National Maritime Museum:
ADM L/G/42: Journal of Lieutenant John Clayson.

London Metropolitan Archives:
MS 11936/389: Sun Fire Office: Insurance Policy for Naval
   Academy.

Printed Sources:
Almack, Edward., *The History of the Second Dragoons: The
   Royal Scots Greys*, London, 1908.
Anderson, Douglas N., *Scots in Uniform,* Holmes
   McDougal, Edinburgh, 1972.
Aspinall, A., *Later Correspondence of George III, 1793–
   1797,* Vol 2, Cambridge University Press, 1963.

Byrn, John, D. (ed), *Naval Courts Martial 1793–1815,* Navy Records Society, Vol 155, Ashgate, 2009.

Coke, David and Borg, Alan., *Vauxhall Gardens: A History,* Yale University Press, 2011.

Corbett, Julian, S., *Private Papers of George, Second Earl Spencer, First Lord of the Admiralty 1794–1801,* Vol 1, Navy Records Society, 1913.

Hickman, William., *Naval Courts Martial,* John Murray, London, 1851.

Lillywhite, Bryant., *London Coffee Houses,* George Allen & Unwin, London, 1962.

List & Index Society Vol 248: Ships' Musters Series I and II: ADM 36 and ADM 37, Part One, Distributed to Subscribers, 1992.

Memorials of Brooks's: From the Foundation of the Club 1764 to the close of the Nineteenth Century: Compiled from the Records of the Club, Ballantyne & Co. Limited, Tavistock Street, London, W.C., MCMVIII.

Strachan, Hew., *British Military Uniforms 1768–96,* Arms & Armour Press, London, 1975.

Online Sources

Bettesworth, John., *A plan of the naval and commercial academy at Ormond-House etc.*

https://www.amazon.com/commercial-Ormond-House-Paradise-Row-Bettesworth-assistants/dp/1170121586 Gale ECCO, Print Editions, 2010. Accessed: 24/08/2019

*Oracle & Public Advertiser, Saturday February 13th, 1796, Issue19 242:*17th & 18th Century Burney Collection

Three Decks Forum: Service Records:

Captain Mosse: 10808
Captain Knight: 1378
Captain Trollope: 4580
Captain Duff: 369
Captain Mansfield: 10216